I0760543

THE HOLLIS TIMEWIRE SERIES
BOOK 1

THE DISEASED ONES

DANIELLE HARRINGTON

FROM THE TINY ACORN...
GROWS THE MIGHTY OAK

The Diseased Ones

First Edition

Book interior design and digital formatting by Debra Cranfield Kennedy.

www.acornpublishingllc.com

Library of Congress Control Number: 2019920566

ISBN—Hardcover 978-1-947392-70-0
ISBN—Paperback 978-1-947392-69-4

"THE WORLD WILL TELL YOU THAT YOUR ABILITY TO FEEL THINGS DEEPLY, YOUR SENSITIVITY, AND YOUR EMPATHY IS A WEAKNESS. IT IS NOT. IT IS A SUPERPOWER. AND THE WORLD NEEDS MORE OF IT."

—Melissa Webb

I

"TODAY, MY LIFE CHANGES FOR THE BETTER. TODAY, I become a citizen of the world."

I grasp the folds of my crisp school blazer and pull the blue fabric taut, swallowing an unpleasant lump. I stuff my hand into the right pocket to feel for my documents. The rough and bumpy surface of the papers centers me. It's okay. I have my documentation. I'm fine.

"Focus, Hollis," I whisper to myself.

I lean back against the seat of the white van and square my shoulders. My eyes travel the length of the vehicle, darting between the windows and the driver.

Nine. Ten. Eleven. Twelve. Twelve bars. I count twelve bars.

I stare down at my feet, desperately trying to keep my voice steady.

"Today I become accountable to the world. Today I pledge my allegiance to the government. I pledge my skills to the service of my place and—and . . ."

My throat constricts as I search for the next word. My hands go numb. I clench them into fists, trembling slightly.

My mother's calm tone blossoms in the back of my mind. "Today I help . . ."

"Today I help change the world."

These words comfort me. My brow furrows and I scold myself, muting my countenance immediately. I shouldn't be squirming like a little one. I'm an adult now. Or at least, I will be in one hour. I shouldn't be so nervous.

I close my eyes and picture my mother's perfect face. Unblemished high cheekbones, a thin nose, placid hazel eyes, and a regal demeanor. There's no fear or anticipation there. It's what I aspire to. Our features are so similar, but my face isn't as controlled as hers. Today is my sixteenth birthday, and my expression keeps slipping in an odd attempt to grimace. It's graduation day. Today I find out if I've lost the genetic lottery.

"Today I grow up," I say.

A thrilling mix of excitement and terror washes over me. I press back the jittery, twisting sensation with all the willpower I have. This is childish. Why am I so nervous? It's ridiculous—absolutely silly. There's no way I won't pass. This is a good day, an honorable day. I should be proud. Besides, it's the government's job to keep everyone safe.

The van lurches forward, rounding a sharp corner. I slide sideways, clutching the edge of my seat, and the smell of the new leather upholstery overpowers me. The odor is sickening.

My mouth twitches. Feeling threatens to spill across my face, but I fight it. I don't know what's come over me. I've never had trouble with this. A blank face is all I've ever practiced.

It must be the importance of today. "Focus, Hollis. You can't let anything slip—not in front of a government official. Not on the day of the Test."

A mistake like that would reflect poorly on my intake to the Area 19 Testing Center.

I hear my mother's soft words. "Obey anything asked of you. This will be over quickly."

I promised her that I'd make her and father proud. She said I was ready, and I'd repeated her words. "I'm ready."

I channel my mother's perfectly collected face. Her muted look is endearing—even soothing. How does she do it?

The van's engine roars, snapping me back to the present. The sound turns my stomach and my poise slips again. I ground myself. The Test is a rite of passage, a symbol of my purity and worth as a citizen of the world. There is no reason to fear.

I breathe through pursed lips. Today I become an adult. Today I'm assigned my place, and I'll show the world my carefully crafted perfection.

"Perfection," I say. "Nothing less."

I relax my face into the blank stare I've come to cherish. Society's standard for absolute composure centers me. I know what's expected of me today—a pristine appearance, flawless self-control, and perfect obedience. That's what I will give them.

I count the colored threads weaving in and out of my blazer's trim. Six. Seven. Eight. Nine. Ten. I don't know why I like to count things, but it keeps me calm.

The vehicle rounds a second corner and bright, obnoxious advertisements blare from screens that line the street transit stops. They flash from either side of the road, keen to entice people to buy the next best product. I disregard the screens out of habit and peer through the tinted window, gazing up at the monument ahead.

The Testing Center looms into view, towering above the city. Its pearly embossed prowess fills the entire street. Columns of richly decorated craftsmanship rise high against the building, set aloft by the dozens of marble steps that lead up to its entrance. Glass doors extend to either side, glittering in the light.

It seems silly to be driven to the Test when I only live a few blocks away from the Capitol City's Testing Center, but it's standard procedure. I wouldn't dare question it. Everyone is escorted to their Test.

The van slows and I slide forward, catching myself on the heels of my burgundy laced boots.

"The path to a perfect society is perfect obedience," I say, gaining a sense of purpose. I grit my teeth, burying my nerves as deep as they will go. Everything will be over soon, and after today, I can truly serve a purpose.

The van stops in front of the steps, and the metal door slides open. My escort, a heavy-set man dressed in a chic white suit, stands aside cautiously, allowing me to emerge from the belly of the vehicle. His face is blank, but not like my mother's. His muted control is business-like and calculated. I understand. After all, he's escorting an untested child to the Testing Center on her sixteenth birthday. I'd be anxious too.

Free of my government-issued prison, I take a deep breath and begin the trek up the stairs.

The silver pronged weapon in my escort's hand glares at me. My mother told me I shouldn't be afraid of the weapon. I know it's just a precaution, but I can't seem to staunch the lump in my throat. I swallow it painfully, shifting my focus to the stairs ahead.

Twenty-seven. Twenty-eight. Twenty-nine. Thirty.

The man follows me closely, and together, we trudge up the last flight, straight to the glass doors.

"Please," he says. "To the reception desk."

"Yes, sir."

I stuff my hand into my pocket to feel for the papers once more, as if they could have magically vanished in the short ride from my dwelling to the intake. I need to stop. I have my documentation. Everything is fine.

I adjust my collar and roll my shoulders back. I've been practicing for this day my entire life, so why am I finding it impossible to stay expressionless?

I catch the glint of the silver weapon, but I look away. I can't dwell on it. There are more important things to focus on.

My escort directs me to the large, curved desk ahead. I walk up to a sharply dressed intake receptionist. A red pen is tucked behind her ear, propped up against her tightly weaved chestnut bun. She looks up from her work, removing the pen from her ear and grasping it between her knobby fingers.

"Ah, Miss Hollis Timewire. Big day," she says. "Your parents must be so proud of you. Coming of age is such an honor."

"Yes, ma'am."

"You will make an incredible addition to society, no doubt."

"Thank you."

"And with your father's recent promotion, you'll have no trouble with your career assignment," she chimes. "I'm sure you'll follow in his footsteps. The commanding officer of Area 19's military elite. Truly inspiring. What a prestigious family."

I bow my head ever so slightly. "You're very kind."

"If I can just see your documents?"

"Of course," I say, slipping my hand into the blazer and withdrawing several pieces of paper. Dirt is smudged on the corner of the top page, and part of the gold lettering from the President's seal is water damaged.

Her piercing green eyes snap to the mistake. My lips quiver as a pang travels through my gut, choking me.

My mother's words come to me again, cutting through the tortured thoughts in my head. "Hollis, today you become an adult."

"I know. It's my mistake."

"We don't make mistakes."

We don't make mistakes. I should have known that the flimsy shelf above my desk was no match for the glimmering fishbowl. I shouldn't have placed my Betta there. I'm fortunate the papers weren't ruined entirely.

"Well, well," the receptionist says, taking the documents from me.

She falters a moment as she looks through the stack, unfolding each paper delicately as if it were something rotten and disgusting. She doesn't grimace, but her posture stiffens and her crooked nose turns slightly upward. My clammy hands clasp together, as if in prayer.

She turns away from me for a moment to write something on a clipboard just beyond my view. The scratching of the red pen is deafening in the resolute silence of the lobby. It echoes off the vaulted marble ceiling.

I'm receiving a bad mark on my intake . . .

Seventeen metal beads. There are seventeen metal beads lining the chain that holds the black pen to the countertop. That's the pen I'll sign my pledge with.

"Well, all seems to be in order," she says, rifling through to the last page. "If I can have you initial here and sign down at the bottom."

I take the black pen, move the chain behind my wrist, and write my name. The receptionist collects the sheet and tucks it neatly into a large file folder.

"Right this way, Miss Timewire," the heavy-set man in the white suit says. He points to a lift at the back center of the lobby, and I fall into step behind him. It opens with a clink, its doors sliding smoothly to either side. I step in.

"Identification please," a soft musical voice says.

The man places his thumb over a small bioscanner directly above the button panel. The lift flashes.

"Identification verified."

There are thirteen polished buttons. The button at the very top is the smallest. It's pure white, standing out of place above the twelve silver ones.

The man pushes the silver button marked for the third floor, and the lift comes alive, zooming up with unsettling speed. My stomach seizes, but I reprimand it viciously.

Why am I freaking out? People don't lose the genetic lottery—not anymore. It's been twelve years since the last incident. Twelve years. I need to stop acting like an undisciplined child. I need to calm down. It's just the Test. Everyone passes the Test. Everyone graduates.

I take several cleansing breaths as the lift halts. It opens with a clink. I step out, and my escort leads me to the first door—the waiting room. He places his palm on the side panel and the door opens.

"Take a seat and wait to be called."

"Yes, sir."

I barely finish my reply before the door slides shut. My escort is rid of me. Must be nice for him.

I stand there a moment before I realize that I ought to sit down. I take the seat nearest me. It's brilliantly white, and as I glance around, I notice everything in here is white—unnaturally white.

Someone coughs and I nearly jump out of my skin. I compose myself quickly and tuck my hands into my lap. I didn't see them at first, but there are seven other intakes patiently waiting, sitting in silence. Their faces are blank, as good children's faces should be, but something lies underneath. We are all thinking the same thing.

What are the odds that I fail this? Do I have the biomarker? Am I the one in ten million?

My stomach is churning again. Today is the one day that I can't rely on anything I've accomplished because this is not a test of my skills or qualities. It's a test of my blood.

Happy birthday everyone, I think to myself, let's hope we all have healthy blood.

I can't imagine what it must have been like for that kid. The incident twelve years ago captured the attention of the world. To test positive? To be labeled a Diseased One? To be considered part of a hateful race of murderous creatures that nearly wiped out all of humanity? I shudder. It's too vile to contemplate. I'm glad the biomarker is nearly gone. Its eradication from the gene pool will be humanity's greatest accomplishment.

My eyes wander to the counter at the end of the waiting room. It's directly next to the intake door. A map of the Testing Center hangs just below the silver clock on the wall. The floor plan is intricate, detailing each level in print too small for me to read at this distance.

The intake door opens, cutting through the quiet of the room like a hot, fiery knife. My heart jumps into my throat.

A plump nurse walks through the door with a clipboard and calls a name.

Calm down. I need to drop my expression right now, but I missed it . . . I missed the name. Did she call my name? Nobody in the room has moved. She must have called my name.

Mustering up all the self-control I can manage, I begin to stand, but to my relief, the curly-haired girl nearest the exit jumps up, tottering slightly, her bony hands balled into fists.

"Please, follow me," the nurse says.

The girl obeys, and I slide back into my seat, feeling faint.

Three. Four. Five. Six. Seven. My shoelaces weave in and out of the metal holes seven times. I trace their crisscrossed path with my eyes.

How silly of me. I came into the room five minutes ago. Of course I'm not next. I'm after everyone who's been sitting here for who knows how long. I just need to be patient.

I cling to my mother's flawless strength and dignity, sitting up in my seat and composing my face to match hers. I think back to her graceful words.

"Remember, Hollis, it's just one day, and after that, you'll never think of it again."

She's right. When this is over, I'm tucking the memory of today as deep as it will go, along with every feeling it has produced. I hate that I'm expressing anything at all. It's juvenile and foolish. I'm putting it away forever after this.

That's what I should focus on—not the pointless, muddled anxiety of passing the Test. Of course I'll pass the Test. That's not supposed to be a question any longer. My senior social studies presentation was on the socio-economic benefits of a Test-free society. The genetic lottery will be obsolete soon because the biomarker is almost gone.

Too bad I missed the cutoff, I think. It would have been nice to receive chemical therapy as an infant. Then I wouldn't have to deal with any of this.

"Miss Hollis Timewire, we're ready for you."

My hands turn cold. The waiting room is empty, and I'm the only one left.

"Please, follow me."

I didn't notice? How is that possible? All of the others have gone. How long have I been sitting here?

"Miss Timewire," the nurse says sharply.

Her tone pulls me to my feet, and after a brief moment, I follow her through the intake door, keeping my gaze above her wide hips.

We walk down a long, cold hallway past seven doors. I count each one while our footsteps echo jarringly off the walls. The nurse directs me to the eighth room. It contains nothing but a smooth table, set pristinely against the back wall.

"Wait in here," she says.

"Yes, ma'am."

The door shuts, and I stand there, hugging myself. I need to wait for the doctor. I sit gingerly on the table, the sterile paper crunching beneath me.

"Everything is going to be okay," I say aloud. "Only one in ten million people have the biomarker. I'm not different. I'm fine. Perfectly fine."

I tap my feet against the edge of the metal table. I want to get this over with so I can take my pledge and go home. I want to show my parents my career assignment. I want to celebrate my success with them and eat a huge bowl of Bolognese. I want to be done.

A new wave of anxiety hits me like a sledgehammer. I feel sick, and a wild thought crosses my mind. Are they testing me now? Are they observing me as I sit here?

I scoff at my foolishness. They have to take my blood. Why

are my mind and body issuing a full-frontal assault on my resolve? I hate this. I hate feeling anything at all. I don't want to feel this—

The door to my room opens.

"Miss Timewire?" The dark-haired doctor's tone is muted with perfect societal control.

"Yes," I say, a little too loudly. I adjust my tone to match his: perfect, emotionless, respectable. "Yes."

"How are we doing today?"

"Fine," I say. I'm lying through my teeth. I'm not fine—not even close.

"I'll just get a sample of your blood, and you'll be on your way."

I nod, trying to maintain my heartbeat as the doctor removes a blue stretchy band from his kit and wraps it tightly above my elbow. He wipes the flat of my arm with a cold cloth, selects a syringe, and sticks me with it. The sample of my blood is surprisingly dark, and the sight of it makes me a bit light-headed, so I look away. I focus on my shoelaces instead.

Seven times. Seven crisscrosses.

He finishes and packs up his equipment.

"I'll be back shortly," he says, holding the medical bag under his arm. "Wait here."

"Yes, sir."

I tuck my left foot behind my right and lean forward on my palms, staring blankly at the floor. A few more minutes, I think, just a few more minutes. But time seems to drag on.

I look up at the door. I feel like I've been waiting forever. Is that normal? It shouldn't take long to run a sample of blood. Maybe it did back in the dark ages when citizens had to wait a few days for their lab results, but it's 2647. Technology has rectified this. I should ask someone if the doctor will be along soon.

I hop off the table, and, against my better judgment, I grab the handle and pull. It's locked. Why is it locked?

My heart does a little pitter-patter as I return to my seat, but the moment I'm back, the door opens, electrifying me. Someone has returned, but it's not the doctor. This man looks different. His wiry hair, rimmed glasses, and grey eyes are unsettling, and he isn't wearing a lab coat. I stand, unable to breathe.

"Miss Timewire?"

"Yes, that's me."

"You passed."

I blink, letting out a sigh of relief. I silently scold myself for the last time—one more exposed feeling. Now I'm an adult. Now I can take my place in society. My shoulders relax, but the man hasn't moved.

"Am I free to go?" I ask.

"Absolutely. Please, follow me. I will escort you out." He holds the door open and gestures me through. "Please, to the left."

I'm confused. The waiting room is to the right.

"Miss Timewire, please."

I nod my apology and swiftly turn to the left. I count twelve more doors. I want to ask him where we're going, but I can't.

The path to a perfect society is perfect obedience. I recite this to myself automatically. Besides, I passed.

The man stops at the thirteenth door. It's larger than the others.

"Please," he says. "In here."

I hesitate for the smallest fraction of a second before taking the handle and pushing the door in. It's heavy, so I lean into it, and now I'm certain. Something is very wrong.

I gasp, my self-control fracturing into jagged pieces. My hand slips from the door. There are a dozen people in front of me. And guns. There are guns.

My escort grabs my upper arm and pushes me into the room. His touch is foreign and unwelcome. Members of society do not touch one another—ever. Panic rises in my chest, choking me. I don't know what to do.

My escort is joined by two men in beige military uniforms. They seize me, pulling me toward what appears to be a strange metal throne.

"B-but I passed," I say, strangled as unfamiliar hands grasp at me, paralyzing me. This form of touch is horrifying.

"Unfortunately, Miss Timewire, you did not pass," the doctor says.

A scientist near the back of the room speaks up. "This is an anomaly. We haven't had a Diseased One in twelve years."

"What?" I say. "No. I'm not a Diseased One. I can't be. This has to be a mistake."

I stand, my body tingling limply in the military men's grip.

"We do not make mistakes, Miss Timewire," the scientist

says. "Will you strap her down, lieutenant? Securely please."

They push me onto the hard metal throne and fasten cuffs to my ankles and wrists. A gun is trained on my head, and my body goes numb. This is a mistake. This can't be real.

"Is this necessary?" someone asks.

"Of course. She's a Diseased One."

"But shouldn't we study her? Couldn't we?"

"No. This is a matter of world security—not one of your science experiments."

"But what about Maddy?"

"No. She must be taken care of. Now."

An icy sensation cascades over me. Taken care of? My face is tingling, and for the first time in my life, emotion, raw and pure, floods to the surface of my being. I have never experienced such a rush—and I'm terrified by the noise that escapes my mouth.

"This is a mistake. I'm not a Diseased One. I hate the Diseased Ones. I hate them!" I cry.

I pull desperately at the cuffs binding me to the metal throne. My heartbeat pumps into my ears and the tingling enters my limbs.

"Let's do this quickly, doctor," the scientist says, disregarding my outburst.

"Of course."

I pull against the restraints, tears falling down my face. They feel unfamiliar against my cheeks, unwanted and terrible, but utterly beyond my control.

"Please. I'm not a Diseased One. I'm not," I say, through

strangled tears. I can barely speak. "I h-hate them!"

The doctor ignores me and withdraws a large needle with green fluid. He flicks the end of it several times and pushes a small amount through the tip. It cascades over the metal and onto the glass rim.

"Let's clean this up quickly."

The needle hovers over my arm and my adrenaline peaks. My fingers stretch out, and in a snap of movement, everyone turns completely still—perfectly rigid, rooted to the spot.

"What are you doing to me?" the doctor with the syringe says. His eyes are bulging. "I can't move."

What?

"We need help in here," he says, panic fracturing his societal control. "We need help."

"No, wait," I say, clenching my right hand into a fist.

The doctor's jaw slams shut as if an invisible hand forced it to do so. I'm overwhelmed with an incredible amount of control.

I'm trembling. "What's happening to me?"

"Sound the alarm," someone says.

No. Something deep within me rears and my hands move in a flash, completely against my will. This time, every jaw in the room snaps shut.

"W-what? I don't know how I'm doing this. I—"

Then I stop dead. Shaking, with power coursing through every pore of my being, I experience the sensation once more: complete and utter control, as if suddenly, I know exactly what to do.

"Let me go," I say, commanding the man nearest me.

A boldness beyond my comprehension surges through my veins. It's as if the man is a puppet attached to the strings of my dancing fingertips. My restraints are gone. I stand. I don't know how much more adrenaline I can take, but something moves me to the door. I step into the hallway, guided by the mysterious force in my hands, and in a moment of clarity, I come to my senses.

I need to get out of here. Right now. But . . . what did I just do?

My mind is racing. Why are my hands tingling? How did I do that? Were they going to kill me? Were they actually going to kill me? I'm more terrified than I've ever been in my life, and everything has turned upside down. But there's one thing I know for sure.

I am a Diseased One, and that's a death sentence.

2

STAY CALM. DROP YOUR EXPRESSION. RIGHT NOW.

I make it to the end of the hall and walk back through the intake door. The next round of patients is waiting there, staring at me with wide eyes. I'm clearly not the nurse.

I mumble something incoherent as I move past them, trying not to show emotion, but the tingling in my palms and the thumping of my heart betray me. My mouth twitches into an expression before I can staunch it, and, against my will, my face transforms. I'm certain everyone in the room can see it.

Panic creeps over me. I have to stop. This isn't allowed.

A scrawny boy nearest the exit gawks at me with huge blue eyes. His muted countenance slips as I approach, and he stands, backing away from me. His control is splintered. I can't believe what I'm seeing. Is he afraid of me? But that thought is brushed aside by another, more sinister voice. It overpowers me, taking control of my mind.

He's in your way, Hollis.

Something moves my arm, and before I know it, my hand is aloft, palm pointing directly at the boy's chest. Fear rips across his face, and he stumbles backward, tripping over a chair.

Alarms explode about the room.

The sound is shrill and terrifying, and the boy jumps, pressing himself flat against the wall. *Move, Hollis. Now*, the voice says. I don't hesitate. I charge the door.

The intercom crackles to life. "Code black. Facility staff, this is a code black. We are in full lockdown. Shoot on sight. Repeat. Shoot on sight."

Go, it says, prodding me forward. I obey, slamming through the door and stumbling into the hall. Where is the lift? Was it to the left? Which way did I come from?

I try to remember my arrival, but the adrenaline pumping through my veins is desensitizing. The alarms are so piercing I can't think, so I clap my hands over my ears and run blindly down the endless hallway.

I round the first corner at breakneck speed and yelp as I crash into a petite, mousy-looking nurse. She screams, and we both end up in a heap on the floor.

"I'm—I'm sorry," I say, scrambling to my feet.

But the moment I'm up, she catches me off guard with a hard kick to the back of my ankle, and I crumple to the floor.

"You're not leaving, Hollis," she says, pulling herself up.

She steps onto my ankle with her full weight, and I scream. Blinding pain shoots up my leg, and the tingling in my hands intensifies.

I'm pinned to the floor, unable to move, and it takes me a

moment to recognize the shiny object that's thrust into my face. I'm staring into the barrel of a gun. The nurse's tiny hand is steady as she points it at my head. A fresh wave of panic rips through me. All I can think to do is throw my arms up to shield myself from the bullet that will end my life. I shut my eyes, cowering on the floor.

A few seconds pass by. Nothing happens, and then I hear the distinct clatter of metal hitting tile. The pressure on my ankle vanishes.

I open my eyes. The nurse is recoiling on the floor, shielding her face from me, as if *I* were the one pointing the gun at her. She is completely still—eerily still.

I lower my arms.

She lowers her arms.

I sit up.

She sits up.

What is happening?

"Demon," she says, spitting at me. Her blank face is flickering in and out of fear. She looks into my eyes, and for a second, we connect on an intimate human level, a shared moment of disquiet. But her emotion vanishes as quickly as it had come. "What are you doing to me?" she asks.

I shake my head. I have no idea. Every inch of my body is pulsating as something monstrous arises from within. The perplexing power surges through me.

"Level three!" the nurse screams. "She's on level three! Level—"

No. The hellish voice in my mind is back, and in a flash of movement, my hand clamps into a fist. The nurse's jaw slams shut like a steel trap. I've silenced her.

Stand up, it says to me. I obey.

"I'm sorry," I say, peering into her terrified eyes. She's completely still, sitting on the floor with her neck tilted up at an awkward angle. "I'm sorry . . . I—"

But I have nothing more to say. I need to move.

I hobble down the next hallway, wincing at the acute pain in my ankle. It thunders up my leg, nearly crippling me. I've never felt pain like this. I've never had to feel pain for long.

My face contorts into a grimace. I can't help it and I can't force it back. Pain promotes emotion. Pain is the enemy of control. But the panel on the wall of my housing unit will take it away. Just a little prick—that's all I need—and then I'll be able to command my features again.

Eyes streaming and palms sweating, I begin to run down the hallway, disregarding my throbbing ankle. A singular thought courses through my mind: I need to find the stairs.

With no regard for the ruckus I'm creating, I pull open every door I come to, hoping against hope that one of them will lead to the stairwell. I find it six doors down and lunge onto the marble steps. My heavy breathing echoes harshly against the walls of the enclosed space.

This is unreal. This has to be some kind of freakish nightmare—some sick joke. I should be home now. I should be celebrating my career assignment with my parents. I should be imagining the incredible future ahead of me. But I'm still here, and I'm running for my life.

I clatter down the remaining flight and burst into the main lobby, only to find several dozen military personnel standing between me and the exit. They're all armed, and every single weapon is pointed at my chest.

Terror rips through me like a jagged knife, crippling any resolve I have left. I'm going to die, and there is nothing I can do about it. What a strange concept—to know the exact moment of your death. It's exhilarating and frightening beyond words.

My palms are vibrating. I stand straight and relax my face. If I'm going to die, I will be standing, strong and without feeling—just as my mother and father taught me. I promised to make them proud, and that's exactly what I'm going to do.

The group of men moves in unison. This is it . . .

But nothing happens. None of them fire. None of them move. Instead, they all drop their guns to their sides and stand straight and proud. They're all standing . . . exactly like me.

A murmur runs through the group.

"I can't move."

"What is she doing to me?"

"Someone shoot her."

"I can't fire, sir."

"I can't move anything."

"Shoot her."

"Somebody shoot her."

Enough, the dark voice says. My hand shoots forward, viciously silencing every mouth in the room. *Walk through them*, it commands, pushing me forward, *now is your chance. Escape, Hollis.*

With an icy shiver, I move toward the men. I can't help myself. Something deep inside compels me. Instinct has become my faithful teacher—pure primal instinct.

You know what to do, so do it. They're in your way.

I yield to the mysterious entity. It directs my hands, and in a fluid motion, I push the men to each side of the room. They part straight down the middle. It's as if they are connected to the bizarre limb-controlling machine of my fingertips.

I walk through their midst, unable to believe it. The men are motionless. I fear that the spell will break and their guns will raise, but the group remains frozen in place, resolutely statuesque.

I lock eyes with the last man between me and the door. His pointed jaw is locked in place and his brown eyes are wide. His face searches mine, and just as with the nurse, we connect for a moment. His look holds genuine fear. He's afraid of me. He's looking at me like I'm a monster. But I'm not . . .

"I'm not a monster," I say.

My brow furrows. I pause in front of him. Looking deep into his watering eyes, I force my expression back to the blank stare I've practiced thousands of times. I want to show him that I'm not a monster. I'm a member of society. I'm just like him.

Get out.

The voice attacks my thoughts, and my hand explodes forward. The jab of movement is unnaturally quick, causing the man to jerk sideways. I've thrown him to the floor with the energy of my tingling palms, and his head slams into the nearest pillar. A resounding crack resonates through the room.

I gasp, clamping my hands over my mouth. The man lies motionless, his body sprawled across the marble.

Run, Hollis, the voice says, *run.*

I'm thrust toward the exit, led by the invisible power. I slam into the push bar and the glass doors fling open with a mighty crash. I don't look back. Running with the crazed frenzy of the command, I pelt down the smooth steps of the Testing Center. I need to get home.

3

THE STREETS ARE EMPTY AND THE SKY IS GRAY. I RUN FOR several blocks before slowing down and coming to a halt near the transit stop. My chest is heaving, and my lungs burn. I gasp for air, trying to ease the stitch in my side by pressing on it firmly with my fingertips.

Advertisements flash onto the screen directly in front of me. The bolded titles of the merchandise are obnoxiously bright. I squint, holding my hand up to shield my eyes.

All New Holo-Tablets. Get this smart and flashy updated hologram technology. More storage! Higher resolution! Better quality!

Flash.

Smart Vacuum. This fantastic cleaning device will dust your dwelling. No operation required. It's a green, mean, do-it-itself cleaning machine.

Flash.

Get your Presto-Fold. Tired of folding the laundry yourself? Then buy this self-folding wonder. It's never been simpler. It's never been faster.

Presto!

Flash.

The advertisements vanish, and my picture appears on the huge screen facing the street. My heart drops into my stomach. I stumble backward, tripping over my feet and falling toward the rough concrete. My hands smack into the pavement with an unpleasant crunch. It's as if someone has punched me in the gut.

I stare at my own face, plain and pallid, my thin blonde hair tucked into a neat bun, my hazel eyes muted with control. It's the photo from my citizen's card.

I panic, scraping across the ground as I stand up. My name is flashing on the screen. The bold red print sneers out at the street, like a viper ready to strike.

Alert. Escaped convict. Extremely dangerous. If sighted, do not approach. Contact your local authority. Any information regarding the whereabouts of Hollis Timewire must be reported immediately.

"No," I say, still fighting to breathe properly. If this alert is on the street screens, that means it's on every screen—everywhere. "I'm not a monster. I'm not like them. This is a mistake."

There must be something wrong with the Test.

"This isn't right." I'm attempting to verbalize the craze of thoughts in my head. "I'm a society member. I can't be diseased. I can't be."

A burst of noise near the end of the block sets my teeth on edge, and I spin around, jumping nearly a foot off the ground. My ankle spasms and I wince, pulling my weight off of it. I peer around the edge of the transit stop. People are walking toward me.

My pulse quickens. I can't be seen. They'll report me.

If I can get to my dwelling, my parents will know what to do. My father can sort this out. He's the head of the military elite. If anyone can help me, it's him. He'll fix this.

"It's alright," I say, desperately trying to keep calm. "Everything will be okay. Just go home."

I take a tentative step forward, and pain thunders up my leg. Gritting my teeth, I begin to limp down the sidewalk, pushing through the throbbing discomfort.

The group is close now, so I keep my head down and tuck my hands into my pockets. I can't run from them and I can't hide. All I can do is stare at my feet and hope they don't recognize me. To my relief, they stop several yards ahead of me and cross the street, whispering to each other in hushed tones and pointing up at the broadcast.

My stomach squirms, but I keep my eyes glued to the sidewalk. I move away from the large screen, and when my back is safely to them, I look up.

My heartbeat spikes with every labored step. Now that the adrenaline has diminished, I can barely walk.

Five minutes later, I hobble up the familiar cobblestone path and slam my hand against the outside panel. It flashes and the door admits me. I slip through, utterly exhausted, and slide down against the polished wood. Salted sweat is pouring from my brow into my eyes, making them sting. I wipe my face with the sleeve of my blazer.

"Hollis? Is that you?"

My mother's soft voice electrifies me and I jump to my feet.

"Mother."

Quickly suppressing my expression, I walk into the living room, and my heart drops. Our wall screen is off. It's not supposed to be. It's never off. Why would she turn it off? My stomach flips. She must have seen the announcement—my face, my citizen's card.

"Hollis."

My mother's tone is slightly elevated. I meet her gaze and hurriedly press my uniform flat. My cream shirt is half untucked from my skirt, and stray wisps of hair tickle my forehead. I brush them aside, squaring my posture to look as proper as possible.

Her thin lips press into a line. I can tell that she's alarmed by my appearance, but her face doesn't flicker. Her control is pristine, and her expressionlessness grounds me.

What can I say to her? I need to tell her. But how?

Her eyes wander to my blackened palms.

"I felt like a run," I say, blurting out the first thing that comes to mind. I push my tone back. It's too emotional. "I tripped and fell."

"It is not becoming of a young lady to run about the streets, Hollis. You are an adult now."

I squint at her, puzzled. Maybe she didn't see the announcement.

"I apologize," I say automatically. "Where is father?"

"He is out on work-related business."

"Out?"

I'm fighting to control my voice, but it's slipping.

"Hollis, go clean yourself up," she says firmly, fussing with the folds of my shirt. She glances at the door and then back to me.

"Yes, but mother," I say, batting her hands away. My voice catches in my throat in an alarming fashion. "I need to tell you something. I need to . . . to tell you something that sounds crazy. I . . ."

I'm making no sense, but how can I possibly say this? I don't know what to do.

My mother's delicate fingertips clasp together, and her brow pulls back ever so slightly. I've seen this look before. I'm expressing too much. Her posture and poise reprimand me.

"Hollis, it is time you learn to control yourself. This kind of behavior was acceptable when you were younger, but now you are sixteen. You've graduated. You should not express so much—even within your own home," she says. "I am disappointed that you have returned from the Test like this. Honestly, I don't know what has gotten into you. Now, go clean yourself up."

She says this with perfect control, her tone clear and directed, but her words have pierced me. She's disappointed in me? But she doesn't understand. She must not have seen the alert. Our wall screen is off. She doesn't know.

My mother glances at the door again, and my heartbeat picks up. I have to tell her, but . . .

"Why is the wall screen off?" I ask.

"That is none of your concern," she says, fidgeting with the sleeves of my blazer. "Obey me at once and go wash up."

"But mother—"

"Hollis—"

"I need to tell you something. It's important."

"If this is about your career assignment, we can discuss it over dinner," she says, looking to the door once again.

I push her hands away. "It's not. Where's father?"

She ignores my question. "Then go wash yourself up."

Hurry. The menacing voice in my head is back, and my fingertips begin to tingle. My heart jumps into my throat, and for a moment, I'm suffocated with adrenaline.

"Mother, please," I say, abandoning my attempts to remain controlled. "I have to tell you something. At the Testing Center, I—"

But before I can say another word, my mother speaks over me in a frightening manner. Her face curls with anger, and her hands tighten into fists.

"Hollis, enough! Enough of this childish behavior. I will not stand here and have you blatantly disobey me. Go wash yourself up this instant."

My mouth parts in shock. Stiffening silence hangs between us for several seconds, and my mother looks away from me. She is clearly appalled with herself, but something about this moment clicks in my mind.

"You keep looking at the door. Where's father?" I say, pulling my mother's hands into my own. I sound terrified and I hate it, but I've lost all societal control.

"Business . . ." she says, mumbling under her breath.

"You're lying to me." I squeeze her hands tightly as my mouth turns dry. "Please. Where is he?"

She says nothing, but her splintered face replaces her words. I've never seen her wear an expression before. She's lost control . . . she doesn't even look like my mother.

"You're scaring me." I drop her hands and back away.

Time's running out, the voice says, and a sudden rushing sensation enters my limbs. The horrible tingling is back. It extends from my chest to my entire body, filling me to the brim.

I have to do it. I have to tell her. Now.

I open my mouth to speak, but a jarring noise cuts me off. It's the sound of metal slamming against hinges—the kind of sound that only comes from one thing. Military trucks.

"No," I say, shaking my head. "No. Please, wait."

I sprint to the front of our dwelling and peer through the window. Half a dozen military trucks are gathered outside. I spin around, stricken, and my voice falls into a tone I've never used before.

"I failed the Test, but you don't understand," I say, speaking rapidly. My eyes are streaming with uncontrolled tears. "There's been a mistake. I'm not a Diseased One. They made a mistake and now they're trying to kill me. Mother, please. You have to help me. Father can help me! He can talk to them! Is that where he is? Is he talking to them?"

She backs away from me. "Hollis, be reasonable. You need to go with them."

"Why?"

"They are here to help you."

"They're going to kill me," I say, running over and clinging to her. My voice is wildly beyond my control, moving through inflections I never thought existed. "They have guns. They're going to shoot me, but it's a mistake. They've made a mistake. Mother, please, you have to help me!"

"Nonsense," she says. "They are going to help you. They are not going to shoot you."

"It's true. Please, you have to believe me. You have to! Please, mother, don't let them take me!"

Boom.

The pounding at the front entrance of my dwelling sends new waves of terror ripping through me. The door is shaking, and my fingertips ignite. My mother, taking the momentary distraction in stride, pulls her hands out of mine and backs away from me once more.

Her eyes, dulled with control, meet my own. "Hollis, you need to go with them. They are here to help you."

I turn toward the door, unable to stop myself. The tingling reaches my face, and I hold my hand out in front of me. The ominous power has overtaken me, and I stand, ready to meet the onslaught of weapons.

The door bursts open. A dozen men in dark camouflage spill into the room, and my mother gasps at the sight of their machine guns. Just as in the Testing Center, every barrel is aimed at my chest. My stance adjusts instinctually, arm aloft and palm forward. I can't stop myself.

The tingling consumes me.

Then, as if in some freakish dream, a girl materializes out of thin air. She stands at my side and grasps my shoulder in a vice-like grip. I don't even have time to gasp before I'm pulled into oblivion, and everything around me is compressed into complete and utter darkness.

4

A BURST OF HARSH, UNYIELDING LIGHT BLINDS ME. MY FEET scrape across the floor, and I stumble forward. I've just been crushed.

I take several heaving breaths, and when I come to my senses, I whirl around to find concrete walls and bright fluorescent lighting in every direction. I am no longer in my dwelling.

I back away from the girl who grabbed me. She looks like she's several years older than me. Her straight black hair cascades from behind her shoulder, and her dark eyes glisten. The expression on her face paints the oddest picture against her olive skin. I press my back against the wall.

"Where am I? Who are you? How . . . how did we . . . ?"

I don't even know what I want to ask.

"My name is Tiffany Chang. You can call me Tiff for short, if you like," she says, panting.

"Wh-what did you do? How did we get here?"

I glance around, half expecting this to be some crazy illusion, but nothing fades away. The tingling in my hands is gone, and I can't feel the strange power anymore.

"I teleported us," she says. "And just in the nick of time too."

"You did . . . you what?" I say, stammering.

I rub my eyes, as if somehow this could wake me up, but nothing happens. I shake my head, staring at the girl. Her face twists into a grimace, and then a strange sort of grin. She's showing emotion. She's expressing herself . . .

My stomach drops. Society members don't do that.

"Are you a . . . a Diseased One?" I ask.

She gives me a sad little smile, cocking her head to the side.

"I had to bring you here," she says. "I'm going to get Jonah. He'll explain everything. I promise. I'll be right back."

She strides to the metal door at the end of the small room and slips through it. It clangs shut, and the sound echoes harshly off the seemingly impenetrable walls. A loud click issues from the handle.

"Hey!" I run to the door and pull. It's locked. "Where am I?"

The acoustics of the room magnify my voice. I've startled myself. I hate yelling. I need to stay controlled. I back away from the door, attempting to gain composure over my thumping pulse. I relax my face, and this simple act gives me an incredible amount of comfort.

She didn't say no. I asked her if she was a Diseased One, and she didn't say no. I run my hands through my hair. This is bad—really bad. There are more Diseased Ones? How many are there? Are they planning a second Terror War? Does the government know?

I shudder. The Terror War left millions dead. A hundred years ago, the Diseased Ones tried to take over the world, and they almost won. I have to get out of here. I have to warn the government. It's my civic duty. People need to know about this before it's too late. History must never repeat itself.

A shiver runs through me, chilling me to the bone. My family is in danger. What am I going to do?

I pace the length of the room, running my hand across the rough wall. My bun has come loose, and I shove the stray blonde wisps out of my face. I turn back toward the door. Maybe I can make a run for it when they come back. I have to get out of here.

I tense my fingers, and for a fraction of a second, I will myself to feel that all-consuming power, but nothing happens.

"What am I doing?"

I stare at my palms, a deep sense of self-loathing emanating from my gut. I'm not like them. I will never be like them. They're evil. Monsters. Murderers. I'm a society member, the government made a mistake, and when I tell them that there are more Diseased Ones, they will forget about my Test. They'll make things right. They'll fix this.

Click.

I jump, backing away from the door and flattening myself against the wall. My desire to run wilts.

Tiffany Chang has returned along with three others: a

dark-haired middle-aged man, a blond boy, and a heavily freckled red-headed girl. The last two look like they're my age. My hands tense up, and for one wild moment, I fear that the group in front of me will go rigid, but nothing happens.

The dark-haired man approaches me, and I shrink back. My heartbeat pounds in my ears, and I'm completely frozen, unable to think.

"My name is Jonah Luxent," he says.

I simply stare at him. The man's face looks kind, and his brown eyes are somber, but his strong features overpower this. His stubble beard catches the harsh lighting, and I look away.

"And this is Ashton Teel and Rosalie Simmons," he says, pointing first to the blond boy on his left and then to the red-headed girl on his right.

I can't speak. It's as if I've been struck dumb.

"I'm sure you have a lot of questions," Jonah says.

My mouth closes. I'm disgusted and terrified. I'm standing in a concrete room with four Diseased Ones, and I'm completely overwhelmed. All of their faces hold deep-laden concern—even worry. They can't control themselves. My heartbeat thunders so violently that tiny stars surface in my peripheral vision.

What are they going to do to me? Torture me? Kill me? Hold me hostage as a pawn in their subversive and murderous political games?

I try to swallow the lump in my throat, but I choke on it.

"You're all Diseased Ones," I say, after several moments of pin-drop silence. It isn't a question. It's a statement.

"There's a lot we must discuss," Jonah says calmly. "I'm just here to talk. I'm not going to hurt you."

"I don't believe you."

I retreat until the cold concrete is at my back, and I lean against it so fervently that I nearly lose my balance. I adjust my footing, all the while keeping my gaze on the man in front of me.

"You don't have to believe me. It won't make it any less true," he says.

"How did I get here?" I ask, my eyes darting about the room.

"I teleported us," Tiffany says, stepping forward.

I snap. "Why did you do that?"

"You're like us," she says. "You have an—"

"I'm not like you," I retort with all the venom I can muster. I scold myself, deadening my tone and changing my face to match. I'm a society member, and I'm going to act like one. I say the next words with so little emotion that even my mother would be proud. "I'll never be like you. You're evil. You're all murderers, and I hate you."

There is a moment of uncomfortable quiet, but Ashton Teel breaks it, stepping between Tiffany and me.

"She just saved your life," he says, interjecting himself into the conversation. "How about a 'thank you'?"

His tone is revolting—so much feeling in it. It's disgusting. His thick eyebrows and haughty features catch my attention, and his watery grey eyes hold a reproachful look. His face is just like his voice—too emotional.

"Like I said, we have many things to discuss with you, Hollis," Jonah says.

My lower lip trembles. "How do you know my name?"

Jonah looks slightly amused. "By now the whole world knows it, if I'm not mistaken."

"I... where am I?" I ask, trying to move past this disconcerting statement. I have more pressing matters to deal with—for one, the fact that there are more Diseased Ones.

"We are in an underground facility, a compound if you will," Jonah says. "This is where we live."

"Why? Planning another round of slaughtering millions of people? Need a secret base to scheme?"

I speak with more daring than I normally would. My ingrained emotional control is broken by the events of today, and I'm finding it increasingly difficult to behave properly. My mother would be ashamed.

"No," Jonah says, quite softly. "Hollis, I'm going to tell you something that will be difficult to hear, and I want you to know that we will respect your reaction. This will take time."

I stare at him for several seconds. Respect my reaction? I'm not going to react. That's what he wants. I've read all about the Diseased Ones in school. They want to suffocate the society member in me by appealing to my emotions. But emotion leads to conflict, and conflict leads to war. Wars have been fought over hate, jealousy, power, wealth—even love. Keeping people neutral guarantees equality and peace. War, conflict, and strife have been eradicated because expressing yourself isn't allowed. Not anymore. Civilization has finally got it right, and I won't let them change me. It's not going to happen.

"What do you want with me?" I say, gritting my teeth to keep my face blank.

Rosalie Simmons answers in Jonah's stead. "We want to tell you the truth."

My eyes move to her pink, freckled face as she tucks a strand of fiery red hair behind her ear.

"All I ask is that you listen to what I have to say," Jonah says.

I shake my head, pressing myself against the cold stone. "I don't want to hear what you have to say. You don't deserve to be heard. You're a Diseased One."

Ashton scoffs. "Well, that's not really up to you, is it?" He leans back against the wall to my left, tucking one leg up and resting his foot against the concrete.

"Ashton," Rosalie says, rebuking him with her tone.

"I hate it when they call us that," he says defensively. "We're not diseased. It's bull—"

"Ashton," Jonah says, cutting him off. "Not now."

Ashton falls silent, folding his arms across his chest and glowering at me.

"Hollis." Jonah's soft tone brings my attention back. "I'm going to tell you something, and it will sound absurd, but all you need to do right now is listen. The government has lied to you. There is a very different story we need to share with you about what happened a hundred years ago."

I blink. He's right. It already sounds absurd—absolutely stupid. I nearly laugh aloud. I took my education seriously, and

I know for a fact that this is a trick.

"You're lying," I say, trying to maintain a calm and confident voice. "I'm not a child. You can't trick me. The government doesn't lie to the citizens of the world. They help us. They protect and defend us against animals like you. I know what you are."

Tiffany's mouth twitches into the sad little smile again. I look away from her.

Jonah continues. "A hundred years ago, there were a lot of people like us, Hollis."

"I know," I say, dead-pan. "You killed eighty-seven million people, in cold blood, and then tried to take over the world."

Jonah disregards my words with a patient pause before continuing. "There were many people like us. People with abilities."

"Abilities?"

Jonah smiles, and my stomach churns. "We're not diseased in the way that you've been taught. It's not simply bad blood. The biomarker is only half of the story."

I scoff out loud, losing my composure. My brow furrows and my lip curls. "Half the story? What are you talking about?"

"We have powers," Ashton says, cutting in with a stiffened reply. "Not bad blood."

This time, I do laugh aloud. The noise is gruesome. I need to stop expressing myself, but I can't help it. Ashton's remark is too absurd, and although I'm afraid, I forge ahead, speaking with boldness.

"I'm not stupid. If you have the biomarker, you have bad

blood. Bad blood affects the brain. Your delusions are an unfortunate side effect of the biomarker."

"That's just what you've been told, but we do have powers. I could show you mine," Rosalie says, taking a few steps forward, her red hair cascading over her shoulders.

My short-lived bravery vanishes like a flimsy puff of smoke. "Get away from me," I say, strangled.

Fresh waves of panic spring up within me. I'm trapped against the wall. Petrified.

"Rosalie," Jonah says, raising his hand up. "Not now."

She retreats a few paces, looking defeated.

Jonah, their elder and clearly the leader of this trio, continues. "It was an exciting time. We were discovering ourselves and what we were capable of."

Like murder.

"Our ancestors had incredible abilities, and this produced something wonderful. In a society completely void of expression, we found feeling and passion beyond anything we could comprehend."

I feel sick. It's because of their bad blood. Feeling is vile. Emotion is bad.

"We lived under the radar for a while, but we could only keep our abilities a secret for so long. Eventually, society noticed that we were different, and that's when things got bad."

"The Terror War," I say.

"There never was a war," Jonah says soberly.

I stare at him, eyes blazing. My hands are balled into fists, and my heartbeat is drumming relentlessly against my chest. "You're a liar."

A strange buzzing enters my limbs, but it's not the same as the tingling in the Testing Center. This sensation is cold and numbing, as if I've been dunked into a pool of icy water. He's lying. I want to say something. I have to.

Jonah's eyes turn somber as he continues. "The government offered to make arrangements with us under false pretenses. They told us they wanted to learn about our kind and help us develop our abilities. That was a lie."

The government doesn't lie. I bite my lower lip, fighting to keep myself collected.

"They rounded us up by the thousands and slaughtered us. No warning," Jonah says, and his expression deepens into something I can't explain.

He looks . . . sad? It has to be an act—a trick.

"Our abilities produce feeling and tremendous power, and that's something the world couldn't have," he says. "We were a mistake of nature that the government couldn't afford to keep."

Well, at least I agree with him on that one. The Diseased Ones are a mistake of nature, an unfortunate evolutionary accident. Bad blood. They went crazy and tried to kill us all. Emotion causes even the most sane and docile of creatures to become violent. It's been scientifically proven. I've been educated. I know better.

"They didn't see us as people, so a hundred years ago, they massacred us . . . a genocide against an entire race of people out of fear."

How could he say such things? How can he slander the government so freely? I want to speak out against this, but I can't find the right words. My voice catches and my chest constricts, suffocating me.

Tiffany joins the conversation, her dark eyes staring into mine. "The people that escaped went into hiding and . . . well, most of us live here now, in this compound. We believe there are only a few hundred of us left. We've been searching for people with abilities ever since—to offer them protection and peace. We've found a few, but . . ."

I shake my head, finding my voice at last, and with it, a small dose of courage. I have to defend my government.

"You're lying. There was a war. The government would never murder. The Diseased Ones murder. You murdered millions of us," I say, the heat rising in my cheeks. "There's documentation. There's evidence. You can't just make up a story like that. There's proof for the Terror War. Footage. Photographs. Things that—"

"Didn't they try to kill you?" Ashton asks. My eyes snap to him. "The doctors in the Testing Center? They were going to inject you. And then they tried to shoot you, right? There were machine guns, Hollis, and they were all pointed at you."

I stand speechless, my mind racing for an explanation.

"How . . . how do you know about . . . no. No, they wouldn't have," I say, standing my ground. My voice fluctuates as I speak. "The government doesn't lie. The government doesn't kill. They protect us."

I have to stand up against these monsters. I have to. But my heartbeat is thundering again. There's so much adrenaline coursing through me that I'm faint.

"Hollis." Tiffany's soft voice cuts at me. "Your parents turned you in. Those men in your dwelling . . . they were going to shoot you for failing the Test. You have the biomarker. You know what that means."

"No," I say, shaking my head fervently. "No. They wouldn't. You're lying. They were going to help me, and you took me away from them."

I'm vibrating from head to foot. The cold, unyielding numbness is working its way into my fingertips and face. Everything is buzzing. My mother's words echo in my mind: "Hollis, you need to go with them. They are here to help you."

Why didn't I listen to her?

"Take me back," I say, staring directly at Tiffany. My tone is alarming, and my face contorts into a new expression. "Take me back, right now."

"Hollis," Tiffany says. "I'm sorry, but I can't."

"Take me back!" I say, half yelling, half choking. "No. Today, my life changes for the better. Today, I become a citizen of the world . . . Today I . . . Today I become accountable . . ."

I don't know how to process such pure emotion. Stars pop in and out of my vision, and I begin to hyperventilate.

"Today I become accountable to the world. Today I pledge my allegiance to the government. I pledge my skills to the service of my place here," I say, clutching my shirt. My knees give out, and I slump to the floor. "Today I help change the world."

I'm trembling, glaring at them in disgust as my eyes stream with angry tears. What is happening to me? Why can't I control myself?

"I think that's enough for today," Jonah says. "This is a lot to take in. You've had an incredibly traumatic day."

His tone is revolting. I flare out my fingertips, but nothing happens. Good. I don't want to feel that strange power ever again. I hate it, and I hate them.

Jonah looks down at me, his brown eyes deepening. His brow wrinkles and a profoundly troubled expression fills his face. I don't know what to call it. I've never seen someone look at me this way. There must be a word for it.

"I'm sorry this happened to you, Hollis. I truly am," he says. "Try to get some rest. I'll have Tiffany and Ashton bring you some food and a mat to sleep on."

There is a brief pause, and then the four of them exit. I hear the harsh click of the lock, and I lean against the wall, completely drained. All of the energy in me has died. I hold my hands on my head and tuck my feet close to my body, making myself as small as possible.

Maybe I'll wake up tomorrow and this will all have been some terrible nightmare. I'll wake up to my mother's gentle, blank face. I'll hear my father's muted tone. I'll wake up to find that I haven't taken the Test yet. No biomarker. No needles. No guns. No Diseased Ones.

But something deep within me recognizes the reality of this moment. I failed the Test, I've been kidnapped by Diseased Ones, and I'm completely at their mercy.

Happy birthday Hollis, I think to myself, you're probably not going to make it to your next one.

5

"SHE'S SEVERELY BRAINWASHED."

My eyes flutter open, and an unpleasant sensation makes my stomach squirm. I wake from my fitful sleep to soft voices issuing from just beyond the door.

The conversation is faint, but I can hear them. Two of my captors are outside. It's Tiffany Chang, the girl who kidnapped me, and Jonah Luxent, the man who spawned the horrific lie about the Terror War.

"We've never rescued anyone straight from society before, have we?" Tiffany asks.

"No," Jonah says. "Everyone we've extracted has been in hiding."

I jump to my feet, and silently make my way to the crevice between the frame and door. I press my ear to it.

"And the people in hiding already know what's going on. They understand the true history of this," Tiffany adds.

"Exactly."

There's a long pause.

"Honestly, I never expected a new person with an ability to manifest. This is a unique situation." Jonah's tone is solemn. "We've never dealt with anything like it before."

"And she doesn't know anything about her ability yet," Tiffany says.

"I know." His tone deepens. "But whatever she has is extremely rare, and quite powerful. I don't know how she managed to escape the military at the Testing Center. There were easily thirty men."

There's another extended pause. I want to hear more, and I loathe myself for it. Curiosity is highly discouraged in school. Don't question things. The path to a perfect society is perfect obedience. It's ingrained in me, but I can't help myself. I need to know what's going on. I readjust my position, practically hugging the door.

"So what do we do?" Tiffany asks. "How do we approach this?"

"We give her time, and we grant her patience," Jonah says. "She's just been ripped away from her life. She's terrified and alone, and on top of that, she's with people like us."

"What do you mean?"

"All her life, we've been painted as evil and murderous. She's known nothing else. From her point of view, we're liars and we're dangerous."

I scoff. Do they actually think I'll believe their story? I know what they are. There's proof—legitimate, historical, documented proof for the Terror War. There are eye-witness accounts. There are pictures. There is street cam footage from the Capitol. I've seen clips of Area 19 in flames—my streets, the shining Capitol itself, burned to the ground. I've seen the photographs of dead bodies—men, women, and children senselessly murdered in cold blood. Of course they're liars—treacherous, hideous, deadly liars.

Tiffany sighs. "That's so sad. Do you think she'll come around?"

"She will likely remain on the defensive for a long time," he says. "She's going to have to learn to do life over again, and to be honest, I don't know if she'll ever change her mind about us."

"But they were going to kill her," Tiffany says. She sounds frustrated. "If I didn't get to her dwelling when I did, they would have shot her."

"It's a miracle she made it to her house."

"There were so many guns, Jonah. I was afraid I was going to get shot. We barely made it out of there in time. Why can't she see that?"

"All we can do is be patient with her. We need to show her kindness and grant her as much time as she needs."

Their footsteps scrape just outside. They're moving closer to me, and I retreat, panicked, but I push the feeling back and approach the door again, holding my head to it. I need to hear this.

"What if we show her what we can do? What if we show her that we're good?" Tiffany asks. I can hear a tinge of desperation in her voice.

"Unfortunately, I don't think it's going to be that easy."

"Let me get Rosalie. Rosalie can show Hollis. I think it might help."

"Tiffany, I'm not sure that—"

"You heard Hollis," she says. "She was going on and on about proof and documentation. That's what she'll respond to. I know it. Please? Rosalie can show her. She can use her ability to help."

Fear floods every inch of my body. I step back from the door. Show me what? I don't want to see it. I don't want any part of it.

"I don't know," Jonah says after a brief moment. "It's possible, but it may be too early for that."

"Jonah, Rosalie's ability is perfect for this. Hollis says she's read about the Terror War. She says she has proof. Well . . . we have proof too."

Tiffany's tone is resolute. The silence that follows this statement sends me into a frenzy. My heart is pounding so loudly I'm surprised they can't hear it.

"Very well, but take Ashton with you. We don't need any unnecessary injuries. Hollis can't control her ability yet. Perhaps, in time, I can teach her to do so, if she is willing."

Is that why they've locked me up? Because they don't know what I can do? Because they think I'll hurt them? I'm covered in sweat, and my clammy hands curl into fists. I don't know what to do. I don't want to see Rosalie. I want to go home. I have to find a way to escape.

I move against the back wall and slide to the floor, hugging my knees. They were going to inject me in the Testing Center, but what if that green syringe was the answer to all of this? Wouldn't the government know what to do if they found someone with the biomarker? They must have a way to restore such a person—to reintegrate them into society.

I shudder, clutching my chest. What if I've lost the only opportunity to return to a normal life? What if I never get to see my parents again? I feel sick. I just want to go home.

Click. The door opens and I jump to my feet.

Tiffany enters, followed by Ashton Teel and Rosalie Simmons, whose unkempt fiery red hair splays playfully around her shoulders.

"Hollis," Tiffany says. "How are you doing?"

I don't answer. I try to keep myself impassive, perfect. I want to be an example. I want to show them what a society member looks like. I won't give in to their feeling. It's vile.

"I know you don't trust us, and you think we're evil. I understand that," she says. "And I know you don't believe us—about the Terror War. And that's okay."

Again, I don't say a word.

"I've been thinking about what you said, about having proof. I respect that. You want the facts. That's admirable."

Flattery. She's trying to flatter me. Horrid creature.

"But we have proof too. We can show—"

I cut across her. "I don't want you to."

"You can see for yourself," Ashton says, staring at me with his watery grey eyes.

See what for myself? Some freak show? Their brain

mutations? Their delusion about having powers? What if they hurt me? I shake my head, backing away from them. I'm terrified, and I'm having difficulty suppressing it. Emotion is collecting in the pit of my stomach, threatening to spill across my face.

Rosalie takes a small step forward. "Let me show you what I can do."

"No," I say, raising my voice. I stop and then speak in a precise, controlled manner. "No, thank you."

"Rosalie, maybe if you tell her what it is first?" Tiffany suggests, brushing her long black hair over her shoulder.

Rosalie nods and then retreats a few paces, giving me space. "I can see people's stories—their life. When I'm around someone, I can absorb their history into my hands."

I stare at her blankly.

"I'm like a history book," she adds. "I collect people's memories, and I hold on to them." Rosalie places her hands out in front of her thin body. Her fingertips dance across the air in a beautiful arc. "And I can show these memories to others."

A golden bird bursts from Rosalie's fingertips. I gasp, nearly toppling over as I watch it soar gleefully around the room. The bird is misty and slightly translucent. It chirps blissfully, moving with a carefree energy.

Rosalie's hands flutter, and a silvery figure materializes. It appears to be a younger Rosalie. She laughs, chasing the misty bird.

I watch, mesmerized by the animal's beauty. I've never seen anything so innocent—so majestic. It's enrapturing. Something powerful wells up within me. I'm exhilarated by the sight of this small creature, but it's not the same exhilaration I experienced at the Testing Center. This is different. It's pure joy. I don't have anything to compare it to.

I walk toward the bird, my hand outstretched. I want to touch it—to appreciate its charm up close. But before I reach it, Rosalie pulls her hands together, and the two translucent figures vanish into her palms.

I drop my hand and stop in my tracks. The feeling has vanished, and my sense of societal obligation returns. I retreat, moving away from Rosalie.

What just happened? What did she do to me? How did she make me feel that . . . that feeling?

"That's one of my memories," she says.

I stand there, speechless. I don't know if I should be amazed or horrified. I don't even know if I've imagined the whole thing. This girl did something to me. But before I can organize my thoughts, she continues.

"I want to show you one of your memories so that you know I'm telling the truth. I show things exactly as they happen, and Hollis, I'm truly sorry that this happened to you."

She lifts her fingers again, and to my surprise, something like black ink spills out into the forms of a dozen military men. Their machine guns are drawn, and they are outside my dwelling.

All of the air is sucked from my lungs, and the room turns icy cold. Rosalie's hands swipe sideways, and my living room materializes, shifting into focus. In a twist of movement, a delicate figure seeps from her palms.

My jaw drops. It's me. I'm staring directly into my own petrified face. A moment later, my mother joins the scene.

I hear myself speak. "Why is the wall screen off?"

"That is none of your concern. Obey me at once and go wash up."

"But mother—"

"Hollis—"

"I need to tell you something. It's important."

I gape at the scene, unable to believe my eyes. I stagger back, completely crippled by the misty figure bearing my resemblance. It's me. That's me. This is my living room. That's my mother. How is this possible? Am I going mad?

"If this is about your career assignment, we can discuss it over dinner," my mother says.

"It's not. Where's father?"

"Then go wash yourself up."

"Mother, please. I have to tell you something. At the Testing Center, I—"

"Hollis, enough! Enough of this childish behavior. I will not stand here and have you blatantly disobey me. Go wash yourself up this instant."

The memory darkens, and Rosalie's fingertips shudder as another dose of black mist spreads into the room. Impending dread hangs in the atmosphere, and I clench my hands together, unable to look away. A horrible sensation creeps into me.

"You keep looking at the door. Where's father?" my translucent twin says.

"Business . . ."

"You're lying to me. Please. Where is he?"

I stare at myself in disbelief. Why am I asking about my father? Why haven't I told her about the Test? I'm wasting time.

"You're scaring me."

The memory shakes, and the temperature of the room drops dramatically. I hear the distinct bang of twisting metal. The military vans are outside my dwelling.

"No." My own voice sends chills down my spine. "No. Please, wait."

The memory grows, breathing like a creature about to attack its prey. The scene appears to unfold on fast-forward. It's surreal—I'm watching myself panic. The misty figure in front of me retains absolutely no control, and it's sickening.

"Hollis, be reasonable. You need to go with them," my mother says.

She's right. I need to go with them.

"Why?"

"They are here to help you."

I watch the memory, helplessly. My mother wouldn't lie to me. She wouldn't, and I'm behaving recklessly beyond control.

The frightened tone that escapes my lips is disgusting. "They're going to kill me. They have guns. They're going to shoot me, but it's a mistake. They've made a mistake. Mother, please, you have to help me!"

My mother's reply is controlled, but frigid. "Nonsense. They are going to help you. They are not going to shoot you."

Why am I refusing to listen to her? What's wrong with me? How have I lost all control?

My misted double clings to my mother. "It's true. Please, you have to believe me. You have to! Please, mother, don't let them take me!"

The room trembles, bringing the temperature down a few more degrees. The cold is unbearable, but something occurs to me. The military men are going to burst into my living room. In a few seconds, I'm going to see what happened. This is it. This will prove that the government wasn't going to hurt me.

My mother's dulled voice issues from the memory. "Hollis, you need to go with them. They are here to help you."

This is it.

The scene swells, overtaking the entire room. The blackened military men flood in, and my translucent doppelganger raises her hand, palm forward, ready to die. The look on my own face is alarming. I've never stared directly at myself, and I've never seen my own expression before. Disheveled blonde hair, a pallid complexion, and deep hazel eyes stare back at me. The extreme feeling plastered on my thin face is gut-wrenching.

The guns raise, my mother gasps, and right on cue, Tiffany's silvery outline appears, grabbing hold of me and vanishing with a pop.

The memory expands like a shock wave, throwing me to the floor with an unpleasant smack.

Boom.

The guns fire, shattering the silver-black mist into a thousand peppery pieces.

I gasp, throwing my hands up to shield myself from the spray of debris, but the mist contracts, slipping back into Rosalie's palms. The memory is gone, and the room is empty.

No one speaks. I'm trembling so violently that I can't stand. They fired the guns? Why? Why did they shoot at me? There's been a mistake. I shake my head. It can't be true. It can't.

"I'm sorry I had to show you that," Rosalie says, hanging her head. "I truly am . . . but now you know I can show you the truth."

My mind is racing at an incomprehensible speed. The memory isn't right. Rosalie changed it. That's not what happened—that's not even my memory. They can't have fired at me because I wasn't there anymore. Tiffany kidnapped me. I never saw them fire . . .

"I can show you what really happened a hundred years ago," Rosalie says. "You want proof, right? Well, you can see it for yourself. I can show you what happened. No tricks. Just the truth."

6

"How?"

The question escapes from me so quickly that I don't have time to stop myself. They have piqued my curiosity. I want to see more. They haven't proven anything, but the inky scene that formed from Rosalie's fingertips is burned into my memory. The military men in my dwelling, my mother's shocked face, Tiffany's sudden appearance—all of it happened, but the ending didn't. They can't have fired at me.

"You changed it," I say, slinking back against the concrete.

"Changed what?" Rosalie asks.

"You changed the memory," I say defiantly. "They didn't shoot at me."

She falters a moment before shaking her head. "I can't do that."

"Typical society member," Ashton says, snarling. He runs his hands through his dirty blond hair. "Brainwashed machine.

I told you this wouldn't work. If she doesn't believe her own memory, you really think she'll believe someone else's?"

"Ashton," Tiffany says, reprimanding him.

He scoffs. "What? You know I'm right. She's been here a week. It's going to take longer than that. Like I said before, this is a waste of time. Can we go now?"

"No," Tiffany says.

He throws his hands up. "Come on."

"Ashton, no," the girls say in unison.

Rosalie glares at him but then turns her attention back to me. "I can't do that. My ability doesn't let me fabricate a memory."

"But I wasn't there. Not at the end." I say. I point at Tiffany. "She took me before anything happened, so how can they have fired?"

Rosalie and Tiffany exchange an understanding look. "It's residual memory," Rosalie says. "I can see what happens in the moments before and after a person's experience."

"How convenient," I retort.

She sighs. "I can show you another one of your memories if you—"

"No," I say, a little louder than I intend to. "I . . . how . . . how can you show me what happened a hundred years ago?"

I regret my question. The spell the memories cast is sickening. I don't want to feel it again. I'm done.

"There's a man who lives here with us," Rosalie says. "His name is Jacob Ganiston. He's a hundred and seventeen years old. He lived through what happened and I've seen his memories."

I blink several times, rubbing my nose with the flat of my hand. "What?"

"He can heal himself," Tiffany says, answering my skeptical look.

"So, he can't die?" I ask. "He'll live forever?"

What am I doing? I shouldn't be interested in this. I'm talking to Diseased Ones. They've kidnapped me. They're murderers. Liars. They don't deserve to be heard.

Rosalie and Tiffany shrug.

"Don't know," Tiffany says. "Never thought about that. But I suppose it's possible."

I'm trembling. Who are these creatures? Can some of them really live forever?

"I want to show you what he remembers," Rosalie says. "Then you can see for yourself. We're telling you the truth. The Terror War never happened."

Something nasty wells up within me. I want to scream at them—to stand up to their slander—but the impulse is quenched by the eerie power I felt at the Testing Center. A strange hunger consumes me, and, as if in a trance, I say, "okay."

The ravenous power is guiding me, just as it did on the day of the Test. There's no doubt about it. The only difference is the strength. The power is muted and fuzzy. I can't quite explain it.

My eyes snap to Ashton, and I tilt my head sideways, staring at him with wolf-like intensity. There's something about this boy—something that's holding me back. For a moment, his face changes from snide to alarmed. His hands are shaking, and the image of the scrawny boy from the waiting room comes to mind. Is Ashton scared of me too?

But just as quickly as it came, the hunger vanishes, and with it, my senses return. Did I just say 'okay'?

"Alright." Rosalie interlaces her hands and stretches them. "I'm going to show you a collage of what he remembers. It comes in bits and pieces, so it will be more disconnected than your memory. Your memory was fresh."

Before I can protest, Rosalie throws her hands forward, and dozens of figures erupt from her fingertips. The horrible cold returns, and with it, a feeling of deep despair. The misty setting forms around us, and someone's living room materializes.

A middle-aged, brown-haired woman and a slender, wide-eyed boy who looks to be about my age appear in the midst of the room. They scurry around like gazelles. I'm pulled into the scene, glued to the action by the magnitude of the memory.

"We have to hurry," the woman says, her tone stricken, and even through the silver memory, her thin face is markedly ashen. "Jacob, grab your things. We have to leave. Now."

"Mom, what's happening? Why are we packing?"

The woman scampers around, stuffing items into a duffle bag and muttering things under her breath.

"Mom?"

"Jacob, your things. Quickly."

He obeys, running over to the corner of the room and grabbing a backpack. He shoves a sweatshirt and a pair of shoes into it. "Mom, what's going on? Talk to me."

"You know the things we can do?" she says, still bustling about. "Our abilities?"

"Of course, what about it?" Jacob asks, helping his mother stuff an oddly shaped blanket into an oblong bag.

She grabs several pairs of woolen socks and dumps them into Jacob's backpack. "We have to hide."

"What? Hide . . . why?"

Jacob's misted face takes on a curious look—almost innocent. His soft, blue eyes mirror his mother's, and his mouth quivers.

"There are people who don't understand what we can do. They're afraid of us."

"Who's afraid of us?" Jacob asks, raising an eyebrow. "Why?"

"Because," she says, running to the kitchen and opening up the cupboards. They slam against each other in a cacophonous chorus, and she dumps several silver packages into the largest duffle bag. "They think we'll hurt people with our abilities."

"But that's not true," he says.

"I know, but that's why we have to hide."

"What if we talk to them? What if we show them that—"

"No. They don't want to listen to us." Mrs. Ganiston stops her frantic packing and looks her son straight in the face. "Jacob, you need to understand something. These people will kill us if they find us. Do you understand what I'm saying? They will kill us. Tell me you understand me."

Jacob's face turns as pale as his mother's. He nods slowly. "I understand."

"They don't see us as people. They think we're monsters, and that's why we need to run."

"But I'm not a monster," Jacobs says. "We're not monsters."

"Of course we're not."

My eyes water as a dark chill sends spasms down my spine and into my stomach. The darkness seizes my chest, paralyzing me.

I'm not a monster . . . I said it to the man I threw into the pillar at the Testing Center, the man I looked in the face, the man I connected with—just for a moment. I said that to him.

The room shakes, and the memory expands as the inky figures of a dozen military men crash through the scene. I gasp, holding my hand over my mouth.

"Mom!"

"Stand behind me." Mrs. Ganiston pushes her son out of the way.

White, icy crystals explode from her fingertips, shattering across the room in all directions. I throw my arms up, forgetting momentarily that I'm simply a witness to the scene. The crystals fly straight through me, but the military men stagger back. Several of them fall over, impaled by the shards.

"Go, Jacob! Run!"

He darts toward the door but hesitates at the threshold, turning just in time to see the silvery prongs of a taser gun fly through the air. They catch Mrs. Ganiston in the shoulder, and she crumples to the floor with a loud thud. Jacob yells.

The memory darkens, rocking the concrete room on its

foundation, and the force of this knocks me to my knees.

Moments later, a second taser gun hits Jacob in the chest and he falls, landing on top of his unconscious mother.

The scene dissolves into a peppery mist and reforms around me. Rosalie's fingers flitter, and hundreds of people slip into existence like water from a faucet. She holds her hands steady, palms in midair, and pulls them apart, zooming in to a large warehouse.

People are chained together, row upon row, one in front of the other. They have hoods over their faces, and one by one, each row is dragged outside. Jacob and his mother are in line with the others.

The military men lead the chained prisoners to the top of a large dirt hill. Its steep slope causes a few of the blindfolded people to fall, but they are yanked back to their feet. I can almost smell the scent of dirt and decay.

Harsh voices echo in the memory, but they're distorted. No distinguishable words are spoken, and as the prisoners reach the top of the hill, they stop, standing shoulder to shoulder.

The military men line up at the base of the hill. The general issues an indistinct command. Dozens of guns raise.

I glance between the prisoners and the gruff face of the general, my eyes streaming. There's a moment of delay, as if the memory were frozen in place . . .

The guns fire, ripping into the prisoners, and blood oozes from the bullet holes. All at once, the line topples over the hill and out of sight. Screams pierce my eardrums, stabbing my senses and sending me into a frenzy. I hold my chest, trying to breathe, but I can't. I can't breathe. I can't even speak.

The scene dissolves and reforms again.

Jacob is lying on the ground behind the hill, his hood askew. He's chained to several others. Blood leaks from his open mouth, pooling in the dirt. His eyes are blank, and his body is still, his limbs at awkward angles.

"No . . ." I say, strangled at the emotion gripping my throat. I look away. "No."

But a strange choking noise pulls me back into the scene. Jacob sputters violently, gasping for air, and I jump about a foot. The scrapes across his arms vanish. New skin stretches over the gashes in his knees, and like some strange mutating metamorphosis, the bullet wounds in his chest disappear. Light returns to his sparkling blue eyes.

Jacob's distressed voice cries out. I've never heard anything like it. The grief in his tone is beyond words.

"Mom . . ."

"Stop," I say. "Stop. I don't want to see anymore."

Jacob calls out again. "Mom!"

"I'm done. Stop," I say, raising my voice.

Rosalie's hands contract, absorbing the inky scene into her palms.

I'm quivering from head to foot, and a rush of violent emotion overwhelms me like an angry wave. This must be some kind of sick joke. It can't be real. It's a lie. They are torturing me, for fun—on purpose. That's what this is. Something like rage fires up inside of me, and I curl my hands into fists and stand to my feet.

I want to cry out. I want to destroy the memories. I want to forget.

"It's a lot to take in," Rosalie says, stepping toward me with her delicate hand outstretched.

"Get away from me!" I snarl at her, shrinking back, crippled with fear.

I jerk my hands forward, flexing my palms. Instinct is telling me what to do. I'm trying to feel the power I felt in the Testing Center, and for a moment, the tingling emerges, but it's snuffed out a second later. Nothing comes. No power courses through me. My hands drop, and I slide down the wall, sitting on the floor. I hate myself, and I hate them.

Faithful societal control has abandoned me. I can't process it. My brain feels like it's on fire. If I truly am a Diseased One, then this is the start of my brain's sickness—my bad blood. Maybe that's why I have emotion now. Maybe that's why I can't suppress it anymore. Bad blood. Maybe I *am* diseased.

"We need to give her space," Tiffany says, backing away.

Rosalie and Ashton follow her lead, and the door clicks behind them. They are gone. I'm all alone. I hug my knees and shut my eyes, willing myself to forget. If I can just forget . . . but all I can see is the line of prisoners toppling back over the hill, and Jacob's cold, dead eyes.

7

THE NEXT FEW WEEKS PASS SLOWLY. THEY BRING ME FOOD, most of which I hardly touch. I'm growing weak. My hair feels dirty, and I can tell by the sagging band of my skirt that I've lost weight. I can only imagine how disheveled I must look. They've offered me new clothes several times, but I don't want anything from these creatures.

They come to clean the toilet in my cell frequently. I'm grateful for this, but every time I see them, I can't help but feel nauseous. I'm still terrified.

There's not much to do when you're a prisoner. I've counted the cracks in the concrete over and over again. Ten little fractures. I've memorized each pattern, tracing the lines with my mind. There are only so many things to count in a bare room, so the odd habit isn't as comforting as I hoped it would be.

My mind wanders to thoughts of escape. There must be a

way out of here. I just need to find it.

They've detained me because of my ability. After Rosalie showed me Jacob's memories, Jonah Luxent came to visit me. He made himself perfectly clear. They don't know what I can do, they don't understand what my power is, and they aren't willing to put any of their own at risk. Until I'm willing to cooperate and learn from them, I'm to be confined.

The smallest part of me concedes to this decision. The satanic voice I experienced at the Testing Center frightened me to my core. I was unstoppable. The wide-eyed man I threw into the pillar is evidence of this. That day, I was a monster.

Tiffany comes and sits with me every day, always accompanied by Ashton. We don't talk much. She says she wants to keep me company. It's baffling. Why would she want to sit in this concrete hole with me? I've already made my feelings toward them apparent. I hate them. They're evil, and although Tiffany, Rosalie, and Ashton are not directly responsible for the Terror War, they're the offspring of those who were. Their ancestors were vile, cold-blooded murderers. Maybe they don't know this?

They must be brainwashed. They don't understand the true history of the world like I do, but the small amount of pity I feel for them is stamped out by anger and fear. I've been taken against my will. I'm a captive, and I can't do anything about it.

At night I dream of my parents. I dream of how my mother would sit at the end of my bed and tell me stories of the government's triumph and goodness. She would lull me to sleep with her soft voice. I dream of my father's words—his perfect advice. He would speak of control, of how to conduct myself like a true citizen of the world. I cherish the memory of his words like costly diamonds. As one of the military elite, he knew just what it took to be blameless in society's eyes. I miss them so much it hurts.

But when I wake, reality crushes me all over again. It's gut-wrenching. Each morning trods on me like I'm dirt underfoot. I'm sick with a disease, and these monsters took me away from home. My parents must be worried out of their minds. Their only child is gone.

One morning, however, something changes. I wake with a curious thought. What if I play along? What if I join their world? What if I believe them, just for now, just to see? If I play along, I can leave this room. I can investigate them. I can even explore my power.

The first time I think this, I am so repulsed by it that I nearly throw up.

No. Absolutely not. I will not abandon my principles. I will not relinquish my beliefs. No . . .

But the thought returns, creeping into each day and weaving itself into the fabric of my mind. If I feign interest in their world, I may even find a way to escape. I can pretend.

This thought thrills me, but also scares me into silence. I never voice this when Tiffany comes and sits with me. I loathe this thought, but no matter what I do, I can't rid myself of it. It's glued to my mind, like a cruel vice, and day upon day, it only grows stronger.

I can do it, I think to myself, I can play along.

The scenes from Rosalie's fingertips compel me. Could they possibly be true? No . . . they can't be. The repercussions are too gruesome to contemplate if they were. Genocide doesn't happen. Not anymore. The world is well past the savage days of our ancestors, but I can't get Jacob's face out of my mind.

It scares me to venture into the realm of hypothetical circumstances. It's new territory. What if it were true? Deep down, I know it's not . . . but, what if I could pretend it was? What if I could leave this prison cell?

My curiosity is getting the best of me, and I can't help myself. I can pretend. I can do it, and if I play my part convincingly, I'll see these Diseased Ones at work. I'm going crazy in this room, and I don't know if I can keep quiet any longer.

"Can you show me?" I ask.

Tiffany looks up from her seat, surprise lighting up her olive complexion.

"Your ability," I say. "Can you show me?"

"Oh," she says, smiling and hopping up. She's keen. She likes that I'm showing interest. "Of course."

She walks to the end of the room, brushing her long black hair out of the way and squaring her shoulders. I keep my eyes trained on her, intent on not missing a thing.

Tiffany vanishes with a pop and reappears at the other wall.

"Can you show me this place?" I ask. I bite the inside of my cheek, lowering my head. I'm coming across too eager. I need to calm down.

Tiffany and Ashton exchange concerned looks.

"I don't know if we can do that," Ashton says.

"And what do you do?" I snap at him. My lips twitch, and the smallest expression flickers over me. "Why are you always hanging around? It's not like you're pleasant company."

Why did I just say that? What's wrong with me? I need them to trust me if I'm ever going to get out of this stone cage, and on top of that, I've just spoken out of turn to a member of the opposite sex—someone my own age. School is segregated by gender, and intermingling is forbidden until adulthood, when someone has passed the Test. I can't lose myself in this quest to fit into their world. I must retain some of my respectability.

Ashton gives me an amused look. "I can suppress another person's ability."

I stare at him, blank-faced. So that's why I haven't felt that horrid power . . .

"We don't know what you can do," Tiffany says, shrugging.

"Well, I don't know what I can do either," I say, trying to mend my little outburst. "I don't know how I did those things back at the Testing Center. It just kind of . . . happened."

"And that, unfortunately, is why I'm here," Ashton says. He folds his arms across his chest. "Don't need any more accidents."

I fight the urge to say something nasty, forcing my face to remain pleasant.

"The most powerful manifestations of our abilities can come during times of extreme stress," Tiffany says. "One time I ended up halfway across the world."

"What made you do that?" I ask.

Tiffany runs a hand across her cheek. "It's a funny story actually."

Ashton rolls his eyes. "*Must* you tell that again?"

"Why do you have to be like that?" She flashes him a disgusted look.

"It's not like I signed up for this stupid babysitting job," he says, peeved. He leans back against the concrete wall.

"Well, tough," Tiffany says, glowering at him. "We need your ability right now, so like it or not, suck it up and do your job."

They've kidnapped me, and now they're complaining about having to watch me? Is this some kind of joke? I clench my teeth together, biting my tongue. Don't retaliate.

"Well I don't have much of a choice, do I?" Ashton says. "With you dragging me into this room every day. I've got better things to do."

I press my tongue against my lower lip, but I can't help it anymore. I glare at Ashton. "I don't like you," I say pointedly. I've done it again. I've spoken to him, but this time, my aggressive response feels justified. "Maybe you should leave."

"Yeah, you'd like that, wouldn't you," he says, raising an eyebrow. He's looking at me like I'm a child.

"I would, actually."

I've completely lost my mind. He's a boy. Stop talking to him.

"That's enough, Ashton," Tiffany says, stepping between us.

There are a few seconds of heated tension, but I forge ahead, turning toward Tiffany. I try my best to keep my voice impassive as I steer the conversation back to my original request.

"Can I see this place?" Tiffany looks worried again, so I point to Ashton. "He can come along. I can't use my ability, and besides, I don't even know how. I'm dying in this room. I want to see everything . . . please?"

She contemplates this for a solid minute—longest minute of my life.

"Okay," she says. "Yeah."

"What?" Ashton says, throwing his arms up. "Come on, really?"

I glower at him, giving in to the emotion. I feel it flourish across my face as my lips press into a tight line and my eyebrows knit together. It's highly satisfying.

"Tiffany," Ashton grumbles, tossing a hand up, "I don't think we can."

"I'll speak with Jonah."

"Come on, Chang, seriously?"

She tilts her head to the side and throws him a vile look. "You're an ass. You know that?"

She dismisses him, turning back to me. I drop my expression. I can't look too pleased.

"I'll speak with Jonah, and then we'll come get you."

I nod. "Fine."

I back away from the door out of habit and sit on the floor. Tiffany and Ashton leave, and the lock clicks. There's a pitter-patter of excitement budding within me. After four weeks, I'm finally getting out of here. If I'm honest with myself, I don't know what to believe about the Terror War anymore, and I don't care. Right now, all I'm thinking about is leaving this room.

I wait for what feels like an hour before the lock clicks and the door opens to reveal Tiffany, Ashton, and Rosalie, whose freckled face shines.

"Let's get this over with," Ashton says sullenly.

Rosalie's eyes widen, and Tiffany sighs.

"Come on," she says, waving me over. "I talked with Jonah. You can join us for dinner in the common room. We have a lot to show you."

I stride to the door and cross through the frame, finally free from my stifling cell. I've stepped beyond the barrier I've come to know so well. It's a strange feeling, and I don't quite know what to do with myself. For the first time since my arrival, unexpected excitement accompanies me. They let me out.

We stroll down the lengthy hallway, our footsteps echoing off the concrete. It ends at a large metal door. Tiffany grabs the handle and yanks it open to reveal the largest room I've ever seen.

The space is nearly as deep as it is long, and easily the size of several massive aircraft hangars. I gaze at its impressive dimensions, unable to believe it. How can the government not know about this?

We step onto the platform of a metal stairway that clings to the giant wall, and I grip the handrail for support. A fall from here would likely be four stories.

"And we're underground?" I ask.

"Yep," Tiffany says, beaming at me. She starts her descent into the room and I follow suit, giving the edge of the staircase a wide berth.

I hug the stone as my eyes cascade over the enormity of it all. The room has three sections.

"What is all this?"

Tiffany points to the first section, "That is the training area where we practice our abilities."

I stare at the giant raised platform. Its grayish blue paint is peeling in places, and a huge cream-colored mat covers its surface. Something unpleasant sinks into the pit of my stomach. Training area? What for? Why do they need to practice their powers? What kind of place are they running? I fight the urge to say something horrible by biting my lip. Not now. Not yet. Instead, I turn the urge into another question, trying to sound innocently curious.

"What do you train for?"

"I'll explain everything. Don't worry."

Tiffany reaches the bottom of the stairs and hooks a left. Rosalie slips past me, catching up to her, while Ashton skulks behind, keeping his distance from me. I quicken my pace, keen to catch up to the girls. This place is unreal.

We continue down the seemingly endless room until we reach the second section. It contains hundreds of tables and chairs, neatly arranged in alternating windows of available space. Red leather booths line the far wall—the kind I used to see in photographs of vintage restaurants in the 'decades gone by' section of my history textbook.

People are scattered everywhere, and I'm acutely aware of the fact that nearly all of them are staring at me. I look down at the floor, but I can still feel their eyes.

"This is the dining area," Rosalie says, bringing my attention back to the tour. "We also have a recreation area just over there."

She points across the sea of wooden tables. It's a smaller subsection with deflated couches, torn and patched recliners, dinged up wall screens, and . . . are those pool tables? They have old-fashioned recreation here? I've seen these types of games before. We learned about them in school. But leisure isn't something that's stressed in society, and idleness is scorned. Children are supposed to focus on their studies so that the school board can determine the most suitable career path for them.

"The parents don't like hanging out in the recreation area." Rosalie chuckles. "Too loud for them."

"Yeah, the adults park themselves at the tables and talk until they're blue in the face."

I follow in Tiffany and Rosalie's wake, still puzzling over the games.

"And this is the kitchen," Tiffany says, pointing to the third section.

The area spans the width of the end of the room. Inside are dozens of stovetops and metal hoods that arc over the space.

Vegetable stew. I can smell it simmering deliciously, and my mouth begins to water.

"Everyone spends most of their time in the common room

because it's pretty cramped everywhere else," Rosalie says.

"Right," I say, not really paying her much attention. I'm eyeing the boiling broth. "Smells good."

"It's dinner time. Come on," Tiffany says. "Let's get in line."

We walk through the maze of tables and I hug my side, shifting my gaze between the floor and Tiffany's back. More and more people have noticed me, so I keep my head down until we make it to the end of the large line.

"Are you Hollis?"

The voice comes from directly behind me, and I jump a foot into the air, spinning around wildly. I slip, and a pair of strong hands catch me. The touch makes my stomach flip with jittery butterflies, a sensation I've never experienced before.

"Oh. Sorry, didn't mean to startle you."

It's a boy who looks to be a couple of years older than me. He brushes his dark hair across his forehead, smiling. His intense blue eyes are piercing. He raises an eyebrow.

"Are you okay?"

"I-I'm . . . I don't—I'm . . ."

I don't know what to do. I don't speak to strangers, let alone a member of the opposite sex—it isn't proper or safe. But I've already broken this rule several times with Ashton.

"I'm Keith," he says, smiling brightly. "Keith Keaton."

I open my mouth, but nothing comes out.

"We're just showing Hollis around," Tiffany says, coming to my rescue. "This is all very new for her."

"I bet," he says. "You'll do fine."

He gives me a reassuring nod, and then turns around, joining the group of people behind us.

Heat crops up all over my face, and a new sensation flitters across my body. What is this . . . this strange sensation? I can still feel the place where his hands caught my shoulders. That's the first time I've ever been touched by a boy. I press my hands to my cheeks, trying to hide the pink color I'm certain is there for everyone to see.

We make our way through the food line. I'm starving and everything looks delicious. I grab two bread rolls, as the squat woman behind the counter ladles a healthy portion of steaming hot stew into my bowl.

I don't even care that this meal was prepared by Diseased Ones. I'm starving and I'm thrilled that I'm not eating alone.

"Let's sit over there." Tiffany leads our group to one of the corner tables, mumbling something about "not as many people."

I grab a chair, pull it out, and sit down. Tiffany and Rosalie sit across from me, but Ashton walks past me, stopping two tables down.

"Ashton, seriously?" Tiffany's eyes narrow.

"I'm still close enough," he says, stuffing a bread roll into his mouth. "She can't use her ability. Relax."

Tiffany lets out a frustrated sigh. "Whatever. Okay, I'm sure you have a lot of questions, so, fire away."

"What do you train for?" I ask, blurting it out. I run a hand through my hair, scolding myself. I need to calm down.

"Well, we train—" Tiffany begins, but she's cut off by Ashton, who interrupts her in a loud voice.

"We're planning on revolting against the government. That's what we train for."

Rosalie chokes on her bread roll, and Tiffany drops her spoon, swearing under her breath. I nearly fall out of my seat. I grip the edges of my chair like a vice. What did he just say? They're planning on what?

"Ashton!" Tiffany roars, her voice dangerous. Her face is stretched taut, eyebrows raised and mouth wide. "I swear, one more comment like that and I'll report you to the Council. Don't think I won't."

He looks taken aback by this, but he shrugs it off. "Whatever, Chang. It was just a joke."

"Not funny," Rosalie says, glaring at him.

"You two are no fun," he says.

"Stop talking," Rosalie adds in an icy tone. "You wanted to sit over there, so butt out of our conversation."

A few tense moments pass before Tiffany and Rosalie turn back to me.

"I'm sorry for that," Tiffany says, shooting a nasty look at Ashton. "We're not. That's not what we train for."

"We train because when we find other people with abilities, we bring them here," Rosalie says. "This place is a safe haven for people like us."

"Yes, and there are definitely more of us out there," Tiffany says.

I stop, mid-sip of juice, and nearly spray it down my front. I cough violently and my eyes start streaming.

"Are you okay?" Rosalie asks.

"Yes, I—sorry, I'm . . . yes, I'm fine," I say. Fear grips my insides. "There are more of you? I mean . . . other than in this compound?"

"Of course," Tiffany says. "Not many, but there are people with abilities hiding all over the world. We train so that when we find someone, we can rescue them. The government doesn't know this place exists, and that's what makes it safe."

"And . . . and you've found other . . . people?" I ask.

It pains me to use the word 'people'. They are creatures—animals. I know this. I've studied them in biology class. But I need to pretend. I need to blend in until I've come to a conclusion on this.

"Absolutely," Rosalie says. "Just this year we've been able to locate and rescue seventeen people."

"But how?"

"We monitor the President's broadcasts, keep up to date on any new Testing Center procedures, and intercept satellite communication," Tiffany says. "We have technology too, you know."

"But I thought the government—"

I stop myself. They will say that the government lied. I don't know what to think yet, but I don't want to hear anything more about the genocide. Not right now.

I reshape my question. "How are you all here?"

The girls look at one another, but Tiffany speaks first. "What do you mean?"

"Well, if the Terror War—"

I stop again, correcting myself and gritting my teeth to try and keep my demeanor calm. I hate this. Pretending that I believe them is going to be harder than I thought. I take a deep breath.

"If the genocide was a hundred years ago, how are you all here? You two certainly weren't alive back then. No one here looks like they were. So . . . how did this place get here?"

"This place has been here for a hundred years," Rosalie says. "Ever since the genocide. Our great grandparents built it. They were the first to hide here."

"But how?" I'm struggling with this point. "A place like this? How could this have been built without anyone noticing?"

"My great-grandpa, Charles Chang," Tiffany says brightly. She lifts both of her hands up, palms open. "He could move the earth. That was his ability. He commanded the very stone in these walls."

"He built this with his ability?" I ask. I grip my spoon tightly. My knuckles are white, and I'm painfully aware of the fact that my cheeks are flushed.

"Yeah. Without him, I don't think our great-grandparents would have survived. He was the reason they were able to escape detection and go into hiding," Tiffany says.

She sips a spoonful of stew, and I stare at her.

"So . . . this was built in a day?" I ask tentatively.

"Less than an hour I think," Rosalie says.

"And there were only fifty-three people here when it was built," Tiffany adds. "Now we have just over four hundred."

My hands turn to ice. "You've found that many people?"

Rosalie laughs. "No, we were born here. A lot of us were."

My pulse is thumping erratically, so I swallow a large gulp of juice to give myself something to do. I regret this immediately as a painful lump travels down the length of my esophagus. My eyes begin to water.

"Hollis, are you alright?" Tiffany asks.

"Fine," I say. "So you were born here?"

"Yep."

They are breeding... repopulating. But something deep inside of me stops this train of thought in its tracks. If I'm pretending, then I really need to pretend.

At the very least, all I'm sure of is that I don't know what to believe anymore. It's a game of who is telling the truth. Who is really brainwashed? Me or them? Perhaps they are telling me the truth—or at least, what they believe to be the truth.

It's too early to decide. I know I don't trust them, but unfortunately, I don't have a choice. I'm stuck here. I'm not on their side, but I need them to know that I'm not hostile to their world.

I change the subject. "I'm the only one like me? I'm the only one you've rescued from society?"

I hate the fact that I'm using the word 'rescued'. 'Kidnapped' is more appropriate.

"Yes," the girls say in unison.

"But what about the boy from twelve years ago?"

There's a brief pause, and Tiffany's brow furrows.

"The Council diligently watches the world news," she says, her tone somber. "We knew someone with an ability could be born to parents without the biomarker. It's rare, but it happens."

"And ever since the World Order, we've been vigilant," Rosalie says. "We knew that the government had developed a genetic test to weed out people with the biomarker."

"What we didn't expect was the chemical therapy," Tiffany adds.

"You know about that?" I ask.

"Of course," Rosalie says. "It's sad, really."

Well, I think it's fantastic. Too bad I missed it.

"And twelve years ago," Tiffany says. "The boy who failed the Test . . . well, the rescue team was too late."

"Too late?" I repeat, shaking my head. "Too late for what?"

"They killed him."

Tiffany buries her head in her hands. "The team couldn't risk exposure because the government thought we were all dead. And I'm the only one here who can teleport, but I was thirteen at the time. I didn't even have my ability yet."

I still don't want to believe it. The government can't have killed him. They wouldn't have. There must be some other explanation.

I look Tiffany in the face and her dark brown eyes meet my hazel ones. I can tell that she's genuine. She doesn't think she's lying, but it can't be true.

"They killed him like they were going to kill you," she says.

I try to process her words, but my brain is failing me. I've received so much information over the past few weeks that my head is spinning. I stare at my spoon for a long time.

"Hollis," Tiffany says softly, and I look up at her. "I know this is a lot. This would be a lot for anyone, and I can't imagine what's going on in your head right now, but . . . I want you to know that we're here for you. And I want you to know that I'm going to do my best to make this transition as easy as possible."

I'm still deep in thought. I don't know what to say to this. She doesn't know me. How can she possibly mean that? I'm a society member, and she's a Diseased One. We're enemies.

Rosalie gives me a warm smile. "We care about you."

I'm overwhelmed. "But you don't know me."

"That's okay," she says. "I'll get to know you."

"And why would you want to do that?"

"Because," Tiffany says, and her words shatter my resolve, chilling me to the bone. "You're one of us."

8

I TAP MY FOOT AGAINST THE LEG OF THE TABLE I'M SITTING on. I'm in the common room near the end of the dining area facing the giant training platform. I start to count the threads protruding from the seam of the mat.

Twenty-four. Twenty-five. Twenty-six. Twenty-seven.

It's my allotted "free" time. An hour a day accompanied by Ashton. They don't trust me yet. It's fine. Smart move on their part. I'm new here and they don't know me.

Thirty-seven. Thirty-eight. Thirty-nine. Forty.

I appreciate the free time. I can barely stand to be locked in that cell. I'm going a little stir crazy, but an hour a day with Ashton is almost cruel. His presence brings the inexplicable urge to smack him in his snide, complaining face—a violent tendency I've never experienced before.

Fifty-one. Fifty-two. Fifty-three. Fifty-four.

I fear that I'm becoming like them. The dark expression

bubbling to the surface of my being is frightening. I can't deny it anymore. I definitely have bad blood, and it's affecting my brain.

Sixty. Sixty-one. Sixty-two. Sixty-three.

The question is, how long can I resist the natural inclinations that come with being a Diseased One? And what kind of monster will I turn into?

"Hey, want to join?"

I look up, startled. It's Keith Keaton, the boy who prevented me from falling in the dinner line. His bright blue eyes flash with his grin, and my stomach does an uncomfortable dance. A strong societal urge overwhelms me. Don't talk to him. I look down hoping that he will take the hint, but to my dismay, he repeats the question.

"Do you want to join?"

"I . . . I don't know. I don't think I should," I say.

"It's just a game. You'll love it," he says. "It's called Marbles."

I don't understand. Games are for children. In society, young adults focus on their career assignments. There's no time for distractions, and I haven't played for fun in a long time. I've never even heard of Marbles.

"I don't know how," I say lamely, glancing over at the group standing on the training platform. They're all looking at me expectantly. I look down again, uncomfortably aware of my fiery cheeks. I don't know how to interact with them. What would I say?

"We'll teach you." Keith brushes back his dark brown hair. "Come on. It'll be fun."

Keith and I lock eyes for a moment. He smiles at me, and

something twirls my stomach into a knot. I open my mouth to say "no thank you," but "okay" comes out instead.

"Great," he says, beaming.

I stand, shaking slightly, and follow him to the edge of the giant training mat. He jumps onto the platform with ease and then turns around.

"Here," he says. "Let me help you up."

He takes my hand and pulls me up to the platform. I gasp as a shock runs through my skin, and I yank my hand back, gaping at him. What was that? My power? His? I curl my hand into a fist, holding it behind my back.

I feel strange—almost ashamed. Touching of any form isn't okay. I know this. I've learned this. It's been drilled into my mind since childhood. It's for your spouse, in your own home—never for strangers.

"You okay?" Keith asks, giving me a confused look.

"Yes," I say.

What else could I possibly say to that? I stand in front of him, frozen in place.

"Hey, not too far away," Ashton says, calling after me.

It's Ashton's voice that jolts me back to life. I dismiss his cross tone and walk straight to the group of people huddled at the other end of the platform. Anything is better than sitting with Ashton—even meeting complete strangers that I believe to be evil.

"Hollis," Keith says. "This is Candice, Darren, Audrey, and Ben."

Everyone says hi to me at the same time, and I'm

overwhelmed. I force a smile and wave at them, attempting to copy their greeting, but the smile is completely foreign.

I drop my expression and stare at my feet, desperately trying to disappear. This was a bad idea.

"Hey," Keith says softly. "Just think of it like school. You meet new people there, right?"

Yes, girls. Schooling is by gender. The campus is split down the center, mirrored on each side so that both genders receive equal resources and opportunities. We would only see the boys during an all-school assembly for presidential announcements.

"Um . . . right. Thanks," I say.

"So, let's play." Ben claps his hands together enthusiastically. I nearly jump out of my skin. I eye him warily. He's a tall, skinny boy with dirty-blond hair, and he's bouncing up and down with an excitement that can only be described as overeager.

"I don't know how to play," I say. This seems to deflate Ben a bit, and he stares at me, nonplussed.

"You don't know how to play Marbles?" he asks. "But it's been around since the eighteen hundreds. In fact, mass production of the game became possible in 1884."

"But it's 2647, and nobody plays childish games anymore," I say.

The girls' mouths drop open, and I regret my comment. Why do I keep saying passive-aggressive things? I need to fit in here. It's a matter of survival. It's the only way to get out of my prison cell—the only way I'll find out the truth. I have to learn all that I can about these creatures.

"It's okay," Keith says. "We can teach you. It's Marbles, but with a twist. Miss Audrey Rye, would you do us the honor?"

"Sure," the shortest girl says.

Her sleek, mousy hair tosses about her shoulders as her tiny hands cut through the air. Both of her fists are stuffed with marbles, and she flings them into the middle of our group. I flinch, expecting to be pelted with the little glass spheres, but to my utter bewilderment, they remain suspended in midair at chest level, glittering in the harsh fluorescents like small twinkling stars.

My eyes widen. "Woah."

"Hey, guys versus girls," Candice says, and she beckons me to her side with a determined grin. "You're with us, Hollis."

I immediately notice Candice's eyes. They're piercing blue like Keith's, and I stare at her as she pulls her hair into a messy bun. She's a pretty girl with thin lips and dark, shiny hair.

"Guys versus girls?" Ben says, grinning broadly. "Oh, it's on."

"You know you're going to lose." Candice stretches her right arm across her chest and tilts her head back and forth.

"You wish."

"Okay." Audrey flicks her fingers. "Let's do this."

The marbles begin to move in rapid, random patterns. A dark blue one whizzes back and forth. I watch it, mesmerized.

"Right, Hollis." Candice points to the circle of animated spheres. "So, the goal is to knock as many marbles from the middle as possible."

"And if you knock a marble from the middle, you get to go again," Audrey says. "And you'll know if you've knocked one out because it will stop floating."

"And we take turns between the two teams," Candice adds. "It's a pretty simple game, but fun."

"Okay. And what do you use to knock the marbles out?" I ask. My pulse quickens. I'm utterly out of my element. Candice gives me a compassionate smile. Great. I've just asked a stupid question.

"Shooter marble," she says. "Right here."

She pushes a large marble toward me, and it floats gracefully across the air. I tap it with my pointer finger, and it bobs like an apple in water, floating directly in front of me. I give the shooter marble back to Candice.

"You can start," I say.

"Alrighty boys, get ready to lose."

Ben smirks. "Yeah, okay Candy. Sure."

Candice grabs the shooter marble and skips it like a stone, knocking one of the center marbles askew. It moves precariously toward the edge of the playing field but remains hanging in the air.

"Ah, tough luck sis," Keith says.

Candice passes the shooter to him with a sigh. "Thought I had that."

"What a bummer," he says, his tone soaked in sarcasm.

Candice huffs. "Yeah Keith, if only you were any good at it."

I look between Keith and Candice, noting the sky blue eyes once more. "You and Candice are siblings?"

"Yep," Candice says, patting Keith on the back. "And, as the little sister, giving Keith a hard time is my full-time job."

Keith grins, folding his arms across his chest. "Yeah Candice, if only you were any good at it."

"Ha. Ha. Ha. Very funny."

Audrey jumps in, pointing to the shooter in Keith's hand. "Well Keith, go on and take a shot. We're waiting."

"Patience," Darren says. He's standing behind Ben and Keith, arms crossed, with a mysterious look on his face. "Let the man take his time."

"You're just as impatient as I am, Darren," Audrey says, picking at her fingernails.

"Ah, but here's the thing," he says, and he dips his head ever so slightly. "I don't show it like you, Miss Competitive."

Audrey opens her mouth to retaliate, but Keith holds his hand up. "Alright, you two, I'll take the shot. Relax."

He flicks the shooter through the air, knocking a marble out of the center and onto the floor. The boys give a whoop of victory.

"And that's how it's done," Ben says, punching Keith on the shoulder.

Audrey huffs. "Now he gets to go again."

"Right."

Keith smiles at me, and my stomach is in knots all over again. I don't feel well. What is he doing? Why is he smiling at me? I'm certainly not going to smile back. Should I say something to him?

"Hollis? Um . . . are you okay?" Candice asks.

"Yeah," I say. They're all staring at me, so I blurt out the only thing I can think of. "So Keith, what do you do?"

He throws the shooter again, missing the middle entirely. "What do I do? What do you mean?"

Audrey beckons the shooter back to center, stifling a snicker. What is she laughing at? I brush past the moment, intent on my question.

"I mean, what's your ability? What can you do?"

"Oh, okay. Yeah." His eyes twinkle. "Take my hands."

I give him a strange look, that sense of societal obligation bubbling up again: no touch. Do I dare break it? On the one hand, I should hold to my values. My virtues are civilized, true, and honorable. I'm not like them. But on the other hand . . . no one from my world would know. I'm all alone, and I'm studying them. I want to learn about their world. As far as I'm concerned, it's the only way to find the truth.

Keith extends both of his hands, and with another twirl of my stomach, I take them. I feel almost . . . scandalous.

He stares into my eyes for several moments, and I wait expectantly. What kind of power will come? But after ten seconds, I furrow my brow.

"What's supposed to happen?" I ask.

He raises an eyebrow and grins. "Look down."

I gasp, my composure shattering away. I grip onto his hands fiercely as my pulse spikes with adrenaline. The two of us are several feet above the training mat.

"You can fly?"

"Sure can."

He sets us back onto the floor. He's still looking at me, so I break eye contact.

"Oh please." Candice rolls her eyes. "Way to charm, Keith."

What does she mean?

"Do you use that with all the ladies or just the mysterious new ones?" Candice asks. She giggles.

I'm confused, but the buzz of thoughts flying through my brain is interrupted by the shooter marble. Audrey holds it up, handing it to me.

"Your turn Hollis," she says.

"Right."

But I don't want to play. I want to see their abilities.

I take the shooter and toss it into the center. It misses by a significant amount, and I cringe. Maybe I should have tried a little harder, but I'm overwhelmed by curiosity. I want to see more. Something deep within me says I shouldn't want this, but I dismiss it. I tuck society's voice away. I don't want to hear it. Not right now.

"It's okay," Audrey says brightly, pulling the marble back with her fingertips. "You'll get it with practice."

"Right, thanks," I say. I turn to Candice, hardly able to control my eagerness. "So, what can you do?"

She grins and holds her hand out, palm to the ceiling. Flames spring to life on her bare skin, dancing into the air—flickering and alive with intense heat. She closes her hand, extinguishing the flames.

"I can produce fire." She looks over at Keith and squares her shoulders. "I think it's cooler than flying, but, you know, that's just me."

I'm half thrilled, half terrified. "Wow . . . that . . . that is incredible."

"I keep forgetting this isn't normal for you," Darren says, tossing the shooter into the middle. He knocks two marbles out, and they fall to the mat with soft thuds.

Ben throws both of his fists into the air. "Nice shot."

"And what about you?" I ask Darren.

Darren tosses the shooter a second time. It misses.

"Ah, man. Close," Ben says.

Darren, without missing a beat, kneels on the training mat and sticks his fist to the floor. It sinks into it as if the mat had melted away.

"Rearrange matter. You know, walk through walls and stuff."

My mouth falls open. Darren pulls his hand out of the mat, stands up, and shrugs. I stare at the place where his fist had been a moment earlier. It looks as good as new.

"Ladies and gentlemen," Keith says, in a brisk announcer voice. "Darren Mitchell, casual as ever, sticks his hand through the floor. It's not a big deal."

"Well, at least I'm not the one who's a show-off," Darren says, glaring at Keith.

"Me?" Keith chuckles. "Ben's the show-off."

Ben nods. "It's true."

Abruptly, there is a torrent of wind, and I step back a few paces, buffeted by some invisible shock wave. Ben is gone. "W-where did he go?"

Someone taps my shoulder. "Right behind you."

"How did you—"

I spin around, caught off guard.

The group laughs as another rush of wind whips my hair

askew, tossing it across my face. I brush it away. Ben is gone again. Keith joins my side, pointing to the opposite end of the massive common room.

"He's over there, waving his hands like an idiot."

I squint through the throngs of people, and sure enough, Ben is standing on top of a table, flailing his arms over his head.

Another rush of wind and Ben is standing right in front of me. I stumble back, tripping over my feet and nearly falling. Keith catches me, and his hands send another jolt through my skin. His touch is still so jarring.

"Careful, Benny boy," Keith says. "You've nearly knocked her over twice now."

"I'm speedy," Ben says. "Really, really speedy. I'm like the Flash."

I must look thoroughly confused because Ben's energy deflates.

"You know? The Flash," he says, gesturing to the room.

I shake my head.

"He was a DC Comics superhero who was introduced in November 1939?"

"Dude," Keith says. "Does she look like she—"

"The Flash's name is really Barry Allen. He got super-speed when lightning hit his forensic lab, dousing him in chemicals. Of course, I was born with my speediness, so I think that makes me cooler than the Flash, but—"

"Okay, Ben, slow down there," Candice says.

Ben looks completely beside himself. "Did you just say 'slow down'? Do you even know me? I'm Ben Bryson, speedy boy wonder. I can't just 'slow down.'"

"Oh, my mistake. So, is 'speedy boy wonder' your official superhero name, or . . . ?"

"Whatever, Candy," he says. "Hollis was going to ask for my ability next, so naturally, I had to put on a show."

He folds his arms across his chest, looking smug. She giggles, rolling her eyes and muttering something about "classic Ben."

"See?" Keith says, looking to Darren. "Show-off."

"Yeah. Yeah." Darren waves his hands. "Your turn to shoot, Audrey. And no cheating. No powers."

Audrey motions the shooter to her side and then flicks it expertly across the middle. It knocks three marbles to the floor. They fall with satisfying thuds.

"And that's how it's done, boys. No powers. Just pure talent."

Audrey dips into a little curtsey, and Candice claps.

I can't explain the surge of expression I'm witnessing. Something about this group is baffling to my core. They act like a family, but only two of them are related. It doesn't make any sense. They're expressing themselves, and embracing each other, and it seems to bring a sense of bliss.

I'm at ease too. I don't feel the horrible tightness in my chest, and I'm not on my guard. Is that a good thing? Was that their plan? The raw emotion that I'm observing is exhilarating—thrilling even. My life has been so formal, but this . . . this is unparalleled. I don't get it. We're just playing a game.

"So, what about you, Hollis?" Keith asks. "What can you do?"

"What?"

"Your ability?"

"Oh I . . . I don't really know," I say.

The strange bliss in the air vanishes, and the unwelcome heat creeps back across my face. I want to disappear again.

"What do you mean?" Candice asks.

Images from the Testing Center flash across my mind. "I . . . I just don't know. I don't know what I did. It only happened once, and I'm not sure how I did it."

"I heard about that," Darren says. "Jonah told us that you were almost killed, but he didn't say much else. What happened out there?"

"I-I don't think . . ." I say, stalling. This is the last thing I want to discuss. I don't even know if I believe the government was trying to kill me. Maybe they were trying to help me. I mean, for all I know, they could have been. Now I'm with Diseased Ones, and I can't decide who is telling the truth.

"Guys, not now," Keith says, sensing my discomfort. "She doesn't have to tell us anything she doesn't want to."

Relief floods me, and the knots disappear. Keith smiles and takes my hand briefly, giving it a little squeeze.

"Hey, time's up," a snide voice says. My heart plummets. It's Ashton. "Time to go back."

"Can't she finish the game?" Candice asks.

"No, let's go."

"But it'll only be five minutes."

"I said no."

Candice glares at him, hops off the training platform, and

walks over to him. "You're just sour that you have to watch Hollis."

"Whatever Candice," he says. "Like I told Tiffany, I didn't sign up for this. So, get out of my way, fireball. Timewire needs to go back to her cell."

Candice's face turns pink. "Fireball?"

"Oh no," Keith mutters under his breath.

"Yeah. Fireball. I think it's cute," he says in a mocking tone. "Now move. Timewire, let's go."

A flicker jumps from Candice's hand, and she holds her fist up, opening her palm. A flame bursts from it and dances between them. It expands rapidly, pushing Ashton back.

"Don't call me cute. Ever."

His expression falters, but only for a moment. A horrible look creeps across his brow. His twisted smile is off-putting. He moves his hand in a high arc, cutting through the air as if he were going to strike her. Immediately, Candice's flames are extinguished.

"Cute trick, fireball."

"Hey!" Keith jumps down from the platform to join his sister. "Don't take her power."

Something huge and vicious seizes my insides, crushing my chest and stealing the air from my lungs. I gasp, staggering backward. It's as if I've been hit by an invisible monster. The force cascades over my hands, and they begin to tingle. My senses heighten, my body numbs, and my jaw tightens.

For the first time since the Testing Center, the evil power emanates from my palms. It fills me to the brim, overpowering every faculty.

I stare at my hands, paralyzed with fear. I need to get away from them. I retreat from the group on the platform, wide-eyed and panic-stricken.

Audrey notices this. "Hollis? What's wrong? Are you alright?"

"No, stay back!" I cry, holding my hands up to keep her away.

My palms surge forward, and Audrey is gripped under the ferocity of the vile power. The tingling in my hands forces her to her knees, and in a tug of movement, I pull her toward me. My fists close, her mouth presses shut, and her eyes bulge.

Visions of the man I threw into the pillar of the Testing Center fly through my mind. Audrey's wide eyes are watering. This can't be happening again.

"Hey!" Darren shouts. "What are you doing to her?"

"I don't know . . . I-I can't control this," I say, stammering and tripping over my feet. "Please. Stay away from me. I don't want to hurt you."

"Let her go," Darren says, charging at me.

My hands jump up to shield myself from Darren, and he is pulled to his knees next to Audrey, perfectly rigid and bound under my power. He's been silenced along with her, and the same horrified look comes across his face.

"Help." My voice is strangled, suffocated by the power I feel. I'm trying not to pass out. My pulse thunders wildly, sending me into a frenzy. "Please, somebody help me. I can't control this. Help."

"Ashton!" Ben bellows. "Get over here. Hollis's power."

Ashton is beside me. His hands cut through the air, and

Audrey and Darren fall forward. They are both on their hands and knees, coughing and sputtering. They're free from my ability, and the tingling vanishes.

"What the hell was that?" Darren says, his face contorted. He lifts Audrey up from the floor, and they back away from me. Audrey is shaking so violently that she can barely stand. Darren grips her fiercely, holding her up.

"I'm sorry," I say, feeling awful for scaring them.

"What did you do to us?" Darren is shivering with anger, and his hands curl into fists.

"I don't know," I say, stricken. "I'm sorry. I'm so sorry."

I want to melt into the floor and never return. What did I do to them? How could that have happened? I'm not evil, but . . . what is this power?

Keith walks up to Ashton and pulls him around by the scruff of his collar. "You took your power off Hollis. Why did you do that?"

"Hey," Ashton says, holding his hands up. "It's not my fault she's some kind of freak. She did that. Not me."

Keith grabs Ashton by the front of his shirt and yanks him forward. Their faces are an inch apart.

"Keith, no!" Candice screams.

Several tense seconds follow this.

"Don't call her a freak," he says, releasing Ashton and pushing him backward. "Just do your damn job."

Keith approaches me.

"No, don't," I say. My hands are jittering. "Please, stay away from me. Please."

"Hey, it's okay," he says softly. "It's okay."

"No, it's not."

"You don't have control over your ability yet." He holds his hand out to me, closing the gap between us. "It's alright. Your ability is gone now. Just take my hand."

I hesitate, utterly terrified, but Keith's soft eyes and gentle voice coax me forward. I grab his hand and move to his side, practically hiding behind his shoulder. All eyes are on me.

"Sorry to break up this tender moment, but it's time to go now," Ashton says.

Keith ignores him. "I'll walk you up."

"I'm sorry," I say, still hiding behind him.

"Everything's alright." Keith turns to Ashton. "I'll walk up with you two."

Ashton scoffs. "Looks like Timewire's got herself a boyfriend. Good for you."

"Just ignore him," Keith says, giving my hand a gentle squeeze.

I hate this power. All it's done is hurt people. I hate feeling whatever this horrible feeling is. Emotion is vile. Society had good reason for ridding itself of it. How could this happen? I'm too overwhelmed to process anything. I need to get back to my cell. I need to be alone, where I can't hurt anyone.

"I want to go back to my room," I say, slightly hysterical. I'm still shaking, unable to think.

Ashton throws his hands up. "What do you think I've been trying to do?"

"That's enough," Keith says, throwing Ashton a disgusted

look. He turns back to me. "It's alright. We'll get you back there. Come on."

9

"I WANT TO LEARN HOW TO CONTROL MY ABILITY."

I hate using the term 'ability'. It's not an ability. It's a disease. But I'll use their term if it gets me what I want. I need to control this.

I pace back and forth in my cell, restlessly running my hands through my hair. Jonah stands patiently in the door frame. Tiffany is at his side, but I ignore her. She's tapping her feet against the concrete, pursing her lips together, and biting her nails. It's annoying. What does she have to be worried about?

"Your ability is particularly powerful," Jonah says, scratching his dark stubble beard.

"I realize that."

"And what happened with Audrey and Darren—"

"Was an accident," I say heatedly. "I need to know how to control this . . . this disease."

There. I used my word for it. They should know how I really feel.

Tiffany takes a few timid steps forward, coming into the room. "Hollis, we know it was an accident. It's not a question of your character. We just want you to realize that—"

"My character?" I repeat. "You don't know anything about my character. You don't know me."

"Hollis—"

"No. You kidnapped me. You don't get to talk right now."

I glare at her. It's a strange expression, but oddly comforting. She retreats back through the door, pulling at her fingers and staring at the floor.

I turn away from Tiffany, giving my full attention to Jonah. I'm angry, and it's seething from me like a vile poison. It's giving me a clarity I thought I would never have, and for the first time, I'm giving in to the feeling. I don't care about controlling my emotions. I need to control my ability, and if anger will help me do that, then I'll invite it in—fully, with no restraint.

"I didn't ask for this."

"We know," Tiffany says solemnly.

I ignore her. My eyes are fixed on Jonah.

"I didn't ask for any of this. I've been kidnapped by creatures with magical powers, and everything's messed up. None of this is normal. You all have bad blood, and bad blood messes up your brain. You're diseased. And now . . . now I'm diseased too. So I want to learn how to control this so that I never have to use it again."

"So that you never have to use it again?" Tiffany says, eyebrows raised. "What?"

I disregard her.

"Whatever I have is evil," I say, imploring Jonah to my plight. My voice catches in my throat. "Please help me. Please. I don't want this. What I did back there—what I did at the Testing Center . . . that's not me. I didn't mean for any of it to happen. I can't control it, and that's what scares me more than any of this nightmare."

"Maybe you need to take a breath," Tiffany suggests.

"Tiffany," Jonah says, holding his hand up.

But I can't ignore her any longer. I snap, rounding on her with a vicious look. My hands ball into fists, and my eyes start to water. I'm completely beside myself.

"Take a breath? Are you kidding? The only reason I'm here is because of your screwed up idea of 'rescuing' me from my life!" I say, hurling my words at her.

Tiffany claps a hand to her forehead. "Hollis, they were going to kill you. They were going to shoot you. You saw it for yourself. Rosalie showed you the memory."

I pace back and forth like a cornered, wounded animal. I don't know what to say regarding Rosalie, but I know what I want. I scowl at her with venom in my tone.

"If you're going to hold me here against my will, then you have an obligation to help me," I say. These words come with more boldness than I thought myself capable of. "I need to learn how to control my ability. I need to. Please help me."

This sinister disease is too much for me to handle. It's

frightening and evil, and I want nothing to do with it. I'm determined to rid myself of it—even if that means learning from the Diseased Ones.

I stare at Jonah, utterly helpless. He's considering me, looking me up and down. He walks a few paces into the room and then stops. I'm taken aback by the look on his face. I don't have a word for it. Why is he looking at me like that?

"Can I ask you something?" he says quietly.

"Fine."

"Does using your ability frighten you?"

I stop pacing and stare at the floor for several moments. I nod slowly. "Yes."

I'm terrified. Deep down, I know that I'm different than them, even in my ability. The Diseased Ones seem to have docile powers—even fanciful ones. My power is cruel and dark. Whatever I have is far worse than they expected. I can see it in Jonah's eyes—in all of their eyes. What I have is a sickness far more depraved than theirs.

"There are a few things I'd like you to be aware of if we attempt to do this, Miss Timewire," Jonah says. "Are you willing to hear me out?"

"Yes."

"First, for you to control your ability, you must learn how to use it. One can't come without the other," he says. "So, are you willing to use your ability, Miss Timewire?"

I am utterly bemused by this. I speak slowly and deliberately. "Yes, sir."

That's a lie. I know for a fact I'm not okay with using it, but right now I don't see any alternatives. I have to do this. It's the only way I'll be free.

Jonah gives me a surveying look. "Are you willing to learn about your ability?"

"Yes."

"It will be difficult."

"That's fine."

"And it will take some time."

"Fine," I say.

Jonah pauses, still scrutinizing me from head to foot. Something behind his look is beyond my comprehension. I stand there, planting my feet and elevating my posture.

"Are you willing to work with me?" he asks.

"Yes."

"Will you put forth your best effort?"

"Yes."

Jonah stops speaking once more and continues to study me. I try to look determined, but I fear he can see something else.

"Are you willing to listen to me?"

"Yes, sir."

"And are you willing to trust me, Miss Timewire?"

I'm befuddled. It's as if he knows me. Every question cuts at me, every word draws me out, and every point pierces my resolve. How does he know what to ask?

I open my mouth, but it remains suspended there. I stand still for several seconds, unable to speak. Am I willing to trust him? Am I willing to voice this? I don't know if I can, but I don't have a choice. I can't do this on my own. I recognize that.

"Yes, I am willing to trust you," I say.

"And are you willing to do whatever I ask of you?"

I hesitate, brushing my face with the back of my hand. "Yes, sir."

"Do you give me your word?"

"I give you my word."

"Very well then," Jonah says. "I'd like to share something with you."

"Okay."

Jonah approaches me, and out of instinct, I shrink back.

"I'm . . . I'm sorry," I say. I move forward again. If he's to become my teacher, I need to learn to control my deep-seated uneasiness.

"I can take on another person's ability when I'm near enough," Jonah says. "I will learn from your ability with you. I learn from everyone as I train them. I work on the nuances of an ability for myself, and I share what I learn with my students."

I stare at him, mouth open. He can take on my power? I shudder. Part of me is horrified by this, but I'm relieved at the same time.

I bite the inside of my cheek before I ask, "Can you show me?" I point to Tiffany. "Can you show me hers?"

Jonah nods, backing away from me to stand against the far wall. With a pop, he vanishes and then reappears next to Tiffany.

My heart drops. He's telling the truth.

"You would do that?" I ask, meeting Jonah's eyes. "You would take this on? To teach me?"

"Yes."

I stare at him. How can he possibly mean that? A strong desire to warn him overcomes me. He doesn't realize what he's offering, and even though I'm desperate to be rid of it, I wouldn't wish my power on anyone—even a Diseased One.

"Jonah, this ability is more than just dark. It's alive." My lower lip quivers. "It's all-consuming. It makes me do things. It . . . it speaks to me."

Jonah considers me for a moment, his brow furrowed. "Hollis, I need to ask you one more time. Are you willing to do whatever I ask of you?"

I look down at the floor, twisting the ball of my foot against the concrete. Am I? I meet his gaze and then nod. "Yes, sir."

"And will you trust me?"

He looks me in the eye, and my heartbeat pounds in my ears.

"I will trust you."

The phrase falls awkwardly on my tongue and leaves a bad taste in my mouth. I've just uttered my biggest lie yet.

"Then, Miss Timewire, I believe you have yourself a teacher."

10

I TOSS FITFULLY IN MY SLEEP. JONAH WANTS TO BEGIN MY training immediately, which means I start tomorrow morning, bright and early. He thinks it's best to train me away from prying eyes, and I'm deeply grateful for this. No one needs to watch. No one needs to see this.

I roll over to face the wall, pulling the blanket over my head and staring blankly ahead. Numbing cold cascades to my toes. I'm wrestling with my tortured thoughts. How is this my reality? Why is this happening to me? What am I going to do? And more importantly, will I ever be free again?

"Mother," I whisper. "I'm scared . . . I'm sorry. You taught me to be brave. But I'm scared right now. I don't know what to do."

The pitch darkness holds nothing but silence. No one is with me. I'm all alone. I hug the blanket fiercely, trying to anchor myself to something real, but all I can picture are the evil deeds this power has forced upon me.

I need to block it out. I need to be the society member my parents trained me to be. I can't let emotion ruin me. My father once said that I'd make a fine military woman. I never wanted to join the military elite, but he saw that pristine control in me. He knew I had what it takes. Father was proud of me—*is* proud of me. He said I could be a military elite. He called me a dedicated and bright individual.

"I have what it takes," I say. "I have what it takes."

But even my father's words can't staunch the vivid visions of Audrey's bulging eyes and Darren's strangled voice, and as I fall into a disturbed sleep, I hear the crack of a skull smacking the marble pillar over and over again—like some sickening beat marching me toward inevitable failure.

■ ■ ■

"Can you tell me what happened?" Jonah asks. "To the best of your recollection."

I'm on the training platform, blurry-eyed and exhausted. Jonah stands across from me, and Ashton leans against the huge mat, wearing a sour look. It's five in the morning. I rub my face, trying to think back to the chaos of that day.

"Everyone just freezes," I say, brushing my hair out of the way. "I don't know how else to describe it. Everyone turns completely still, and there's this voice that guides me and . . ."

I stop speaking, exhaling sharply. I probably sound insane, even by their standards.

Jonah contemplates this, standing at the other end of the training platform. He takes his time before replying.

"Could you make them do what you wanted?"

A chill shoots down my spine, icing me to the core. I stare at him, a little unnerved.

"Yes," I say.

"Did anyone copy you?"

My heart drops into my stomach, thundering uncomfortably. Did he watch the Testing Center's screen footage? How could he possibly know that?

"Yes." My hands begin to shake.

"Can you be specific?"

"There was a nurse," I say. "She had a gun pointed at me, but when I covered my face, she dropped the gun and covered her face. She was cowering. It was like I was the one pointing the gun at her. She looked exactly like me."

I'm fighting with my own words. I try to clear my throat, adjusting my shoulders and folding my hands together. I need to calm down. We're just talking.

"Did anything else like this happen?" he asks.

"Yes. The military men at the entrance of the Testing Center," I say. "When I came down to the lobby, they were blocking the entrance and they . . ."

My throat closes, completely stifling me. My face turns hot, and my eyes begin to water.

"Take your time," Jonah says, giving me an encouraging look.

I swallow a painful lump and start again.

"They had guns, and when they pointed the guns at me . . . I thought . . ."

I falter. Do I really want to say something I don't believe is true? My hands are cold and clammy, drenched with sweat. Jonah waits patiently, keeping his eyes on me. I take a deep breath.

"I thought that they were going to shoot me," I say. "So I stood up straight because I wanted my parents to be . . . to be proud of me and . . . they were standing like me. All of them."

Jonah begins to pace back and forth, his hand to his chin.

"And did you tell anyone what to do?" he asks.

"Like giving an order?"

"Yes."

I rub my hands together, letting air out between pursed lips. That day feels like a messy canvas of one nightmare after another, and as I reflect on it, I recognize that the Diseased Ones' narrative of a murderous government has merit. But I'm not sold. Not yet. There's still too much to learn and too many questions left unanswered.

"Yes," I say. "When they cuffed me to the metal throne, I told them to let me go."

"And they did?"

"Yes."

"Very well then," Jonah says, clapping his hands together. "I think I've learned all that I can with my questions. Now it's time for you to try."

Adrenaline hits me like a bus, crippling every sinew in my body. It takes me a moment to speak.

"Try to use my ability? Right now?" I shake my head, backing away from him. I can't do this. I don't want to.

"Your ability is directly connected to other people," Jonah says. "So I would like you to use your ability on me."

"But I . . . I can't. I'll hurt you," I say. "You don't understand. When it happens, it's vicious. It's completely out of my control. It doesn't care that I don't want to hurt anyone. It just grabs people and . . . No. I can't. Jonah, I'll hurt you."

"Ashton is here to suppress your ability if anything gets out of hand," Jonah says, pointing to him. "I need to see your ability for myself to fully understand it."

I stare at Jonah, perplexed. He's willing to become a victim. He's standing on the training mat, perfectly relaxed. He just asked me to attack him. How is he so calm?

"So, you don't know what I have yet?" I ask.

Jonah smiles. "I have an idea, but I can't be sure. Not yet."

I shake my head. "This is crazy. You want me to attack you? I can't control this."

"I want you to use your ability on me," Jonah says, correcting me. "You don't need to attack me to do that."

"I don't know if I'll hurt you."

"Hollis, you said you would trust me," Jonah says gently. "Right now, all you need to do is focus on using your ability. That's it."

I look down at my feet. The cold sweat has reached my forehead. I don't know what to expect, but I don't have a choice.

"Okay," I say.

"Alright." Jonah holds his hand up. "Ashton, you can take your power off her now."

Ashton gives Jonah a stiff nod and then swipes his hand through the air. I flinch, expecting to be enveloped by the tingling, but nothing happens. I don't feel a thing. I hold both of my hands up, squinting at them.

"All you need to do is try," Jonah says.

"Okay."

I hold my palms up, pointing them at Jonah, feeling absurd. I flex my fingertips. Nothing happens. I wave my hand and push it forward. Nothing.

Ashton snickers, stifling his glee by pulling his collar up over his mouth. I must look completely stupid waving my hand at thin air.

"It's not working," I say, feeling deflated. "Why isn't it working?"

"Up to this point, you've only used your ability under times of extreme stress," Jonah says. "Now you must learn to use it without this trigger."

Without stress? He must be joking.

"How?" I ask. I shift my weight back and forth. "I don't know where to start."

"You need to relax," Jonah says. I fight the urge to laugh. "Close your eyes and take a few deep breaths."

"Okay."

I obey and close my eyes, taking a moment to calm the knotted feeling in my gut. I can do this.

"Remember what your ability feels like. How does it make your fingertips feel? How does it make *you* feel?"

What a strange request. Never in my life have I been asked

to dwell on my feelings. An overwhelming societal urge springs up within me. I can't do that. I'm not supposed to do that. It'll only make things worse. But once again, I recall the stark reality of my position. Jonah said he would teach me, and that's my only option.

I take a few long, deep breaths, thinking back to the Testing Center. How did I do that? I just . . . did it. But what exactly did I do?

Something comes to mind. There was a moment in the lobby—the moment I yielded to the power in me. It was as if primal instinct burst forth like an overflowing fountain. It was invigorating. Transformative. I was so scared, but I had never felt more alive. That power was incredible—liberating.

I feel it. I open my eyes. My fingers are tingling, and I raise my hand toward Jonah. His body stiffens, and in a single twitch of my fingertips, he is perfectly still.

"I did it."

"This is incredible," Jonah says. "I can't move."

The moment of victory is short-lived. Fear grips me, strangling my voice. "I-I don't like this," I say, shaking my head and retreating from him. "I want to stop."

"You're not hurting me," Jonah says calmly. "I just can't move. It's alright."

I want to get this over with. "Okay. What's my ability?"

"I have a theory. Can you try to control my actions?"

I nod, moving my other palm up and aiming it at Jonah. The vibrations move through my arm to the end of my hand. I feel an incredible amount of control.

"Just try anything," Jonah says.

"Okay."

I shoot my left hand straight toward the ceiling, and Jonah's arm copies mine, moving at the same speed.

I gasp. "Woah."

I lower my arm slowly, holding it parallel to the floor. Jonah's arm follows this, perfectly synced. What kind of power is this?

"Now," Jonah says, still completely stiff. "Can you make me move without moving yourself?"

"I can try."

"First, imagine the movement you want me to do," he instructs. "And then use your ability, not your body."

"Okay."

I imagine Jonah kneeling. It's the only thing I can think of, and after contemplating this, I flare out my fingertips. Nothing happens.

Come on. Kneel.

I push my hand forward, but Jonah remains frozen with his arm extended parallel to the floor. My entire hand is pulsing. Why isn't this working?

Kneel, I think again. Kneel. But Jonah remains still.

"I can't do it," I say, dropping my hands and scuffing the mat with the sole of my shoe.

"That's alright," Jonah says. "I didn't expect you'd be able to. You still have a lot to learn about your ability. You did very well. Now, I want you to remove your power, so I can move again."

My pulse spikes. That's something I've never done. I haven't been able to stop. This power holds someone until it's done. I've never had a choice in the matter.

"I don't think I can."

"Try," he says. "Focus your mind. You control it. It doesn't control you."

I shake my head. "Jonah, I don't know how. I've never been able to stop." I turn to Ashton. "Suppress my ability. Please."

"Hollis, look at me," Jonah says, his tone even. I turn back to him, and we lock eyes. "You don't need Ashton to take away your ability. You can do it. Let me go."

I catch Ashton's sneering look. He's clearly having a good laugh at my expense. He calls out to me, a cocky grin smeared across his pointed face. "Hey Timewire, just relax your shoulders. You're too tense."

Of course I'm tense. I have a person frozen under my crazy power. I shoot him a dirty look—something I learned from Tiffany—and surprisingly, it calms me down.

I relax my hands, and my arms go limp. To my relief, Jonah's frame relaxes as well, and he appears to fall out of his rigid form. He takes a few steps forward to catch his balance.

"Thank goodness," I say under my breath. "I did it. I actually did it."

No screaming. No bulging eyes. No silent pleading. No cruel voice. No vicious attacks. I did it, and no one got hurt in the process. A small ray of hope crops up within me. Maybe I can beat this.

"Well done," Jonah says. "Honestly, you did an incredible

job. Not many people start off using their ability with the proficiency you just demonstrated."

"What did I do though? What's my ability? I can make statues out of people? Control them? I mean, it's a little... unnerving."

Jonah walks over to me, closing the distance between us. Something is off. He looks muted—like he's trying to hide what he's really thinking. I recognize this right away because concealing expressions is my specialty. That's how I've been raised, and something sends an eerie shock down to my toes. Jonah's not very good at suppressing his emotions. So, what could I possibly have that would make him attempt to do so?

"Your ability is rare, Hollis," he says. "I didn't want to say anything until I was completely certain."

"What is it? What do I have?"

"Hollis Timewire," Jonah says, and my full name rings strangely in my ears. "You're a puppet master."

II

"I'M A PUPPET MASTER?"

The term sounds intriguing, but I can't think of a more frightening name for the monster hiding beneath my fingertips.

"What does that mean?" I ask.

"You can control everything about a person," Jonah says.

An unpleasant sensation settles in my stomach. "I can make people do what I want? Anything I want?"

"It would seem so. People become puppets to your power." Jonah scratches his chin and starts to pace. "Your ability is extremely rare."

I don't like the sound of that. It's bad enough that my power seems to have a mind of its own, but the fact that it's rare is concerning. I can tell that Jonah hasn't come across my ability before. What if he can't help me?

"How do you know it's rare?" I ask.

Jonah pauses, staring at the mat. "I'd like to teach you a little about ability types," he says. "There are two broad categories that abilities fall into. Abilities that only require something of yourself, and abilities that require something of others."

"Two types," I say.

"Yes," he says. "Type one abilities don't require other people to work, but type two abilities do. I know that your ability is rare because you're a type two. You can only use your power when other people are around you."

"Okay." I squint at him. "So Tiffany is a type one?"

"Yes, she can teleport herself regardless of whether she's around others."

I'm trying to keep myself composed. I understand. So if I were alone, I couldn't hurt anyone. Part of me is relieved to hear this, but my heart sinks. I don't want to be alone. I don't want to be locked up in that cell, cut off from any kind of interaction. Is this why they've kept me so isolated?

"And there aren't many type twos?" I ask.

"Out of the four hundred people here, we have six, including you."

I look up at Jonah, eyes wide. "You and Ashton?"

Jonah nods. "Yes, we are both type two."

I tap my foot against the mat, scuffing the underside of my shoe. My stomach squirms. "Are type twos somehow . . . more powerful?"

"Typically, yes," Jonah says. "And while there are some powerful type one abilities, type twos are superior in many ways."

"How so?"

"Stamina, for one," Jonah says. "Type two abilities require so much of a person's energy and focus—more so than type one. I've also found that type twos learn to command their ability faster than type ones, and from what I've seen, you seem to be a quick study."

"I was the top student in my class," I say. "I liked school."

I pause, and a strange thought occurs to me. For the first time since my arrival, I shared something personal. School always gave me a sense of purpose and direction. Studying hard made me feel like I could accomplish anything I wanted to. But this power seems like an insurmountable task.

Jonah looks me in the eye. "I will admit, I've studied many abilities over the years. I've encountered duplicate abilities, but your power is something I haven't seen before. I've only heard of complete control-based type twos in theory. I never thought I'd actually meet one."

Chilling cold cascades through my chest and into my limbs.

"But I can teach you if you're willing to learn," he says.

"I am."

"You don't have to do this alone."

I let my head droop. All of the energy in me vanishes, and a deep sense of helplessness replaces my curiosity. Now that Jonah knows what I am, will I ever be set free? I want to ask him, but I fear that I already know the answer. Of course they won't let me out. I'm a stranger from society, cursed with an ability that's more powerful than any of them anticipated. My ability is too volatile—too new. I'm unpracticed and undertrained.

I bury my face in my hands.

"Hollis." Jonah's soft voice sends nervous jitters down to my toes. "What is it?"

My hands are shaking, and my chest tightens. I feel like I'm going to cry. I look up at him, taking a deep breath. I need to pull myself together. Blowing air out through pursed lips, I begin twisting a lock of my hair through my fingertips, trying to find the right words.

"Will the Council let me out of my cell? Now that we know more about my ability?" I ask.

My heartbeat thunders in my chest, and my pulse beats wildly, pounding up through my head. I'm beginning to feel faint.

Jonah smiles. "Hollis, today you demonstrated to me that you're capable of using your ability without a trigger, and more importantly, you showed me that you're willing to listen to me and work with me. I'll have to talk with the Council, and we'll need to set up some ground rules, but I think it's time that you join the rest of us."

My eyes are streaming. "You're letting me out?"

"Pending Eli Stone's approval, yes, I'm letting you out."

"Eli Stone?"

"Our lead Council member."

Relief, like a wave, washes over me, and a single tear traces the side of my face. I'm getting out. I'm actually getting out of that terrible room, and even though I'm still a prisoner of this underground world, I'm no longer alone.

"Thank you," I say. I wipe my face with the back of my

hand, collecting myself and straightening my posture. I don't want to appear weepy. I've lost much of my societal control, but I still have some dignity left.

"You did well today," Jonah says. "We have a long way to go, but now that I know what I'm working with, I'm confident we'll get there."

"Okay."

"Take it one day at a time."

I swallow the lump in my throat. "Yes, sir."

There's a deep sense of disquiet in my spirit. Somehow, the victory today feels hollow. Jonah figured out what I have, but that doesn't mean I'm any closer to controlling it. If anything, this ability has proven time and time again that it's capable of controlling me.

"I think that will do for today," Jonah says. "Let's get you back. I'll meet with the Council, and then we can assign you a proper room."

"Thank you."

Jonah jumps off the training platform and motions me to his side. I follow him, and as I step off the large, discolored mat, my uneasiness is replaced with a budding excitement. I'm getting out of that horrid cell.

12

TIFFANY AND I WALK BRISKLY DOWN A LONG CONCRETE hallway. She's moving so rapidly I have to jog to keep up with her. She's positively trembling with excitement.

"My room is just down here," she says.

I count the doors that we pass. Twelve. Thirteen. Fourteen. Fifteen. Sixteen.

This underground compound is a bit of a maze, and I'm shocked by the size. I'm still getting my bearings around here.

It's been a week since my first training lesson with Jonah, and to my great relief, Ashton no longer has to accompany me everywhere I go. I can control the most basic aspect of my ability. This accomplishment has allowed me freedom. Jonah has put an incredible amount of faith in me. He says he's extending his trust toward me so that I can extend my trust toward them.

I've also been assigned a room now, and can come and go as

I please. This privilege has returned a sense of normalcy to my life, and I'm deeply grateful for it.

"Not so fast, Tiffany," I say, skipping in step behind her rapid pace.

"Just down here," she says.

Seventeen. Eighteen. Nineteen. Twenty.

"I still can't believe I got this room," Tiffany chimes. "Space is pretty limited down here, but the Council drew my name."

"Drew your name?"

"Oh, there were a few empty rooms being used for storage, but the Council decided to open them up, so I entered my name into a drawing," she says. "Don't get me wrong, I love my parents and all, but it's nice to finally have my own space. Almost everyone has to live with their family, but I figured, why not give the extra room a shot? And I got lucky!"

We reach the very last door in the hall. Tiffany opens it and spills inside, bubbling over with enthusiasm. She waves me through. "Here it is, in all its splendor."

I glance around the modest arrangement. The room is simple. It contains two cots, a wooden stand between the cots, two dressers, and a lamp.

"It's not all that fancy," she concedes. "I just like to make a grand entrance."

"Looks like my room," I say.

"Yeah, great-grandpa Chang went for practicality rather than style when he made this place. Everything's the same in here."

"Oh, that's right. Charles Chang was your great-grandfather."

"Yep. My family has been here since the massacre."

A little jolt runs its course through my limbs. Not that topic again. But for the first time, it occurs to me that I hardly know anything about the girl standing in front of me. She can teleport, and her grandfather built this compound with his ability. If I'm really going to be a part of their world, if I'm going to learn the truth about what happened a hundred years ago, I need to start studying. Maybe I'll learn something useful—something tangible.

I point to the cot. "May I sit?"

"Of course," she says, moving to the cot and folding herself up, crisscrossed. I join her, sitting at the foot and leaning against the wall.

"So, do you have any siblings?" I ask. It's the first question that comes to my mind.

"No, just me," she says. "What about you?"

"It's just me too," I say. "My parents were allowed to have one more, but they were happy with me."

Tiffany gives me a strange look. "Allowed?"

"Oh . . . um, family units are allowed to have two kids," I say. "To replace the parents. It's a population thing. It's . . ." I'm uncomfortable. I don't really want to talk about my world. I want to talk about hers. I try to brush past the moment. "So, what are your parents' abilities?"

"My mom has super strength, and my dad doesn't have an ability," she says.

My interest peaks and I sit straight.

"Your father doesn't have an ability?" I ask, staring at her.

"How?"

Tiffany scratches her nose. "He wasn't born with one. It's kind of like you. You were born to parents who don't have abilities. It's pretty rare both ways, but it's just about the biomarker. You either have it or you don't."

"Right," I say.

Tiffany's comment has sparked a thought. I wonder if there's a way for someone with an ability to lose it permanently? I open my mouth and then shut it immediately. I can't ask that. I reroute my question, steering the conversation in a different direction.

"Hey, what happened that time you ended up halfway around the world? You were going to tell me a while back, but Ashton was—"

I stop myself. Ashton was an ass. I don't say this out loud because I don't want to say anything aggressive.

"Oh yeah," she says, lighting up. "It was pretty terrifying. But it's funny looking back on it now that I'm older."

I give Tiffany the smallest fraction of a smile. It still feels foreign, and I probably look absurd, but I'm making an effort. I've been experimenting with facial expressions. It's strange. Part of me wants to reject the effort entirely. I know that emotion is bad. I've not forgotten my carefully forged education. But I figure that since I'm here—since I don't have a choice—I might as well try. I'll learn more this way. It's like trying on a sweater. I don't have to keep it if I don't like it. I can always go back to the blank stare I know I've mastered.

"So what happened?" I ask.

"It happened when I was seventeen. I was still learning how to use my ability," she says. "In fact, for a while, my parents didn't think I had an ability."

"Why?"

"I was a late bloomer," she says, grabbing a pillow and squashing it under her feet. "We thought I was like my dad because when I turned sixteen, nothing happened. I didn't exhibit any power."

"Really?"

"Yeah. It doesn't happen often," she says. "Oh, and people can exhibit their ability before sixteen too—but that's crazy rare. I've only heard of one case, but I'm pretty sure it's a myth."

"Well, the biomarker is just a result of gene expression," I say. "I learned about it in biology class."

"Gene expression?" Tiffany asks, perplexed.

"It's like a light switch," I explain. "Some genes in our body only turn on at certain times. That's why the government tests people at sixteen. It's when the gene that produces the biomarker turns on. I guess it's when someone's biologically mature enough."

"So if someone's gene turns on early, they get their powers early?"

"I suppose so," I say.

Tiffany shrugs. "Anyway, nothing happened for me that entire year, so I'd accepted the fact that I didn't have an ability—well, to be honest, I was a little disappointed—but I was proud to be like my dad," she adds. "But one day, I was eating dinner with my folks, and I sneezed so violently that I ended up halfway across the common room."

I laugh. "You sneeze-teleported yourself?"

"I sure did," she says, very matter-of-fact. "And my parents were like, 'she has an ability!' They were so excited."

I lean back against the wall, folding myself up like Tiffany and resting my head on my hand. I feel strangely at home.

"So how did you teleport halfway across the world?" I ask.

"Well, once we figured out I had an ability, I started training with Jonah. But I had this problem where I would randomly teleport," she says.

"Oh no."

"Exactly."

"Could you teleport on purpose?"

"Oh, I could teleport on purpose," she says. "But I would also teleport for no good reason. I couldn't control it."

I nod. That's exactly how I feel. "Interesting."

"And I was also very skittish—still am. You can get a good scare out of me if you time it right," she continues, glaring at the air as if someone stood directly in front of her.

"Oh no," I say. "What happened?"

"Ben—that speedy little mischievous thing." She squints. "He thought it would be funny if he zipped up to me with his super-speed and blew in my ear. Scared me so badly that I vanished into thin air. He thought he'd killed me."

I gasp, snorting and covering my mouth with my hand. A wonderful emotion overcomes me. I'm smiling. I'm actually smiling. I drop my hand and embrace the expression.

"And where did you go?"

"Some field in Area Five," she says. "I think I landed in—oh, what did it used to be called—Romania! Have you ever heard of Romania?"

I nod. "Yeah, I've heard of Romania."

It's strange hearing a term from my ancient history class. The world used to be divided into countries, and each country had a name, but that was done away with in 2276. Now the world is sectioned into areas, and each area has a number. At least the Diseased Ones have some kind of education system.

"So what did you do?" I ask.

She readjusts the pillow, pulling it out from under her feet and hugging it.

"Well, at first I freaked out. But after I calmed down, I used what Jonah taught me and concentrated on the common room. I teleported back." Her face lights up. She rubs her hands together, as if scheming something fantastic.

"Wow."

"*And* I appeared right in front of Ben, *and*—" Tiffany wears a satisfied look. "He fell right over. Like one of those fainting goats."

I stare at her, thoroughly confused. "Like a what?"

"You know, a fainting goat?" Tiffany repeats.

I shake my head. "Sorry, no."

Her mouth drops open. She looks incredulous—like I had never heard of the concept of breathing air.

"So," she says, grinning broadly. "It's just like a normal goat, but when it gets really scared, its legs lock up and it just falls over."

I imagine Ben's legs locking up, and the vision of him keeling over on the spot gives me an incredible amount of satisfaction. "That's a great story."

"Serves him right," she says, folding her arms across her chest. She's knotted her limbs together so tightly that I don't know if she'll ever unfold herself.

I smile. Ben nearly made me fall over too. But my expression falls as Audrey and Darren replace all thoughts of Ben and Tiffany. I could never have a story like that—not as long as I have this disease. I drop my gaze down to the folds of the blanket I'm sitting on.

"Hollis, are you alright?"

"I didn't mean to do that to them," I say slowly. "It just happened."

"I know you didn't. It's alright. Jonah talked with them."

"He did?" I say, picking my head up slightly. "Are they alright?"

"Yes, of course."

"Good."

I shift my legs up, tucking myself into a ball. I want to disappear again.

Tiffany smiles, holding her hand out and placing it on the cot right in front of me. "I think you just caught everyone off guard. That's all. But it's alright. That kind of thing happens more often than you might think."

"Really?" I can't help but feel that's she's just telling me this to make me feel better.

"Didn't you hear my story?" she asks, chuckling. "I couldn't control my ability at first either. You'll get it with practice. Don't worry. We all start out like this."

Yes, except her disease doesn't attack other people. Mine does. "I suppose."

"You'll see," she says, encouraging me. "Jonah thinks you're doing an incredible job."

I look down at my hands and then back up to Tiffany. Do I dare voice what I'm thinking? The same question has cropped up again. Is it possible to get rid of an ability . . . for good? I want to know what she thinks, and before I can stop myself, I've asked the question.

Tiffany blinks, staring at me.

I can't believe I just asked. Did I really say that out loud? Of course I did. She wouldn't be looking at me like that if I hadn't.

"You mean permanently?" she says.

"I . . . well, yes."

My heart is ramming against my ribcage, like an animal attempting to free itself from a trap. I tuck my hands under the blanket to hide my nerves.

Tiffany cocks her head to the side. "Huh. I don't know. I don't think so. Why?"

"I don't know."

I can't think of anything to say. I'm certainly not going to tell her why I've asked this. That's my business.

"That's an interesting question." Tiffany scratches her chin. "I've never thought about that before."

I shrug, thinking quickly. "I guess I was just curious. I don't know much about your world yet and . . . and I'm trying to learn."

Tiffany raises an eyebrow, but she smiles and puts her hand on my shoulder. The touch still feels unfamiliar, but I don't pull away. I don't even flinch. Her touch is strangely comforting—almost like coming home.

"I'm glad," she says. "I can't imagine how hard this is for you, but I'm happy that you're trying to adjust. It must be very difficult."

"Yeah."

Of course she can't imagine what it must be like for me. I've been ripped away from my life, and I may never see my parents again. It's more than difficult. It's impossible.

"And about your ability," she says. "I know it's terrifying, but your power is part of who you are now. It makes you an amazing, incredible person. It gives you a history, and more importantly, an identity. You're one of us now—family."

I've moved back to the defensive, pulling my walls up again. "Everyone keeps saying that, but you don't know me. You don't know where I've come from—*my* history, *my* mother and father, *my* world. You don't know anything."

"I know," she says, nodding. "And you're right, I don't know where you've come from, or what you've gone through, but I do know that everyone in this compound will be here for you, whenever you're ready."

I stare at her. What is she talking about?

"But I don't understand," I say. "I'm a society member, and apparently, I've been brainwashed. My life is a lie—or so you've told me." I shake my head, trying to find the right words. "You already know what I think of you. I've made myself perfectly clear, so how can you say you'll be here for me and truly mean it? You have nothing to gain."

Tiffany gives me a sad little smile. "I'm not trying to gain anything from you, Hollis."

"I find that very hard to believe."

"That's okay." She tucks a strand of her black hair behind her ear. "I'm not expecting you to change your worldview overnight. I mean . . . discovering you have powers? Living underground? Learning about the massacre? That'd be enough to overwhelm anyone. I'm just . . . I'm glad you're trying. It's amazing. Most people would give up, or cry themselves to sleep every night, but I don't see that in you. You're wrestling with it, and that's a good thing."

I don't know how to respond to this. Does Tiffany mean that? Is she sincere? Do the Diseased Ones actually see me as family? I don't know. I simply don't know. This grand, universal acceptance is beyond my experience.

Just then, a bell chimes down the hallway.

"That'll be dinner," Tiffany says. "Come on. We don't want to be late. Why don't you join me and Rosalie?"

She hops off of the cot and walks to the door, turning around expectantly. "Coming?"

I hesitate, but only for a moment. "Sure. Why not."

13

THE HUSTLE AND BUSTLE OF DINNER RINGS OUT AGAINST the high concrete walls. I'm sitting with Tiffany, Rosalie, Ben, and Candice. Ben is telling a story, and he's speaking so rapidly that I'm having a hard time catching everything.

"And I was like, 'Jonah, you just can't keep up with me, old man. I'm too speedy.'" Ben says, munching on a stick of celery. He uses it to point toward the middle of the table. "And, it's not even because of my ability. I'm just speedy. It's sleight of hand. He just can't catch it. No one can."

"Ben's gotten himself into magic," Candice says, lowering her voice so that Ben can't hear. She snickers, holding her hand up to her face and rolling her eyes.

"Like old-fashioned magic?" I ask.

Ben glances between Candice and me several times, looking smug. "Magic has been around since twenty-seven hundred BC," he says. "It's the oldest form of performing arts."

"I like history too," I say. "It was my favorite subject in school."

I pause a moment, contemplating what I've said. I just shared something personal, like it was normal.

"Hey Ben. We're all magicians. We just have different acts," Candice says, her tone smug.

"Hey there, missy," he says, whipping the stick of celery toward her. "I'm a grand magician. Like I said, my sleight of hand is impeccable. You can't catch it."

"Ah, but we already have people here who can make things disappear," Candace says, grinning and leaning back in her chair. She puts her hands behind her head, mirroring Ben's countenance.

He looks affronted. "Whatever, Candy. I'm expanding my horizons, and by horizons, I mean abilities, and by abilities, I mean *magical* abilities—not normal abilities."

He crunches on the stick of celery, chewing it viciously.

Candice snickers. "Thank you, Ben, for that line of clarification."

"Okay," I say, turning to Ben. "Show me this magic you speak of. I want to see it. I'm curious."

He looks thrilled. "See Candy? Hollis is interested in my magic."

Candice rolls her eyes. "That's because she doesn't know any better."

Ben disregards her, pulling out a match and standing up from the table, his chair scraping across the floor. He backs away a few paces and then waves his other hand dramatically.

He clears his throat, speaking loudly in his best spooky voice.

"And now, the amazing Ben Bryson will make this match vanish into thin air. Watch closely."

He holds the match between his thumb and index finger and bobs his hand up and down three times. Then, with a final flourish, he flicks his hand out, palm extended. I gasp. The match is gone.

"And now, I shall conjure it back." He reaches up with his splayed hand and appears to pick the match out of the air. "Ta-da!"

He takes a deep bow and our group gives him scattered applause. Tiffany, Rosalie, and Candice exchange looks, giggling.

"Not too shabby," Candice says. "You know, for a beginner."

Ben's mouth thins out into a line, and Candice smirks.

"How did you do that?" I ask.

"A magician never reveals his secrets," Ben says, putting his finger up to his lips.

The three girls are huddled in a group, whispering to one another.

Ben walks over to them. "What are you—"

But he's cut off as Candice stands up dramatically, nudging him out of the way. She walks over to where Ben had been standing moments before. She flourishes her hand, mimicking Ben in a serious and commanding tone.

"And now, the amazing Candice Keaton will create fire from thin air. Watch closely."

She holds her hand up, and a small flame bursts to life on the tip of her index finger. It dances there for a moment before vanishing. She takes an exaggerated bow, and Tiffany and Rosalie cheer at the top of their lungs, clapping way too loudly. Ben looks sour. He folds himself up into a chair, glaring at Candice.

"You guys don't appreciate the art and precision of my craft." He slumps down in his seat, sulking.

"Oh Ben," Tiffany says, chuckling. "You know we're just giving you a hard time."

Candice nods vigorously. "Oh, totally."

"Yeah, well, let's see you pull a trick like that."

Candice opens her mouth, gasping and placing a hand over her heart. "Did you not *just* see my magnificent fire act?" She's completely indignant. "It was absolutely stunning."

"It truly was," Rosalie adds.

"Indeed," says Tiffany.

Ben stands up, nearly knocking over his chair. "You're all *so* hilarious."

"Well . . . I want to see another one," I say.

Ben looks a little taken aback but pleased nonetheless. He straightens his shoulders, rolling his head to either side and stretching his hands. He looks like he's gearing up to take a shot at the marble game.

Just then, Keith walks up to the table, directly behind Ben. We lock eyes, and I look down at my feet. My stomach squirms.

"What are you guys up to?" Keith asks.

"Ben's going to do some magic," Candice says, snickering.

Keith takes a seat next to his sister, grinning broadly. "Well then, let's see it."

"Alright," Ben says. "A card trick it is."

"Fantastic," Keith says.

Ben fumbles in the folds of his jacket and withdraws a deck of playing cards. He casts his eye about the crowd. A small spattering of adults joins in to watch. He's clearly putting on a show. He hands the deck to Candice.

"Give that a good shuffle for me, will you, Candy?"

She grins. "Sure thing."

She shuffles the cards gracefully, pulling them into a cascading bridge. She repeats this several times. I've never seen playing cards before. It's mesmerizing.

"Hollis, will you be my assistant?" Ben asks, giving me a large, goofy grin.

Ben beckons me to his side, and my hands go numb. He wants me to stand up? "Um . . ."

"Come on, all magicians need a good assistant," he says.

"Okay." I stand sheepishly. I have no idea what I've just signed up for. I'm not familiar with card magic—or any kind of magic for that matter. The whole idea of powers is already overwhelming enough.

Ben holds his hand out to Candice, and she returns the deck.

"Now, ladies and gentlemen, may I have your attention please," Ben calls out to the crowd. More people join, and all eyes are on me. I know the reason. I'm the new girl. I'm famous down here. "I will now have the lovely Hollis pick out a card."

I stand there, painfully aware of how many onlookers have gathered. "Okay."

"Pick a card. Any card you like." Ben fans the deck, and I select one from the pile.

The face of a strange-looking woman is printed on it. She stares at me with a complacent look, her heavily lidded eyes drooping with a soft smile.

"Show it around, Miss Timewire," Ben says. "But don't let me see it."

I hold the card up so that the crowd can see.

"Excellent," Candice murmurs.

Ben withdraws a black pen from the pocket of his jeans and hands it to me. "Kindly sign your name on it."

"On the card?" I ask, thinking I may have heard him wrong. "But that will ruin it."

A skinny, doe-eyed girl snickers from the front row of the crowd. This was a bad idea. I just had to ask for another trick, didn't I?

"Don't worry about the card," Ben says, waving his hands. "Just your name. Nice and large."

I scribble my name in loopy letters and hand the pen back. I want to sit down, but before I can do so, he takes the card I've signed, folds it up, and hands it back to me.

"Now, place the card in your mouth."

I squint at him, but he nods vigorously. I look between the folded card and Ben's overeager expression several times before raising my hand and placing it between my lips.

"All the way in," Ben says.

I bite down on the card. This is the most absurd thing I think I've ever done. My arms dangle like noodles, and I've become hyper-aware of every sensation around me.

Ben takes a second card from the deck and holds it aloft. "And now I'll sign my own card." He writes on it, caps the pen, and folds it up in the same manner as he had done mine. "And now, the magic."

Waving his hand dramatically, he traces a pattern through the air and places the folded card bearing his signature in his mouth.

Then several things happen at once: Ben flourishes his hand high over his head, Keith and I look at each other, heat crops up in my face, and Ben kisses me full on the mouth.

Gasps bounce around the room, followed by a smattering of laughter and whistling. I stare at him, my eyes wide. Did he just kiss me?

Several people get to their feet, keen to know what has caused the vocal upheaval. My eyes dart away from Keith's. I want to melt into the floor and cease to exist. My body feels like it's on fire. I now fully appreciate how wonderful it would have been to *not* be chosen for this little trick.

"Kindly take the card out of your mouth and open it up for everyone," Ben says, positively glowing. His tone is as casual as if he had asked me about that afternoon's weather forecast.

I reach for the card, pulling it out of my mouth. My jittering hands fumble with it for several clumsy moments before I'm finally able to pry it open.

"Hold it up, nice and high," Ben instructs.

I obey, holding up the card to reveal not my own signature, but Ben's. Ben holds up his card, showing the crowd my loopy scrawlings. There is a crash of applause and many 'whoops' directly behind me. Some of the girls are giggling, making flirty catcalls through the din.

"Another round of applause for my lovely assistant," Ben says, stepping back and putting me in the spotlight once more. Seriously?

Candice leans over to Tiffany and Rosalie, dropping her voice. "Boy, he has some nerve. Can you believe that?"

She crosses her arms and glares at Ben.

"Are you kidding me?" Rosalie says. "Of course. It's Ben."

"She makes a valid point," Tiffany adds, giggling.

Candice huffs. "Some nerve."

"Why do you care?" Rosalie asks.

Candice's face turns pink. "I don't."

Rosalie tilts her head to the side. "Sure you don't."

"Shut up," Candice hisses.

The applause dies out and I sit down, trying to make myself as small as possible. I wish I could turn invisible. That would be a useful and practical disease—not some freakish, controlling puppet-mastery.

Ben drops down in the seat directly next to Candice, leaning back and propping one foot up against his knee. "What about *that*, Candy?" he says.

"Oh, absolutely amazing," she says, a hint of sarcasm interfused in her tone. "Never seen anything like it. Truly spectacular."

Ben, clearly having missed Candice's hushed exchange between the two girls, beams from ear to ear—smug as ever. He looks as if he's just won a medal.

Candice turns back to Tiffany, Rosalie, and Keith. "What *are* we going to do with that boy?"

Keith shrugs. "Beats me."

14

"DOES BEN LIKE ME?" I ASK, RUNNING A SPONGE ACROSS the bowl of sticky pasta I'm washing in the back of the kitchen area.

The phrase falls awkwardly from my lips. I've never experienced someone's affection in that manner before. He kissed me. He actually kissed me, and it was shocking.

Tiffany rinses several bowls in the sink next to me, running them under the faucet. I continue scrubbing at a particularly stubborn bit of dried noodle that has latched onto the side of a frying pan. It's dish duty. I have finally been assigned my tasks as a fully functioning member of this underground society. I have obligations now. It's quite strange. I didn't expect to be integrated and welcomed in so quickly, but I suppose that an extra set of helping hands lightens the workload for others—small though it may be.

"No, he was putting on a show," she says, matter-of-fact.

"But he kissed me."

I've been struggling with this point. Kissing is an open act of passion. I'd never considered kissing to be an activity in which I could participate—even here. It's supposed to be for your spouse in your family unit. It's personal and connecting, even pleasurable—or so I've heard. I don't know what to make of it. And up to this point, I've only ever been around girls. I was never integrated because integration happens after the Test.

"I know," Tiffany says. "He had some nerve. That must have been quite a shock. I never would've expected that, but then again . . ." She pauses, as if considering something compelling.

"Then again what?"

She shrugs. "It *is* Ben." She grabs another bowl and scrubs at it, dunking it under the soapy water.

That's not an explanation. "What do you mean?"

"It's Ben," she says again, as if it were obvious.

"I don't know what that means," I say, feeling slightly annoyed.

"I mean that Ben has always been a prankster, always joking around. It's how he acts, even when he was a little kid. Always getting into things he shouldn't. He's a real laugh most of the time, but if he went too far, I can speak to him for you."

"No!" I say, way louder than I intend to. I don't need the attention, and the last thing I want is to make Ben feel uncomfortable around me. It's bad enough that Darren and Audrey are still on edge. I mean, I don't blame them. The incident at the marble game is seared into my brain.

Tiffany gives me an 'are-you-okay' look.

"Sorry," I say, turning back to the frying pan. "It's fine. You don't have to talk to him."

I scold myself silently. Even in my experimentation, there's no reason for a verbal outburst of any kind. I still need to foster control.

I wipe the suds off of my hand and brush my forehead to move the stray wisps of hair from my face.

"So, how's training with Jonah going?" Tiffany asks, changing the subject.

I'm incredibly relieved. She's sensed my discomfort and wants to gloss over the topic. Fine by me.

"It's going alright," I say.

"Can you make him do an action without doing it yourself?"

"Not yet."

"You'll get there," she says, smiling at me. "You've come so far already. I'm proud of you."

Proud of me. Does she mean that? "Um . . . thanks."

I smile back at her. I'm getting used to the expression. It isn't as jarring anymore. It's almost . . . familiar. Everyone here does it, and because I'm trying to fit in, I've adopted it as well.

"Of course," Tiffany says.

I glance up at the clock hanging over the large countertop. I jump. "Shoot, I'm late," I say, turning the water off and drying my hands on the nearest dish towel.

"For training?" Tiffany asks.

"Yes, I was supposed to meet Jonah ten minutes ago," I say, noting a hint of distress in my tone. How strange. I'm not in any kind of life-threatening situation, so why am I feeling panicked?

I look around at all the unwashed dishes. Time must have gotten away from me. I should have finished this a while ago. I hold my hand to my face.

"I'll finish up," Tiffany says.

"Are you sure?"

"I'm sure." She smiles. "Go. Get out of here. It's okay."

"Thanks," I say, turning away from the mess and racing down the gigantic length of the common room. I arrive at the training platform three minutes later, panting and flustered, my blonde strands askew across my nose and eyes. I wipe them away.

"You're late," Jonah says. He doesn't sound angry, but something about him commands respect.

"I know. I apologize, I was—"

I stop myself. It doesn't matter what I was doing. I'm late. It's my mistake.

"Punctuality is very important, Hollis," Jonah says. His kind tone pierces me.

"Yes, sir. I understand. I won't let it happen again."

"Alright, let's begin," he says.

I assume the usual position, standing directly across from Jonah and holding my hands up. I will myself to feel the tingling power, and Jonah stiffens—a perfect statue, unable to move a muscle.

"Alright," Jonah says. "We're going to work on your fine

motor skills today. As I've discussed with you previously, these include small tasks that require purposeful movements in your fingertips. You need to be able to control me by doing these tasks yourself."

"Yes, sir," I say.

The concept sounds a lot easier than it's going to be. That's what I've discovered in our short time together. This power isn't easy by any means, but I'm encouraged by the progress I've seen. Every training session has taught me deeper control, an experience that's familiar to me. It's comforting to know that it's still in my life—just in a different capacity.

"Try tying my shoelaces," Jonah says.

I look down, almost grinning. Jonah's laces lie open. That man is always prepared. I tense my fingers and take a deep breath, concentrating on my limbs. I kneel and hover my hand over my shoe. Jonah mirrors my actions, as if we were a pair of synchronized dancers. My fingers fumble in midair, scraping hopelessly at his left shoe and missing the laces entirely.

"Remember what it feels like to tie your own shoes," Jonah says. "Focus on that."

"Right."

My fingers move again, this time a little more deliberately. Jonah's fingers pick at the laces, but after several moments, they end up in an intense knot.

Jonah chuckles. "Try untying the knot."

I concentrate, channeling everything I have into my fingertips and grasping at the laces, but all I manage to do is create a larger, more complicated knot.

"I can't."

I sigh, standing up and scuffing my shoes across the mat. I'm just trying to tie a shoelace. But somehow, the simple skill I've known since childhood has deserted me. I don't get it.

I wave my hand, and Jonah's body relaxes. He falls forward, released from the prison of my power.

"That was an excellent first attempt," he says.

"Well, what about making you do actions that I don't have to do myself?" I ask. "Then I could just say, 'Hey, tie your shoelace,' and you'd have to do it."

"Fine motor skills are crucial to your ability," Jonah says. "You need to master this aspect first."

"But if I could just tell someone to do something, then—"

"What about when you can't?" Jonah says.

"What do you mean?" I stare at him, my brow furrowing.

When I can't control someone? Maybe he's missed the point. I don't want to. I'm only training to control this disease so that I can be done with it.

"Your ability is volatile," Jonah says. "It's eruptive and powerful, and the only way for you to truly gain control over it is to master every part of it."

"I suppose so," I say, my eyes shifting between the mat and the edge of the platform. I can tell that Jonah senses a touch of argument in me.

"While your desire to gain control over the most powerful parts of your ability is admirable, it can be dangerous if you don't master the elemental parts."

"And tying a shoelace is elemental?" I ask. I don't think

Jonah fully appreciates the difficulty of this small request.

"Yes. Tying a shoelace is elemental," he says good-naturedly.

"Right," I say. "What's next?"

Jonah smiles and then points to the corner of the training platform. "How about cutting a loaf of bread?"

To my horror, he pulls out a large knife. It glistens in the bright lighting, and my stomach turns. I take a few steps back.

"Are you crazy? I could cut you with that," I say, slightly panicked. "I don't have full control of this yet. What if it . . . grabs you and—" I stop. I can't even bring myself to say it. The man from the Testing Center swims into my view. "Jonah, I could hurt you."

"All the more incentive to focus on your ability and hone your fine motor skills," he says.

I peer at him, confused. The fact that this man has put so much faith in me, so much trust, is utterly disconcerting. He doesn't seem to be worried at all.

"You may begin whenever you're ready," he says in a calm and conversational tone.

I shake my head and fold my arms across my chest. "I could cut you."

"You won't cut me."

"But Jonah, I—"

"Hollis."

I open my mouth to continue, but my protest fizzles out. "Okay." I take a deep breath, closing my eyes and centering myself. I can do this.

My fingers tense as I move toward Jonah, encasing him under my control. I kneel and grasp at the air, Jonah matching my every movement. He picks up the fork from the side of the dinner plate, and I make a stabbing motion. The fork skewers the hardened loaf a little too forcefully. It scrapes against the porcelain, creating a harsh, high-pitched noise. I wince.

Moving more cautiously now, I hold Jonah's other hand above the floor. His knife moves down and touches the bread. I motion back and forth, cutting a slice, and after a minute, it's free from the rest of the loaf.

"I did it." I exhale sharply, quite happy that nothing terrible happened.

"Well done," Jonah says. "Now, I'd like to try a bite."

I laugh out loud. I flick my hand, leaving him frozen in the crouched position above the dinner plate.

"And what about your eyes? What happens when I accidentally jab you with that fork? I can't," I say. "I won't."

"And what about your promise, Hollis? Your word."

"My word?"

"When I agreed to help you learn about your ability, you said that you would listen to me and trust me," Jonah says. "You promised to do whatever I asked of you. I'm growing tired of your stubborn and obstinate attitude."

Again, Jonah's demeanor isn't angry or shaming, but his words cut across my resolve as sharply as the knife he's clutching in his stiffened fist. He's right. I gave him my word.

I set my fingers in place, kneeling to Jonah's level. I take his fork hand and stab at the slice, carrying it as carefully as I can to his mouth. He bites the piece and I pull the fork away.

"Delicious," he says. "Thank you."

I swipe my hands and release him again. He stands up and walks over to me. "That was excellent. You did it."

I remain silent. I feel ashamed of arguing with Jonah. He's the teacher. I'm the student. And even though I'm scared of hurting him, I know there's no way to learn about this power other than practice.

"I think that will do for today," Jonah says. "I will see you tomorrow?"

I nod. "Yes, sir. Tomorrow. And I'll be punctual. I promise."

"Good," he says. "And how are you settling into your work rotation?"

"Fine," I say, peering over my shoulder. "I think Tiffany still has some dishes left. I should help her."

"Alright, well then, I release you." He smiles. "You may rejoin Tiffany in the kitchen. That's quite a lot of dishes for one person to tackle."

"Yes, sir," I say. "Thank you for the lesson."

"You're welcome."

I jump from the platform and begin to jog down the length of the room when a curious thought stops me in my tracks. It hits me with such force that I'm dumbfounded, and clarity comes to me. In my quest to learn about this world, I need to include one very important person—my teacher. It's the only way I'll beat this thing. I turn on my heels, running back the way I had come.

"Jonah!" I call up to the platform.

He turns, surprised to see me. "Yes?"

I hop up, crossing the distance between us in three strides, heart in my throat. I don't know quite how to say this, so I dive in.

"I think the reason I'm hesitant to listen to you is because you don't know what this power feels like. At least, not the way I do." I stare at the floor, my hands clasping together. "So far, I've only used my power on you. You've never commanded it yourself. We haven't tried that yet."

My lower lip quivers, and my knees begin to tingle, as if they could give out at any moment.

"You don't know what it's like. At least, not fully. I'm alone. Jonah, you said it before. You've never seen an ability like mine, and I'm terrified when we train because I don't know when I'll snap—when it will wake up. This . . . thing inside."

I pause, taking in deep breaths. I lock eyes with Jonah, and I begin to tear up.

"It takes over. At least that's what it did back at the Testing Center."

The hair-raising voice crops up in the back of my mind. I continue, struggling with my words.

"So I want to ask you to take on my power. Make *me* freeze, so that you know what this monster feels like. Please?" I say. "You're the only one who can understand it like I do, but you have to take it on—just once."

Jonah looks at me, compassion in his eyes, and just from his expression, I can tell that he understands. "Of course," he says. "Can you move back?"

I obey him and leave some distance between us.

He walks to the center of the platform, and I follow him with my eyes. He stops and turns to face me. I stand there, watching his hands and waiting for the moment to happen.

Jonah's palms extend forward, his fingers flare, and I gasp. I am rooted to the spot, completely still, unable to move a thing. It feels like I'm being suffocated by a huge object, pressed in on all sides.

Jonah shudders, and his hands begin to tremble, buffeted by the overwhelming power coursing through his veins. He takes a step back, struggling with it.

Something like fire springs up within my chest, and I'm seized with terror. It scorches me, clawing at my lungs, punishing me. I want it to stop. I open my mouth to scream, but in a jerk of movement, Jonah's fist clamps shut, and my lips press together.

Wide-eyed and helpless, I watch as Jonah staggers forward, his face contorted. I'm trapped under my own ability, but after several moments, Jonah folds his hands together and drops his arms. The power vanishes, and with it, my chest expands. He's released me.

I fall to my hands and knees, sputtering and gulping for air. Sweat springs up across my forehead.

"Hollis, are you alright?" Jonah asks, running to me.

I'm panting heavily on all fours. "Did you feel it?" I ask.

He kneels beside me. "Are you hurt?"

"There's this . . . hunger," I say, batting his hands away. "Like giving into it would be exhilarating. You felt it, right?"

"I felt it," Jonah says. "Hollis, are you okay?"

"Yes."

We both sit on the floor, looking at each other, and as I stare into Jonah's dark brown eyes, I can tell that he finally understands me.

He scratches the side of his face. "I didn't mean to close your—"

"I know."

Jonah offers his hand to me and I take it. He pulls me to my feet, and for several moments, neither of us speak. My brain is whirling. He felt it, and for a fraction of a second, he lost control of it. He closed my mouth. Now he knows what I'm talking about.

"It's vicious," Jonah says. "Somehow, it's alive. I understand. Thank you for showing me."

"You're welcome." I hang my head. "And I'm sorry."

Remorse overcomes me. It's different than the rigid apologies I've given in the past. I feel this in my gut.

"For what?" Jonah asks.

"For not trusting you," I say. "I'll trust you from now on. I'll listen to you. I promise."

"I'm glad to hear it. And you are forgiven." Jonah tilts his head to the side, and his dark hair and stubble beard catch the glint of the fluorescent lighting. "We'll tackle this together. Okay?"

"Okay," I say. "Thank you."

"Now hurry along. Tiffany will still need that helping hand, no doubt."

I smile. "Yes, sir."

15

EVER SINCE JONAH TRIED ON MY POWER, MY ATTITUDE has changed, and with it, my countenance. Experimenting with emotion, learning about these powers, interacting with these . . . people—it's not anything like I expected.

I'm grappling with concepts I'd never been taught in school. These Diseased Ones aren't as I anticipated them to be, but I'm not ready to fully commit myself and say that the government is evil. I still believe the Terror War happened, but maybe the Diseased Ones have changed for the better. I simply don't know. I have to continue my investigation into this enlightening place.

"Hey Hollis, wait up."

I turn around, halting my brisk walk, and catch sight of Keith. He's slightly breathless as he jogs up to me. My mind moves back to the previous week. The card trick. The kiss. The staring eyes. I blush.

Why does this always happen around Keith? I must look like an idiot. I don't like these pitter-patters in my stomach. It feels like I'm taking an exam. That's the only feeling I can compare it to. I force a smile, perhaps a little too hard, because Keith's face changes from excitement to concern.

"Are you alright?" he asks.

"Yes, sorry," I say. "I'm just . . . what's up?"

"Where are you headed?"

"To bed," I say. "I just finished training with Jonah."

"Want to join us for a game of Cutthroat?" he asks, pointing to the pool tables at the far end of the common room.

"A game of what?" I ask, taken aback by the violence of the name.

"Cutthroat," he says. "It's a type of game you play with a pool table."

"Oh," I say. "Um . . . okay. Who's there?"

"The usual gang: Ben, Candice, Audrey, and Darren."

I hesitate. I've seen Audrey and Darren in passing, but I haven't spent any time with them since the marble game incident. "Will they be okay with that?"

"Audrey and Darren?"

"Yeah."

Keith smiles. "Absolutely. They'll be great."

"Are you sure?" I ask. "I wouldn't want to cause any trouble."

"I promise," Keith says. "It'll be fun."

"Okay. It might be fun for a little bit."

"That's the spirit."

He holds his hand out, and I take it, feeling happy. We walk down the room, hand in hand. What an odd sensation. I like this form of touch. It isn't anything earth-shattering, but it's nice. It's like receiving a compliment or opening a gift—unexpected, and completely wonderful.

"So, how do you play this 'Cutthroat' game?" I ask.

"Do you know how to play pool?"

I squint. "Yes, but only because I've been watching people play."

"Great," he says. "So Cutthroat is played the exact opposite of pool."

"So . . . ?" I trail, hoping that he will elaborate.

"Essentially, you want to hit everyone else's balls into the pockets, and you want your own balls to remain on the table," he says. "And that's how you win."

"Okay. Sounds simple enough."

I keep pace with Keith as we move down the side of the room. We're almost there. The group is just ahead, and a terrible pang of nerves wallops me in the stomach. I know that Keith said Audrey and Darren would be fine, but I can't get their petrified eyes out of my head. What do I do if they say something about it? Maybe Keith would know. They're his friends. But before I can say anything, Candice bounds up to me.

"Hey, glad you could join us Hollis," she says, pulling me into the center of the group. I catch sight of Ben, and my cheeks ignite. Thankfully, no one notices.

"So, who wants to break?" Darren asks, looking around, pool stick in hand. I step back, standing behind Keith.

"I will," Ben says, snatching the stick from Darren and sizing up the table.

Candice scoffs loudly. She puts her hands on her hips. "And what about all that talk of 'ladies first' and 'chivalry,' my dear sir Ben?"

"Chivalry was born in the fourteen hundreds," Ben says, smirking. He points to me. "And, as Hollis ever so correctly said, the year is 2647."

"I knew it," Candice says. "Chivalry is dead."

"Only," Ben says theatrically, twirling the pool stick, "when there is a game of Cutthroat to be played."

Candice huffs, popping a flame onto her pointer finger and gazing at it intently. Audrey tosses the cue ball into the air, suspending it there with her fingertips. It spins like a shiny white planet, glistening in the light.

"Cue ball, please?" Ben says, holding his hand out.

"Fine."

Audrey flicks the ball over to him, and it lands neatly into his outstretched hand. Ben places the cue on the table, lining it up to hit the triangle, and with a fantastic shot, the balls scatter in every direction. Number twelve sinks into the pocket nearest me.

"Well ladies," Ben says, "looks like Darren and I will be taking numbers one through five. Sound good to you?"

"Absolutely." Darren moves forward and takes the stick from Ben.

Keith leans over to me. "That means if we sink balls one through five, Darren and Ben lose."

"Got it," I say, grateful that Keith is trying to keep me in the loop. I'm still no good at games, even though I've been here two and a half months now.

Darren aims at ball number fifteen, stretching himself awkwardly across the table. "Can't seem to get it," he mutters under his breath.

"It's a hard shot," Audrey says.

I watch intently, keen to see if he'll make it into the corner pocket. I certainly couldn't.

Darren leans over, almost laying on the table. "Well, maybe if I just . . ."

I gasp as he passes right through the playing field. I've seen his power before, but it's still so shocking.

"Woah, woah, woah," Audrey says, marching up to the side of the table. "No powers, that's cheating."

"But I'm not even touching the balls," he says innocently.

The boys roar with laughter, but Audrey furrows her brow, waving her arms at him as if she were shooing away a bird. "Get out of the table," she demands. "Get out!"

"Alright, alright," Darren says, grinning at her. "Miss Competitive over here."

Audrey folds her arms across her chest, glaring at him. "Damn right I am. It's Cutthroat, not Pet the Bunnies."

The boys exchange amused looks.

"That's not even a real game," Darren adds, reclining against the side of the table. He looks so strange, half enveloped by the green felt. I can't help but stare.

"Get out of the table!"

"As you wish," Darren says, stepping backward and

disentangling himself from the center of the game. He aims again, but the ball misses the corner pocket by about a centimeter. "Damn."

"Ha!" Audrey looks immensely pleased.

"Bummer," Candice says dryly. "Our turn."

Darren hands the pool stick to Candice and then turns to the rest of the group. "Hey, so I heard we may have found someone else."

"Really? That's great." Audrey's face lights up. "Where?"

"Move," Candice says, waving Darren aside. He shuffles over, and she sinks balls four and three in one shot. "Audrey and I will take six through ten," she announces.

Audrey gives Candice a high five. "Nice shot."

Darren forces a cough. "Anyway, as I was saying, apparently there have been these huge electrical storms near Area Two."

"And the Council thinks that someone with an ability is causing it," Ben adds.

My hearing becomes razor sharp. "Someone else with an ability is out there?" I ask.

"It's got to be someone with an ability," Candice says, folding over the table to make a second shot. She misses.

"I'll take that," Keith says, grabbing the pool stick.

Ben nods. "Yeah, Darren and I overheard the Council talking about it. And during the meeting, Jonah was saying—"

"You were spying on the Council?" Audrey asks, knotting her arms together and raising an eyebrow.

Ben holds his hands up. "Not spying. Just happened to overhear, that's all."

"Well, you better not get caught 'overhearing' things," Audrey says. "You know that's not allowed. You're not on the Council."

"Whatever," Ben says, rolling his eyes. "It's just a bunch of adults who meet to talk about where we're going to grow our food next year and what chores to give us."

"And you don't think that's important?"

Ben shrugs.

Audrey looks affronted. She points at Ben's chest. "That right there is why I'll be on the Council one day and you won't."

"I don't want to be on the Council," Ben says.

"You know they do more than that, right?" Audrey scowls at him. "They pick the best people to go on rescue missions, they keep us updated on the world news, they figure out how we're going to stay safe and hidden from the government, they—"

"Alright, alright!" Ben says. "They're important. Geez. Lay off."

An awkward moment stifles the atmosphere of the game, and Keith, taking the argument in stride, steps up to the pool table. "I'll just take my shot," he says. "Hollis and I are eleven through fifteen."

"All that to say, I'm too speedy," Ben says, a goofy grin replacing his frustrated look. "Fine. I was spying. Whatever. It's not like they could catch me."

"And electricity is a powerful ability," Candice adds, steering the conversation back. "I mean, if this person can produce it themselves instead of taking it from a preexisting source . . . That's a really powerful type one."

"Yeah, no kidding." Darren looks out across the common room. "You know, I wonder what it was—that secret weapon thing from a hundred years ago."

My ears perk up. The sudden randomness of this statement is puzzling. Secret weapon? What is he talking about? I open my mouth, but before I can ask, Keith interjects himself.

"There was no secret weapon."

Darren looks at Keith. "How do you know? Were you there a hundred years ago? I mean, there were some pretty powerful abilities back then. How do you suppose the government found all the people they massacred?"

"I don't know," Keith says, tapping the heel of his right shoe against his left. "You're right, I wasn't there, but neither were you. It's a myth."

I'm intent on every word, completely consumed by the conversation. I stare at the floor, holding my breath.

"All I'm saying is that there were some really powerful abilities a hundred years ago. Like this mystery electrical person. That's what got me thinking about it." Darren fiddles with the sleeve on his sweater. "And you're telling me that the government tracked them *all* down and killed them without any kind of help?"

Keith looks amused. "And *you're* saying that all of the government's military elite from all corners of the globe isn't enough to find people? They didn't need a weapon."

"They haven't found us," Darren says smugly.

Keith rolls his eyes. "It's a myth. Probably instigated by the government to make us fear them even more than we already do."

A strange buzzing enters my limbs, but it's not from my ability. My mind is racing, and my heartbeat has picked up significantly. The government has a secret weapon against the Diseased Ones? Why would they need one if these people are telling me the truth about the Terror War?

"But what if it's not a myth?" Ben says.

Keith throws a hand up. "You're encouraging him?"

Ben shrugs. "I mean, we hear about it a lot from some of the older people. They've schemed up all sorts of things—and not just the idea that this weapon could find us."

"But they weren't alive back then either. So that's not proof for—"

But Candice interrupts her brother. "Well, if the secret weapon *was* real, then I wonder what kinds of things it could do. I mean, I've heard a bunch of theories too, but—"

"Probably something awful," Audrey says. Her voice sounds distressed. "Like take away a person's ability or something."

"Is that possible?" I blurt out. My body is flooded with a strange kind of adrenaline. I didn't mean to say it so loudly.

"Taking away an ability?" Candice picks at her fingernails. "I don't know. I don't think so. I mean, it's a biomarker, right? It's not like they could remove that from a person's body, could they?"

Ben takes the pool stick from Keith, twirling it in a high arc. "No, I don't think so. I mean, maybe. There's always a possibility of something like that. The world's got crazy technology now, but that sounds impossible to me."

"But that's just terrible," Audrey says. "Terrible."

"That would be pretty awful, now that I think about it," Darren admits.

I disagree. None of them have the affliction I do. None of them have an evil entity hidden in the fibers of their own ability. Having the biomarker removed would be a blessing. Then I could go back home.

A gut-wrenching pang hits me. Home. I miss my parents. My heart aches at the thought of them. They must think I'm dead. I can't imagine what they've done with themselves over the past two and a half months. I feel sick just thinking about it.

"But guys, there's no such thing as the secret weapon of a hundred years ago," Keith says, sighing. "It's a rumor at best."

"Well, even if you're right, it's still fun to talk about," Ben says.

"Fun?" Audrey looks shocked. "It's not fun. It's a terrible thing to talk about. I don't know what I'd do without my ability. It makes me who I am." She inhales sharply. "Let's change the subject. I don't want to talk about this anymore."

"Great idea," Keith says. "Ben and Darren, it's your turn."

"Right," Darren says, grabbing the stick from Ben. "Anyone down for a game of cards after this?"

The idea is met with great enthusiasm. Even I agree with more gusto than usual, but my mind is far away from the foolishness of gameplay now.

The secret weapon. This shining possibility. Can I dare to hope? What if this myth is real? What if the rumor is true? What if there exists such a device—one that could remove a person's ability?

Until now, I had almost accepted the fact that there was nothing I could do but learn to control my power. But what if I could get rid of it for good?

Suddenly, I see myself, plain and normal, returning to my parents, returning to my school, restored to my life, my ability removed, my sense of self-loathing forgotten, and my emotions quenched.

My heart swells at the idea of going home. The very thought of it thrills me, but these glorious imaginings halt in their tracks as a cold reality comes crashing down on me: they were going to kill me in the Testing Center, weren't they?

16

THAT NIGHT I TOSS FITFULLY. DREAMS OF GREEN NEEDLES and armored military men lay siege to my mind, holding me hostage, and the secret weapon intertwines with my broken sleep.

Over the next week, I find myself trapped by torturous thoughts. Although I'm no longer a prisoner in this underground world, I'm still not free. I can't leave. Should I investigate? Do I dare get my hopes up? A strong part of me screams no. This place has turned into a strange kind of home. There is comfort here, and I can tell that these people care about me—something that I still can't comprehend.

But another, more sinister part of me laps at my resolve to know the truth—to know for certain. If the secret weapon is just a myth, I can accept my lot in life and bear it as best I can. But if it's true, if it exists, I could never forgive myself. What if I hurt someone else? What if the monster inside me returns?

Darren's musings make sense to me. If the massacre is true, how could the government capture and kill people with type two abilities if they didn't have some kind of advantage?

During Cutthroat, a horrid thought occurred to me. Now that I have a basic understanding of my power, no one can stop me. I can control everything about a person. If I really wanted to get away from these people, I could.

But fear has stalled this idea. I don't know where I am, or what I'm capable of. I don't want to hurt them, and I'm still not sold on who's telling the truth.

If this secret weapon idea has merit, then I need to stay—at least until I figure out what these people know. How many theories are there? Can it track people with abilities? Can it remove my power? Could there be such a thing?

I believe that Keith and the others don't know if the secret weapon exists, but what about the Council? Could their leaders be the Diseased Ones I have spent my life learning to hate? Are they training me to use me for their own agenda? Is that why they collect powerful abilities via "rescue" missions? Whoever this person with electricity is, they probably don't want to be found, but it seems that these people have other plans. Something doesn't feel right.

What bothers me most are the memories I've seen from Rosalie. They hover in the back of my mind, constantly nagging me. If the events of a hundred years ago happened as Rosalie portrayed, could the government have reasons for committing such an atrocity? It is possible to justify something like that? It can't be . . . The government I've grown to cherish isn't anything like what I've been told down here. So how could the massacre be true?

I have so many questions, I'm bursting at the seams, and I'm finding it increasingly difficult to quietly observe. I need to ask someone—someone older. It's eating at my insides.

If there's truly no way of removing my ability, then this underground world must become my life. But if I can go home, if I can slay the monster under my skin, then I'll take the chance.

▪ ▪ ▪

"We are going to work on your ability to control more than one person at a time," Jonah says. It's early morning and I'm standing on the training platform, blurry-eyed and groggy. "Tiffany has kindly volunteered for this lesson."

"I've been curious," she says, looking sheepish.

"Curious?"

Tiffany shrugs. "About what it feels like to be all frozen. It's a unique ability."

"Unique isn't the word I'd use," I say, trying my best to smile.

She *wants* to be put under my power? My stomach turns uncomfortably.

"Can you describe what it felt like at the Testing Center?" Jonah asks. "When you walked into the lobby and put the men under your power, what happened?"

"It was incredible," I say. "I felt like I could control everything. There were a lot of men, but it didn't feel like that.

It was like all of them were one."

"How many people were there?"

"I don't know." I scratch my head, thinking back. "Maybe two dozen. Possibly more. I can't be sure. I wasn't paying attention because . . . they had guns."

"And you made everyone freeze?" Jonah asks.

"Yes."

Jonah paces back and forth, considering me. I hug myself as my eyes burn from the lack of sleep. The sensation feels out of place because my brain is electrified with apprehension.

"Yes," he says. "You demonstrated a particularly powerful aspect of your ability that day."

"What's that?"

"Mass control."

My stomach twists itself into a knot. I don't like the sound of that.

"Under normal circumstances, it would be extremely difficult to put that many people under your power," Jonah says. "That part of your ability requires practice and a great amount of focus."

"But I was under a lot of stress," I say. "It's different here."

"I agree."

"So what now?" I fold my hands, squeezing them together so tightly they hurt.

"You need to start channeling intention behind the use of your ability," Jonah says. "Every part of your ability."

"Right . . ." I don't know how to do that. "So, do I just go for it?"

Jonah chuckles. "That would be a good way of phrasing it."

I stand there, limp and helpless, facing the two of them. I'm completely out of my element. Tiffany gives me a thumbs up, but this only makes me feel worse.

"Whenever you're ready." Jonah's tone is soft and confident. He thinks I can do this. Well, that makes one of us.

I tense my fingers and the coursing power springs to life. Taking a deep breath, I throw my hands forward, as if scattering a handful of dust. Tiffany stiffens. Jonah, however, remains unaffected.

"Woah," Tiffany says, her voice catching in her throat. "This is so weird."

I flare my fingertips to make Jonah still, and Tiffany falls out of her pose. Jonah is frozen now. I twitch my hands and the switch occurs again.

"Come on," I mutter.

Flick.

They switch once more. I swipe my hands sideways, extinguishing my power.

"What do you think?" I ask, looking to Jonah.

Ever since Jonah tried my ability, I no longer feel the urge to question him. Now I yearn to hear his input. He alone understands the dark force emanating from within me. Working with Jonah gives me a sense of freedom. I'm still trapped here, but my ability has less power over me. I have a teacher.

"I think you need to focus less on trying to freeze us both individually and more on freezing us as a unit," he says. "You said that 'all of them were one' at the Testing Center. Use that."

"Right," I say. "A unit."

"It's like a picture. You're zoomed in too close. You're focusing on one small detail. You need to step back and look at the entire image."

"Okay," I say, nodding. "That makes sense."

"Let's try again."

I square my shoulders and step back, taking in the scene. Tiffany tilts her head to the side, patiently waiting. Jonah gives me a nod. I close my eyes and the buzzing in my fingertips ignites. I don't act. Not yet. I want to feel it fully before I put them under.

Keeping my breathing even, I give in to the overwhelming sensation. It travels up my arms and into my chest, filling me to the brim with thundering warmth. I open my eyes and raise my hand, pointing it directly at Jonah's chest. Stillness encapsulates both of them, and I grin, relishing the victorious moment.

"Good," Jonah says. "Well done."

I release them and let out a huge sigh of relief. I did it.

Tiffany beams at me. "Great job."

"Now, this is important," Jonah says. "How did it feel?"

I run my hand through my hair, thinking back to the vibrant tingling that consumed me mere moments ago. "I had to use more of myself."

"Can you be more descriptive?"

"I had to pour out more of my ability. Like a cup of water. I had to use more of myself, and I . . . I had to . . ." I'm struggling to find the right words. I stand there, holding my hands up to my face. "Does that make any sense?"

"Yes," Jonah says. "That's a good analogy."

"I couldn't move." Tiffany rocks back and forth on her heels. "But then I felt like I could have, if I really tried."

"Like . . . break out of my power?" I ask.

"Yeah."

Jonah nods. "Yes, I felt that too."

"It was weaker than the first time you made me freeze," Tiffany adds.

"You put both of us under, Hollis," Jonah says. He's noticed my defeated look. "You did it successfully. The strength of it will come with practice."

"Yes, sir," I say.

"And your description of pouring out more of yourself is apt," he continues. "I think it's something to focus on next time you attempt this skill. I noticed that you waited a moment before using your ability. Why?"

"I was . . ." I trail off. I can't believe I'm going to admit to this. Part of me hates that I'm giving in to this. "I was letting the power fill me."

Jonah puts a hand to his chin. "Did it travel to your chest?"

"Yes."

"Okay. Good."

The early morning stretches on until the hustle and bustle of breakfast fills the massive room. The intensity of the lesson has left me weak, hungry, and ready to be done for the day. I can't wait to eat. I'm starving, and my hands are shaking.

"Well done," Jonah says. "We will work on mass control again, but for now, I want you to continue to work on your fine motor skills. Perhaps with a partner."

"I'll do it," Tiffany says, without missing a beat. "I'd love to help."

"Thank you, Tiffany," Jonah says. "Well, that's all for today. I release you two to breakfast." He waves his hand.

Just then, the breakfast bell rings, and Tiffany jumps, clutching her chest as if she'd just been punched. Jonah and I laugh.

"Still a bit skittish there, Tiff?" I ask.

"Whatever." She stifles her grin behind her hand. "Come on, breakfast is ready."

"You go on," I say, shooing her.

"You're not getting food? After all that?"

"I am, I just . . . I'll catch up with you in a minute. Save me a spot in line?"

She gives me a bewildered look but shrugs it off. "Okay. See you."

She vanishes with a distinct pop, clearly keen to get in line as fast as possible.

I turn to Jonah, and my confidence plunges like a rock that's been thrown into the sea. My mouth turns dry, a pit forms in my stomach, and hunger makes my head spin. Why am I so nervous? I clear my throat.

"Jonah?"

"Something is troubling you."

"No," I say. "Well . . . yes."

"What is it?"

"I was just wondering about something."

"Yes?"

I take a deep breath. "Well," I say. My mind is firing rapidly. I want to word this as delicately as I can. "I overheard some of the guys talking about this . . . and well . . . I wanted to ask you what you think."

Jonah scratches his chin. "Very well. What is it?"

My jaw stiffens. "They said there was a secret weapon that the government used for the massacre a hundred years ago."

Understanding blossoms over Jonah's face. "Ah, the secret weapon. Yes. A rumor long perpetuated among people with abilities."

"So, it's true?" I try to suppress my tone, fearful that he may guess my intentions. "Is there a secret weapon?"

"Hollis, you're not the first person to ask this question. Many have wondered about it."

"But is it real? Or is it just a rumor?"

Jonah shrugs. "Honestly, I don't know."

My heart plummets. I'm disappointed, but I act indifferent. I need to be careful. How I portray myself matters. I don't want to seem too eager. "Well . . . what's your guess?"

He chuckles. "I think it's likely that the government used the idea as a scare tactic."

"So you think it was just a rumor?"

"Well, there could be elements of truth to it. The rumor caught on like wildfire. There was so much death, so much carnage. It was the perfect way to strike fear into the hearts of our people."

I pause, biting my lip and thinking of what to say next. I know what I want to ask, but I can't be too forthright. Jonah knows more than he's letting on. I can feel it.

"So . . . what did the rumor say?" I ask. "What could this weapon do? Supposedly."

I don't make eye contact with him. I can sense that this question has revealed my true longing. I may have gone one step too far. I hold my breath as the clinking of breakfast plates chime through the massive room.

"There have been many theories," Jonah says. "Some say the weapon was used to torture people with abilities, some say it was used to track and find people with abilities, and others say it could do something far worse than that."

"Like remove someone's ability?"

The phrase slips from my lips so quickly that I can't catch it. I stare at Jonah, hands trembling. What is wrong with me? Why did I just say that? How could I let that slip?

"I suppose," he says. His brow furrows. "Hollis?"

"Yes?"

My pulse thunders, and a fresh wave of lightheadedness crashes over me. I try to look innocent, but I can't manage it.

"It's not wise for you to dwell on this," he says.

"Yes, of course. I was just . . . I was curious."

"Curiosity is not a bad quality, Hollis," Jonah says gently. "But I want to caution you. Curiosity can turn into something dark if left unchecked."

"Yes, sir."

The conversation is over. I dare not ask anything more. I look at Jonah, trying to read his thoughts from his face, but to my surprise, his expression is steeped in compassion.

"I know that this transition must be difficult for you."

I don't speak, and my head drops to my chest until I'm staring at my feet. I'm ashamed. What a strange feeling. I don't understand. I shouldn't feel this way.

"Hollis." Jonah's tender voice picks my head up. "Remember, we're learning about this ability together. You're not alone. It might seem overwhelming now, but you're going to get this, and when you do, it won't seem so frightening."

I can't fathom why Jonah would place so much faith in me. It doesn't make any sense. I'm a society member. I've been trained to hate him. I don't trust the Diseased Ones. I've been educated, primed to suppress emotion, raised to avoid touch, and drilled to achieve perfection. I'm an adult. But down here, I feel like a child, cursed with an ability far too powerful to master. I'm a mouse caught in a monstrous trap.

"It won't always be this hard," Jonah says. "I promise."

"Yes, sir." It's all I can manage to say.

"You better run along to breakfast," he says. "I expect Tiffany has saved you a seat."

17

THE DELICIOUS SCENT OF MAPLE SYRUP ENVELOPS THE packed dining area. I sit beside Tiffany, who is chatting rapidly with Rosalie, Audrey, and Candice. Keith sits on my other side, shoveling down food as if he hadn't eaten in days.

"Hey Ben," Candice calls, jumping to her feet. "Seat next to me is open."

Ben, laden with a tray of fruit and pancakes, makes his way over to us.

"Heads up," Candice says, giggling.

I look up from my plate just in time to catch Ben's reaction as a flying dollop of whipped cream hits him squarely in the face. I let out a snort, stifling it behind my hand. Scattered laughter accompanies the tense moment.

Ben walks up to her, sets his tray down, and wipes the cream from his face. He grins. With lightning speed, he dips his fingers into the tub of white dessert sitting in the center of the group.

Several things happen at once. Candice dives beneath the table, Ben flings his hand, and there is a collective gasp as the whipped cream lands directly on top of the girl seated at the table behind ours.

I hold my breath as Ben swears under his.

"I'm sorry!" he yelps, walking over to the girl, stumbling a bit. "I meant that for Candice, I—"

The girl's hand is on her head, pulling the thick glob from her hair with an air of annoyance. She swings around, and I clap my hand over my mouth as her vibrantly white hair changes to a candy apple red. Her alabaster pale skin is offset by her piercing, silvery eyes.

"Oh . . . Vianne," Ben says weakly. All of the color drains from his face. "Unbelievable," he mutters through tight lips.

"You know," she says, in a tone much gentler than I was expecting. "I absolutely *love* my new hair accessory. I really do. I feel bad that you don't have one."

Ben looks confused. "That I . . . that I don't have whipped cream in my hair?" he asks. "I mean, I guess I could put some there if you like."

"Can I do it?" Candice says, popping up from under the table with a delighted glimmer in her eye.

Vianne's silver eyes are glued to Ben's. "No, not whipped cream," she says. "I have something else in mind."

She holds her hand up and snaps her fingers. Ben's hair turns a vibrant hue of bubblegum pink. The table erupts with laughter, and Ben's hands fly to his head.

"What did she do to me?"

Candice, who can barely keep herself above the table, clutches her stomach, snorting with mirth. "Hey, cotton candy boy. Love the new do!"

"Aw, come on, take it back," Ben says, looking to Vianne, a desperate note in his tone. "I'm sorry. It was an accident. Change me back."

She considers him for a moment and then dips her finger into the whipped cream residing on her bright locks. She licks it off.

"Naw, I think you can manage that color for a day." Her hair flickers to a lovely teal. "The pink suits you. I was done eating anyway."

She jumps up from her table and stalks off, leaving an incredibly pink Ben in her wake.

"Come on," Ben says, calling after her, but she doesn't turn around.

"It does suit you," Keith says, after a few moments.

"It complements your eyes," Audrey adds.

Candice buries her head into her hands, cackling. Just then, Darren arrives with a tray of food. Taking one look at Ben, he sits down and pushes his chair back to get a better view.

"What happened to you?" he asks. "Get kidnapped by a slumber party?"

Candice falls out of her chair, and Ben scowls, dropping himself into the seat next to Keith. "It's not my fault I keep bumping into her."

"'Bumping' into her?" Audrey repeats, raising an eyebrow. "What about last week when she nearly face-planted from tripping over you. You just *had* to race to get in line for food, didn't you?"

"I was hungry."

"Or when you zipped by and blew all her papers onto the floor because you were showing off your speediness to Rachel Vanellope?" Keith adds, patting Ben on the back.

"That was an accident," Ben says, shoving Keith's hand away.

"Or when you shoulder checked her jumping off the training platform?" Rosalie says.

Ben shakes his head, holding up his pointer finger. "That was Pierce Bodegard. Not Vianne—Pierce. And he's so tall. It's not my fault."

"Oh, and what about that time you spilled your drink down her front when you forgot to use your eyes while walking?" Darren asks, smirking and leaning back in his seat.

"See?" Ben says, looking around the table, as if Darren's comment drew a conclusion too obvious to miss.

"See what?" Keith asks.

"See, I bumped into her that time!" he exclaims.

"You know," Candice says, resurfacing to join the group. "I'm surprised she hasn't forced you to sprout a tail or changed your nose into a duck's bill or something."

"Wait . . . Vianne can do that?" Ben says, clearly taken aback. His hands move to his backside, as if shielding himself from the appendage.

Audrey leans forward, resting her head on her hand. "Poor Vianne Evolet, always in the wrong place at the wrong time."

"Poor Vianne Evolet?" Ben repeats, nonplussed. He stands up from the table, his chair scraping across the concrete. He points to his hair. "I'm the one wearing the pixie-colored fashion statement, and I'm pretty sure I can't pull it off like she does."

I can detect a hint of reverence in Ben's tone.

"I'm sorry," I say, finally entering the conversation. "What exactly is Vianne's ability?"

Everyone looks around at each other, but no one speaks. I squint, confused. Do they not know her? I thought everyone knew everyone down here.

"She can . . ." Tiffany begins. "Well, actually . . . I don't know."

"How?" I'm thoroughly puzzled. "What I mean is . . . well, don't you all know each other?"

"She's new," Rosalie says. "We rescued her a few weeks after you got here."

My heartbeat picks up. New? What kind of new? From society new? What if she's like me? It's as if Tiffany can read my thoughts.

"Not from society," she says softly. "She didn't fail the Test. She was in hiding. Out there, you know?"

"Oh." I deflate, slumping down in my chair.

A few seconds pass. It seems that no one knows what to say to me. I must look disappointed. I smother my expression, pulling back the emotion. I shouldn't show them that I'm upset. It's childish.

"Well, I know she can change the color of objects at will,"

Candice says, starting the conversation up again. "And I'm pretty sure she can transform bits of herself."

"Like what?" I inquire, keen to brush past my display of feeling. I look at Ben. "Grow a tail?"

Ben frowns, and Candice giggles. "Yeah. Like grow a tail."

"I've seen her ears go all cat-like before," Rosalie adds. "I think she can hear better when she does that."

"Oh, you know what?" Keith says, sitting up straight. "I think she's a metamorph."

"Oh, I've heard of those," Candice says.

"What's that?" I ask.

"She can't fully transform herself," Keith explains. "Not like a true shape-shifter. But she can partially shape-shift. And alter the appearance of others too."

Candice grins, looking at Ben's hair. "Cool."

"Would you stop staring at it?" he says, clearly annoyed.

"Nope. Not a chance."

The meal finishes, and the mass of people get up to clear the tables. It's dish duty for me and Tiffany again, and half an hour later, I'm scrubbing at the remains of dried bread and caked syrup. I don't mind it though. The hot water is soothing on my hands, and after a while, my mind drifts out of focus and into the realm of daydream.

Who is this girl? This Vianne Evolet? Did she come here of her own accord or did these people force her? What's her story? Why was she in hiding? Was she ever a part of society? Does she know anything about the rumor?

My mind wanders back to the secret weapon, and my

conversation with Jonah resurfaces. Was Jonah telling me the truth about what he knows? About what the weapon could do? Or was he concealing something? And if so, what are his reasons for lying to me?

A hand is waving back and forth in front of my face. "Hey, earth to Hollis."

"What? Oh, sorry. I'm just . . ."

"I lost you there for a minute."

"Yes," I say. "Sorry, I'm really tired. It's been a long day. The training session this morning really took it out of me."

Tiffany blows a strand of her black hair from her face. "Gotcha."

"Yeah, I'm not really—"

I stop talking. An inspiring thought comes to me so abruptly that I drop the pot I'm holding. It clunks into the sink sending water flying in every direction. Hot suds splash both of us, and Tiffany squeals, throwing her arms up.

"Jacob," I say.

"Jacob?" Tiffany looks utterly confused. She shakes the water from her arms and wipes it from her face. "What are you—"

"Can I talk to Jacob?" I ask. "Jacob Ganiston. From the memory. I want to talk to him."

Exhilaration is pumping through me, electrifying every sinew. I feel alive, and for the briefest moment, my ability rears up in my fingertips, and the buzzing enters my limbs.

"Well, I guess so," Tiffany says, giving me an 'are-you-okay' look.

"Brilliant."

"He doesn't come out of his room much. He isn't as young as he used to be. But I suppose it would be fine."

"Great."

"You should probably ask Jonah about it though," she says. "Jacob doesn't like company. He doesn't take visitors, but maybe Jonah can speak to him."

I come crashing back down. Jonah. Right. This may be a problem. If I ask Jonah about Jacob, he'll know it's because of the rumor. Something in my gut tells me that my last conversation with him wasn't entirely truthful.

"Why do you want to talk to Jacob?" Tiffany asks. She stops washing dishes and perches herself on the countertop.

"I want to ask him about the massacre," I say, choosing my words carefully.

This is not, strictly speaking, a lie. I do want to ask him about the massacre, but I also want to know what these people aren't telling me. I want to know about the secret weapon. Maybe he saw it? Maybe he heard the original version of the rumor? My heart leaps. Jacob Ganiston could be the key. Maybe he can confirm that the secret weapon is real. I must know.

"I understand," Tiffany says.

"What?"

"You grew up being taught a complete lie. I understand the need to talk to someone who was actually there, to investigate the truth. I totally get it." She smiles. "It's like I said when you got here. You want the facts—the evidence. That's an admirable pursuit."

"I . . . yeah, I need to investigate," I say. I'm momentarily speechless. I didn't expect her to understand. I expected her to protest my little venture, but she hasn't condemned my curiosity.

"Just talk to Jonah first."

"Right."

Tiffany gives me a thumbs up. "And Hollis?"

"Yes?"

"Please be tactful. You're asking Jacob to share about something deeply personal and traumatic. Just . . . be gentle in your pursuit of the truth. Jonah may have some suggestions for how to approach him."

"Of course," I say, making a mental note to heed this bit of advice.

I turn back to the pile of dishes, attacking it with new fervor. Determination fills me.

"There are so many dishes," Tiffany says, groaning in defeat.

I laugh. "Seriously. Hey Tiff?"

"Yeah?"

"Thanks."

She shrugs. "What are friends for?"

18

I LEAVE DISH DUTY WITH A SKIP IN MY STEP. I'M GOING TO find Jacob and get some answers. Finally. I can hardly contain myself.

I don't want to ask Jonah. This is my quest to find the truth. Jonah acted like my curiosity was dangerous, but it felt like he didn't want me to know the truth. So I've made up my mind. I'm going to talk to an eyewitness, without Jonah's permission.

All I need to do now is ask someone where Jacob's room is. I walk down the vast length of the common room, hoping to bump into someone I know.

I spot Keith a few minutes later, and I jog to catch up with him.

"Hey Keith, wait up."

He turns, a sweet smile lighting up his face. "Well hi there."

My cheeks flush. "Hi."

"What's up?"

I open my mouth, but my brain blanks. I gaze at Keith, taking in his deep blue eyes and dark hair. I shake my head, snapping out of it.

"What do you like to do?" I ask.

Keith chuckles. "That's a strange response to 'what's up?'"

I fold my arms across my chest, squinting. "Well, I don't know much about you, do I?"

"I suppose you're right," he says. "Let's see. You know I like to play games. I'm always down for that."

"I guess I know one thing about you."

"And you know I can fly." He grins.

"Fine, I guess I know two things about you."

I'm smiling like an idiot. I feel that pitter-patter again, but it's picked up. It's exhilarating. There's a word for what I'm doing, and it's strictly prohibited in society: flirting. I've never done this before, but wow . . . it's like an ability all unto itself.

Keith puts a hand to his chin. "Hmm. I like a nicely cooked, medium-rare piece of steak. Only had it once, but man was it good. Oh, and I like to put ketchup on my popcorn," he adds. "There. Now you know four things."

"You like what?" I ask, scrunching up my nose. I shake my head. "That's gross."

"Yep, ketchup on my popcorn," he says. "You should try it."

"No way. Not a chance."

"You're missing out," he says.

I look down at my feet. I don't know why I'm nervous

around Keith, but the butterflies in my stomach remind me that I have a task to complete. I need to find Jacob's room. But before I can say another word, Keith taps my shoulder.

"Let's see," he says. "I know you like to watch games."

I almost say "that's because I don't know how to play," but I keep my mouth shut. I want to hear more.

"And I know you have a super intense ability," he adds. "A really powerful one."

My smile slips a little. I don't like this unfortunate fact, but I keep my face impassive.

I change the subject. "I like the cornbread here. And I like the color teal, like Vianne's hair. It's my favorite color."

"Well, now I know two more things about you," Keith says, extending his hand to me. "Can I show you something?"

My heart skips a beat. I hesitate, but only for the briefest moment. Something about Keith's boyish charm makes my mission to talk to Jacob seem less urgent.

"Sure."

"Do you trust me?"

Keith and I lock eyes, and I grab his hand. "Yes."

"Hold on tightly."

"Okay."

Keith lifts me off my feet, and I grip him fiercely. We're flying up to the vaulted stone ceiling above, and my stomach does several flips.

"It's alright. I've got you," he says.

I'm clinging to his arms, gazing up at the vast ceiling, when something catches my eye. We're flying toward a small crevice in the side of the rock, and as we approach, it widens until, very gracefully, Keith drops us into the opening of what appears to be a small cave. My feet scrape across the rocky outcropping, but I'm still vice-like upon Keith's arm. I'm not fond of heights.

"Woah," I say, catching my balance.

"Here." Keith moves us away from the edge.

"I would have never seen this from the floor," I say. I look around. The cave is just large enough to accommodate us. "What is this place?"

"I think Charles Chang was a bit more creative than people gave him credit for," Keith says. "He hid a bunch of spots like this throughout the compound. For the adventurous people, you know? I think he built them to get away from it all. It must've been hard to adjust to living underground."

"Oh."

I give the edge a wide berth. The fall would likely be five stories. I'm still clinging to Keith, unable to take my eyes away from the massive depth of the room.

He gives my hand a gentle squeeze and then lets go, sitting down to dangle his legs over the outcropping. He taps his hand on the concrete to his left, inviting me to take a seat.

I shake my head. "Are you crazy? Do you have a death wish? What if you fall? What if I fall?"

Keith gives me an endearing look, chuckling under his breath. "I can fly, Hollis. And besides, I would catch you."

I blush. How absurd of me. Of course he doesn't fear dangling his legs over the edge. I creep forward and sit next to him, grabbing his arm to suppress my nerves. I look down, and my stomach twists in on itself.

"Not a fan of heights?" he asks.

"Not particularly."

"It'll grow on you," he says. "Give it a minute."

"So, what do you do up here?" I ask.

Keith leans back on his palms, gazing out at the arched ceiling a few feet above us. "I come up here to think. It's peaceful."

I look back over the edge, noting that the outcropping is a few yards higher than the metal stairs that cling to the walls all about the room.

"And no one can see your feet?" I ask.

Keith peers down. "Well, they could, but they'd have to be looking for them."

I snicker.

"What's so funny?"

"It's just funny." I rub my nose with the back of my hand. "The thought of looking up and seeing someone's feet."

"I guess so."

Keith stares at me with those shocking blue eyes, and I'm lost for a moment. I don't know what to do with myself, and my arms feel like noodles. I've never interacted with a boy like this. It's uncharted territory.

"What do you come up here to think about?" I ask.

"Oh, a little of this and a little of that," he says, giving me a boyish wink. He brushes his hair out of his face and turns back toward the open expanse of the room.

I give him a stern look, but it's more playful than anything else. "And what is the 'this' and 'that' you are referring to? It sounds incredibly riveting."

"Hollis Timewire, are you actually being sarcastic?"

I grin. "I've been around Ben and Candice long enough to pick up 'a little of this and a little of that,'" I say, mimicking Keith's tone.

"You're funny."

"Why, thank you."

We gaze down together, observing the room below. It's soothing to be removed from the crowded atmosphere. I lean back on my palms, copying Keith.

"But really, what do you think about?"

"You really want to know?"

"Yeah."

I turn to him, watching his face attentively. Something's changed. I can tell that he's trying to gather his thoughts. He doesn't look upset, but his brow furrows and his eyes soften.

"I think about the way the world is."

"What do you mean?"

"I wish it were different," he says simply. "I wish the world wasn't like this."

"Like what?"

"Unfeeling. Cold."

Is he talking about the Test? The massacre? The Terror War? I know that society has expelled emotion, but I don't think that's a bad thing. The world has achieved peace. There's no more war. No more death. Nothing to struggle for. The

Terror War is over, and the Diseased Ones have been eradicated. That is, if what I've been taught is true, but I don't know anymore.

"There's just so much darkness out there," Keith says soberly. He shakes his head. "And the worst part of it is . . . no one knows the truth. The world doesn't know."

"And what's the truth?" I ask.

Keith looks at me, his expression deepening. "Almost everyone with an ability was murdered . . . and there's only a few hundred of us left."

Something inside of me breaks. I stare at Keith, and I feel compassion—a connection I never thought possible. He's a Diseased One, and I'm a society member. But when it comes down to it, the only difference I can think of is how we were raised. He grew up believing one thing about the world, and I grew up believing another. But I don't care about that now. I reach for his hand, intertwining my fingers with his. He looks back out at the room.

"I just wish I could do something, like my parents did," he says. "I wish that . . . I wish that the world could change. Maybe one day things will be different. Who knows? Maybe we won't have to hide forever."

"Maybe," I say, barely audible.

"My parents believed that. They thought we'd be able to rejoin society one day. It's just hard to keep believing that the world will get better . . . especially now that the government's started chemical therapy with infants. You know? To get rid of the Test."

"Yeah." I squeeze his hand, chewing on my lower lip. I look up at him.

Keith's face has changed once more, and I study it, trying to discern what's underneath. He looks older, as if the weight of the world rested on his shoulders.

"Keith?"

"It's hard now that it's just me and Candice."

My heart drops. "Your parents?"

He nods slowly. "It happened on a rescue mission . . . I'm proud to be their son."

"Keith . . ." My own voice chokes me.

"And now it's just me and my little sister. She's my world. I'd do anything for her."

I nod, leaning closer to him, and for several minutes, we sit in silence, watching the bustle of people below. I can't imagine what Keith and Candice must have gone through. I can't see my parents, but at least I know they're still alive. How can he believe that the world might change? It doesn't make any sense—especially if his version of history is true.

"Being here," I say. "Being with you, seeing all this . . . It's just so different from what I've been taught. It's . . ."

"It's what?"

"Unexpected."

Keith smiles, and his bright blue eyes find mine. He speaks softly. "Maybe we're not the Diseased Ones you've learned about from the pages of your history books."

I move closer to him. "Maybe," I whisper.

A new desire blooms within me. Keith and I hold each

other's gaze, and for the first time in my life, I throw away the part of my conscience telling me not to feel.

I lean forward and press my lips to his. I kiss him slowly at first, and then with fierce passion in an unexpected surge of abandonment. His strong hands run through my hair, and the scent of his skin pulls me in deeper. A thrill of electrifying power that has nothing to do with my ability courses through me, filling every sinew and lighting up my soul. All the years of no touch are forgotten, all the voices in my head vanish, and nothing else exists but Keith and the feel of his lips against mine.

After several intense moments, we break apart. I'm breathless, and Keith's face is flushed.

"I've never done that before," I say, feeling the heat rise in my cheeks. I'm elated, delighted beyond words.

"You've never kissed anyone before?" Keith asks, amused. "Ben would have to disagree."

"He kissed me," I say. "But I kissed you, and I've never done that before. I've never been allowed to. It's against the rules. It's—"

I'm invigorated. I feel . . . scandalous, filled to the brim with uncontainable energy. I want more of this wonderful connection.

"What's against the rules?" Keith asks. "Kissing?"

"Well . . . yes," I say. "And holding hands, and hugging, and pretty much any form of touch. It's not allowed."

I haven't spoken to Keith about my life, but having just experienced the power that touch can create, I don't mind. I want to share with him.

"That doesn't sound very nice."

"It wasn't."

"Doesn't sound like home," Keith says.

My euphoria crumbles. But it was my home . . . and the 'no touch' rule didn't apply within the family unit. My stomach turns, and homesickness overtakes me. I miss my parents. I want to see them. I never asked for any of this. But this . . . is so incredible.

"Are you alright?"

I give a little start. "Yes, I'm just . . . thank you for showing me this. This was nice."

"Of course."

I grin. Tossing all inhibition aside, I lean in and kiss him once more. We sink into another few moments of bliss, and I'm enchanted all over again.

"Well, Hollis Timewire," Keith says, grabbing both of my hands. "I think I know one more thing about you."

"And what's that?"

He grips me fervently, and without warning, pulls me over the edge of the outcropping and into the expanse of the room. I gasp, clinging to him, and we float down to the floor in a mesmerizing descent.

"You're a fantastic kisser."

There I go again, smiling like an idiot.

19

ONCE AGAIN, MY MISSION TO TALK TO JACOB IS ON hold. I'm standing on the training platform ready to practice, but this time I'm greeted by more than my teacher. The gang of seven is here, all peering at me with curious eyes.

"Today we will be working on mass control again," Jonah says. "But I've made it more difficult. You'll need to put all eight of us under your control."

"Right," I say weakly.

Tiffany and Rosalie give me a thumbs up, and I try to smile, but it only makes me feel worse. I don't like this. What if something goes wrong?

Keith catches my eye, and our scandalous excursion rises to the surface of my attention. I hold my hands up to my face, attempting to staunch the uncomfortable heat creeping across my cheeks.

"Remember the big picture analogy," Jonah says. "And

don't worry, your friends have all volunteered for this."

"I didn't," a sulky voice says.

I spin around to see Ashton lurking in the corner of the platform looking sour. The girls give him a stern look.

"What is *he* doing here?" I ask, turning back to Jonah.

As if these lessons aren't hard enough. Now I've got to listen to his snide, antagonistic—

"He's here if we need him."

"For his ability?"

"Yes."

My heart sinks. That can only mean one thing. My hands begin to shake, and my voice constricts. "Do you think I'll lose control?"

"This part of your ability is extremely volatile, Hollis," Jonah says gently. "And while I have full confidence in you, your power is another matter entirely. I want to take every precaution as we're exploring this."

I'm relieved. Jonah trusts me, but not my ability. We both understand that it's something more than just power—it's alive—and even though I can't stand Ashton, it makes sense for Jonah to include him.

"Okay," I say.

"Whenever you're ready."

I take a deep breath, channeling my ability into my fingertips. The tingling works its way through my limbs and into my chest. I direct my hands toward the group, but only Ben and Candice freeze. They both gasp, and Ben starts swearing at the top of his lungs.

I release them, dropping my hands. "Did I just hurt you?"

"No, s-sorry," Ben says, stammering. He looks sheepish, giving Jonah an apologetic look. "Sorry, that was just—wow—that was . . . wow."

I grimace.

"Just ignore him. He's fine," Candice says, rolling her eyes. She murmurs under her breath, "big baby."

Ben shoots her a dirty look.

"Try it again," Jonah says.

I nod, backing up to take in the group. Eight people. That's a lot of people.

Holding my hands aloft, I make a second attempt, but this time only three people freeze. I center myself, focusing my power and pouring it into the group in front of me, but I can't reach all of them. A few of them keep slipping out of my grasp. I swipe my hands, and everyone relaxes.

"That was an excellent attempt," Jonah says. "You had five of us at one point, I believe."

"There's too many of you," I say. "I don't have enough of my ability to pour out."

Jonah shakes his head. "Of course you do. That much is clear from your encounters at the Testing Center. The trick is accessing that reservoir of power."

I cross my arms. "Okay, and how do I do that?"

"Can you do something for me?"

"Sure." I brush a strand of hair out of my face.

"Your ability is closely tied to the way you feel," Jonah says. "For example, at the Testing Center you were scared and running on adrenaline. Fear is what allowed you to use more of your ability."

I furrow my brow. "Okay, but I can't access it like that anymore."

"I agree, but we can use a different feeling," Jonah says. "You need to think of something equally as powerful."

I nod. An emotion as powerful as fear? I don't know about that.

"What about your time here?" Jonah asks.

"What about it?"

"You've been allowed to express emotion."

"Yes."

"Have you experienced anything you can use?"

I bite my lip, thinking back to the previous night. That kiss. A wonderful tingling sensation makes my stomach jump. That kiss was more powerful than fear. I keep my face impassive. "Yes."

"Good. You don't need to tell me what it is," Jonah says. "I want you to focus on the way it compelled you. What did it feel like? And when you're ready, let that experience help you pour out your ability."

I close my eyes, envisioning the kiss that made me feel alive, and my fingertips buzz with incredible energy. It's as if I've been shocked by a dose of electricity. I give in to the elation and let the power fill me. I hold my hands up, and this time, all eight people are under my perfect control. I have them. I can feel it.

I stand there, breathless and victorious, a grin spreading

across my face. My hands cut through the air, and a few of my friends stagger forward to catch themselves.

"Incredible," Tiffany says.

"It worked." I pump my fist into the air. "And I felt like I had enough power. Even more to spare."

"Good," Jonah says. "That's where you should be, with power to spare."

"Nice job," Tiffany says.

"Now, I want to see your fine motor skills." Jonah rolls up his sleeves and kneels to untie his left shoe. "You've been working on them, I trust?"

I grimace. I completely forgot. My obsession with the secret weapon, my desire to see Jacob, and my outing with Keith have left me little time to work on tying shoelaces and cutting up bread.

I hesitate, trying to think of an excuse that's not 'I was investigating what you told me not to investigate.' Panic sets in, but Tiffany steps forward and tugs on my arm.

"We can show Jonah the shoelaces," she says.

I give her a 'what-are-you-doing' look, but she clears her throat, bends down, and unties her shoelaces. She looks up expectantly.

"Alright, just like we practiced," she says.

I breathe through pursed lips. "Right."

I flare my fingertips and encase Tiffany. Kneeling down to her level, I grab my left shoe, and with the tiniest flick, I release her from my control. I watch her like a hawk, copying each movement, which we pass off rather convincingly. A moment later, she is back under my control, and we rise together, like polished clockwork.

I free her, feeling terribly guilty about deceiving Jonah. I don't want to lie to him, but I can't tell him that I've been distracted with my quest to see Jacob—and my outing with Keith is my own business.

Tiffany catches my eye and I try to pass off a 'thank you' without being too obvious.

"Alright," Jonah says. "I think it's time that you graduate."

My stomach drops. "Graduate? What do you mean, graduate?"

Jonah shakes his head. "My apologies. Poor choice of words—nothing like the Test. I think you're ready to work on the more challenging aspect of your ability: the command aspect."

Relief floods me. "Like giving someone an order? Like I did with the military men?"

"Exactly." Jonah turns to the group behind him. "Thank you all for helping Hollis with this lesson. You may go now. I'd like to work with her privately."

My friends obey, dismissing themselves and hopping off the platform. Tiffany and Keith wave at me. I wave back, and for the briefest moment, Keith catches my eye. I stifle a rosy-cheeked smile.

Ashton, jumping at the chance to leave, brushes past me, purposefully bumping into my shoulder as he hurdles off the platform.

"Hey," I say. "What's your problem?"

"Not you, Ashton," Jonah says. "Back up here."

"What? Are you serious?" He glares at Jonah. "I can't go?"

"No."

His demeanor turns, if possible, even more sour. "Well, she's done freezing the whole group, so why can't I—"

"Because we still need you," Jonah says crossly, quelling Ashton's next protest with a severe look. "Now please, come back up."

He pulls himself up and moves to the corner of the platform, glowering at me. I don't look at him, but I can feel his staring, watery eyes.

"Hollis."

I shake my head, giving my attention back to Jonah. "Yes, sorry."

"Are you ready?"

I grimace. Despite my underlying dislike of this ability, the command aspect has captured my interest. I can tell people what to do, and my ability forces them to do it. It's terrifying but intriguing.

"I don't really know what to do," I admit.

Jonah smiles. "Well, in your own words, just go for it."

I flick my hand and Jonah stiffens. "Right. What should I try?"

"Why don't you do something simple first?" Jonah says. "Have me walk to your side."

"Okay."

Squinting in the harsh fluorescents, I focus on Jonah's silhouette. The buzzing in my hands intensifies, and with the smallest twitch, I think 'walk over to me.' Nothing happens.

I try again, but Jonah remains rooted to the spot. I ground myself, pulling more of the power into my hands and channeling it into Jonah.

He takes a big step forward, but then stiffens, sprawled into a half split. I wave my hand and Jonah falls.

"Sorry," I say sheepishly.

"That's alright." He stands up. "I have a suggestion."

"Yes?"

"Try using a verbal command."

"Okay."

I encase Jonah once more. A powerful surge ignites my ability, and it spills forth, like ink from a bottle. I speak in a loud voice. "Come stand next to me."

Jonah quivers, taking several mechanical steps. He falters and then stops halfway across the platform. I sigh, utterly frustrated. It's not enough. Why can't I get this? Why isn't it working? I've done it before.

"Jonah, I'm not sure if—"

A wave of power overcomes me, and instinct throws my hands forward so violently that I nearly lose my footing. I gasp, stepping forward to catch myself.

"Stand next to me."

Jonah obeys, closing the gap between us in a jerk of movement. I drop my hands. They fall limply to my sides. The tingling ceases, and with it, Jonah comes out from under my power.

"What's wrong?" he asks.

"Nothing. It's just . . ."

"How did it feel?"

I stand there, considering the question, but the answer comes quickly, and fear crushes my determination. "It felt . . . easy."

"What do you mean?"

"Like it was second nature." I shake my head, staring at my hands. "I felt this powerful surge of energy and then . . . it was easy."

I wring my hands out, as if I've just washed them. Why was that so easy? Then a second question pierces me. And why did I like it?

I begin to pace back and forth, a strange pitter-patter thumping through me. That surge of energy was incredible.

"You're getting better at this," Jonah says. "What else did you notice?"

I stop pacing. "I think the fact that you were willing to do what I asked made it easier. I think it would be much harder to command someone who was resisting me."

"A very intelligent observation," he says. "I will keep that in mind for future lessons."

I agree without really listening. I'm still deep in thought about what I just experienced. Whatever this power is, it came to life again. I look down at my hands and notice that they are shaking. I stuff them under my armpits and out of sight.

"I think it's time to call it a night." Jonah turns to Ashton. "Thank you for your time. You may go."

"Finally," Ashton says. He jumps down from the platform,

muttering something to the effect of "didn't need me anyway." He stalks off without so much as a backward glance.

"You should get some rest, young lady," Jonah says.

"Yes, sir."

I stare off into the massive room, my mind tangled with uneasy thoughts. Tonight was like the Testing Center. Something within me emerged to direct my path, and I'm terrified by it. What if it gets stronger and I lose control? And as my mind wanders, my obsession returns. Jacob. I need to talk to him.

"Don't let Ashton's bad attitude discourage you," Jonah says.

"What?" I snap out of it. "Oh, it's fine. He doesn't bother me."

Jonah gives me a look, but I don't meet his gaze. "Get some rest."

"Jonah?"

"Yes?"

"Thank you."

"My pleasure."

I wave over my shoulder as I jump from the platform, sprinting down the room. I am determined to find Jacob this time.

I scan the recreation area, spotting Keith and the gang at the furthest pool table. I weave in between the scattered chairs, murmuring "excuse me" under my breath, and when I'm right behind Keith, I tap him on the shoulder.

He spins around. "Oh, hi."

"Hi."

"Want to join?"

"No, I'm okay." I hook his arm to pull him away from the group. "Can I talk to you for a minute?"

"Sure." He begins to walk with me. "Is everything alright?"

Keeping my face unreadable, I nod. "Yes. Of course. I was just wondering if you knew where Jacob Ganiston's room is?"

"Yeah, sure," he says, pointing behind me. "It's up the stairs, all the way in the corner of the common room, past the training platform. And it'll be the second to last room on the right."

"Perfect. Thanks," I say. I turn to walk away, but Keith catches my shoulder. A little flutter hits my stomach.

"What's up?" he asks.

"I just need to speak with him," I say, panic springing up in my chest. "I'll explain later." I hold my breath, hoping my vague answer will suffice.

He shrugs. "Alright. Want to join the game later?"

"Sure," I say. "See you."

Keith squeezes my arm gently, smiling at me. "See you."

I speed off, running to the last set of metal stairs with excitement bounding in my heart. I take them two at a time, climbing to the top and pulling the heavy door open. I jog to the end of the hall, stopping at the second to last door on the right.

"This is it." I'm panting and clutching the stitch in my side. "This is it."

My hand hovers in front of the door, tentatively. I don't

want to get my hopes up, but something tells me that Jacob Ganiston will have the answer to my burning question.

Well, here goes nothing. I take a deep breath and knock three times.

20

NOTHING HAPPENS.

I press my ear to the door and knock again, striking the surface in even beats. Silence. I'm disappointed. The room is probably empty, but I can't leave until I know for sure. Tentatively, I crack the door ajar.

"Mary, I'm not in the mood for company today."

I jump, panicking. I grab the handle to steady myself, and, taking care to stay out of sight, I speak loudly through the sliver.

"Sir, my name is Hollis Timewire. I need to speak with you."

I wait there for several seconds. I grimace, adrenaline kick-starting my pulse. What if he tells me to go away? I hold my breath, straining to hear his response.

"Come in."

I step inside. My heart is beating so furiously that I'm beginning to feel lightheaded.

It takes my eyes a moment to adjust to the lack of light. Candles are set about, and the bright fluorescents are off. I squint, taking a few timid steps forward. An ancient-looking man is sitting on the only cot in the room, tucked into his blankets and propped up with nearly a dozen small pillows. I stand there, unsure of how to proceed.

"I've never seen you before," Jacob says gruffly.

He peers at me with a curious expression, his face entrenched in wrinkles. I stare at him. I can't help it. He looks so incredibly old that it's hard to imagine he's a real person.

"I'm new," I say. "I've been here about four months." Jacob doesn't speak. He looks me over as if I were something peculiar. I hesitate but then continue in a calm and collected manner. "Sir, I want to ask you something."

Jacob grabs the nearest blanket and pulls it closer to his chest. "If it's about the massacre, I'm not interested. You can see yourself out."

He waves me away, curling forward with a deep bout of coughing. Cold numbness douses my hands and feet. I'm rooted to the spot, looking at him with wide-eyed incredulity. After a few seconds, I regain my composure.

"But sir, I need to know something. You've got to hear me out."

"Got to?" Jacob laughs, shaking his head. "I haven't got to do anything."

"Please sir," I say, desperately trying to keep my tone respectful. "I need to ask you about the massacre because—"

"It was a hundred years ago," he says, cutting me off.

"Ancient history. And I don't like digging up the past. We live here now, safe and protected, completely under the government's nose. It's over, and it has been for a long time."

"But it's not over," I say.

"What do you mean, girl?" he asks, pulling himself into a sitting position with more strength than I anticipated.

"I mean that the government is still hunting down people with abilities," I say. "People like you and me."

I don't know if I actually believe that, but if it will get Jacob talking, then I'll play whatever part is necessary.

"So?" Jacob says, raising an eyebrow. "What does that matter? Like I said, we're here now. They won't ever find us."

"Have you heard of the Test?" I ask, knotting my hands together.

"Of course I've heard of the Test," he says irritably. "Don't play me for an ignorant fool. I've lived more than seven of your lifetimes, I daresay."

I'm feeling defiant. A reckless sense of daring is spurring me forward. I'm going to say it. I can't believe I'm going to say it . . .

"Well, I failed the Test four months ago. The government tried to kill me, just like they tried to kill you on that dirt hill."

Jacob's countenance turns ashen. His wrinkled hands grip the blanket, and his knuckles turn white. "How do you know about the hill?"

"Rosalie showed me."

Understanding lights behind his eyes. "Rosalie Simmons. The storyteller. The memory catcher. But then, you've already seen what happened. Why do you need to speak with me?"

I wring my hands together, frustrated. I almost blurt out 'because of the secret weapon,' but I panic. I don't want Jacob to ask me to leave, so I say the one thing I know will keep him talking. "Because I've grown up my entire life being taught that people with abilities are evil," I say. "I learned about the Terror War—not the massacre. I was told that people like you murdered people like me. I was educated on the government's triumph over a hateful race of creatures—an evolutionary accident. A mutated brain. Bad blood."

Jacob scoffs. "Rubbish."

"But how could I possibly know that?" Anger infuses into my voice. "Yes, Rosalie showed me the memories. But that's not what I'm interested in."

"Well then, what could you possibly be interested in? You've already seen the worst of the massacre from that girl's hands. What else is there?"

"The rumor," I say, treading lightly now. "The one about the secret weapon, and what it does."

Jacob looks at me with alarm, but he collects himself, clearing his throat and grasping the blanket once more. "That rumor makes no difference to anything."

"But—"

"We're safe."

"No one with abilities is safe," I say. "Not where I come from."

Jacob fights through another fit of coughing, keeling forward and covering his mouth with a cloth. Several moments pass before he is able to speak.

"But that's no matter," he says brusquely. "You're not up

there anymore. You're down here. Forget about the massacre or the Terror War—whatever you'd like to call it. It doesn't matter anymore. Forget about your old life. Forget about the rumors of what's already past."

I grit my teeth. "I can't."

"Build a new life." Deep somber fills his features. "Don't let the pain of what happened to you consume you."

I shake my head. "No. It doesn't work like that."

"But it should," he says, as if speaking to himself. "It will save you the trouble of many years of misery. The Test is over. You've had a nasty dose of reality—coming down here and learning the truth. So, do yourself a favor and forget about all this."

"No. Not yet." I fold my arms across my chest. "I still need an answer."

Jacob simply looks at me. His face is unreadable, nearly as perfect as a society member's, but after a few moments, his brow furrows, and he addresses me softly.

"What were you hoping to hear from me, child? Something to solve your problems?" He peers at me curiously. "Something to make you believe? Because I'm afraid that no one can do that for you. That's a choice you'll have to make yourself."

My breathing is uneven, echoing off the concrete in an eerie rhythm.

"This isn't about believing," I say. "This is about knowing. I want to know about the secret weapon. Is it real? Do you know what it can do? Do you know anything about it?"

I stand there expectantly, heart pounding in my ears. If the weapon is real, then I have a chance of getting rid of this disease. If it's real, then maybe I can go home. I can reintegrate myself into society and forget about all of this. I can see my parents again. I can go back to my life, and I don't have to live with the ever-present possibility of hurting others.

"You are not the first person to ask me this," he says. "But you're also not the first person I will turn away. Go back to your friends, child. Forget about this."

Raw emotion washes over me, and I let it in without restraint. "But I can't go back! I need to know. I must know."

"Why? What gives you the right to know?"

"Because I was on the government's side barely four months ago." My tone rises in an unexpected manner. "I believed the Diseased Ones were evil. I hated people like you. That was my life. But now I'm down here, *with* you, and people keep telling me all these stories about the government and the massacre and the secret weapon, and I can't tell if any of it is real! I don't know what the truth is anymore, and it's a damn sight harder changing my entire worldview if no one is willing to answer *all* of my questions. You lived it. You were an eyewitness. You were there. So please, can you tell me what you know? Is everything I've been told down here true?"

Jacob's ancient face falls into a sad little smile. He looks at me with tired eyes and points to the foot of the cot. "Come over here and sit."

I obey and walk to him, sitting gingerly at his feet. My heart is thudding uncomfortably, and I clasp my hands together, looking down at my lap, hoping against hope that Jacob will concede to my request.

"Child, what is it that you're truly after?"

I bite my lower lip. If I can concede to his version of history, if I can pretend that I believe him, he may be inclined to tell me what I so desperately want to know. I choose my words carefully.

"The truth," I say simply. "I'm after the truth."

Jacob sighs. "The truth is a tricky business."

"I want it to make sense," I say. "If the massacre happened—if the Terror War is a lie—I need to know. I have to know your history. All of it."

"Do you imagine that knowing about the secret weapon will change your circumstances?"

I look up, meeting the old man's gaze. I shake my head. "No, nothing like that. I just . . . I've spent my whole life being taught one thing, and now everything I thought I knew is . . ."

"A lie?" Jacob says.

I pause, looking at him with watering eyes. "I don't know."

Jacob shakes his head, and crushing defeat stabs me. It seems that I've taken on a fool's errand, but I have to ask again—one more time.

"Please sir, you were alive back then. You know the truth, and to have someone who knows the truth . . ."

But the rest of my sentence dies, and with it, all hope of ever knowing if the secret weapon exists, because if Jacob Ganiston won't speak about it, no one else can. He's the last one—the only eyewitness left—and after that, everything dies with him.

My head falls to my chest. "I'm sorry to have bothered you, sir."

I stand up, breathing heavily and fighting the urge to cry. It's a curious sensation—my face hot with the threat of tears. Frustration and sadness seize me. It's not fair, and I can't do a thing about it.

But Jacob's quiet voice stops me in my tracks. "Wait."

I turn around, barely able to breathe. Adrenaline drowns me, and stars pop in and out of my peripheral.

"Sit down." He ushers me back to his side with a shriveled hand.

I walk back to him as if in a trance, taking my seat again.

"Let me tell you something, young woman," he says. "I can see the pain you carry. This must be an incredibly difficult circumstance to bear. But I can also see that you're a truth seeker—a rare thing indeed. I admire those who seek the truth, and that alone has convinced me . . ."

I cling to the fabric of my sweater, and my entire body stiffens, as if I were under my own power.

"I will share what I know," Jacob says. "But I must have your word that you will not broadcast this to your friends."

"Yes, sir," I say. "Of course."

"The Council has enough to worry about as it is," Jacob adds, his eyes piercing me. "Scouring the globe to find more of us is no small task. They don't need to worry about anything else."

"You have my word."

Jacob stares at me, as if measuring my worthiness through my countenance.

"I haven't spoken of this for a long time," he says. "These are . . . difficult memories for me."

I nod, patiently waiting for him to begin. His story is the key to my burning desire to know if I can rid myself of this horrid power. Nothing else matters.

He begins. "A few weeks before my mother and I were taken, my childhood friend vanished. He could command the weather. He could make it snow or rain or hail violently. A truly amazing individual."

Jacob takes several labored breaths.

"Before the brunt of the massacre, people with extremely powerful abilities were vanishing without a trace, and we didn't recognize it for what it was. We didn't run when we had the chance."

His voice cracks, and a horrible feeling settles in the pit of my stomach.

"Our neighbors disappeared next," he says. "The woman could make objects burst into flame, and the man could communicate with technology. He would create the most wonderful things. I remember he made me a watch for my tenth birthday. 'Double digits', he said, 'a young man that's turned double digits should own a watch'."

Jacob smiles, as if the man who made the watch were standing in front of him. His face is utterly disconcerting, and his blue eyes glaze over. He continues in a trance-like state.

"That morning, I remember thinking that if someone as powerful as my friend could disappear, then what chance did my mother and I have? How could we escape whatever was capturing the most supernatural of our kind?"

Pain is building behind Jacob's brow, but he pushes

forward, mesmerized by his own words.

"We were being hunted," he whispers. "My mother didn't want to believe it. She always saw the best in people—poor woman. And we decided to go into hiding too late. We were trapped."

Jacob's eyes well with tears, and his voice trembles.

"And my mother told me to run, but I didn't. I tried to protect her, and they took us both," he says. "And then I was chained together with my comrades, waiting to die . . ."

He stops, overwhelmed. He puts an ancient hand to his worn face, bowing his head and shaking. My heart breaks, and I reach out to place my hand on his. He looks at me through glassy eyes, and says, "the day my mother died, I saw it."

My lower lip begins to quiver. "You saw it?"

"In the warehouse, where they kept us chained in lines. A huge, glass-like coffin with an intricate button panel. I saw it when my hood slipped. And that sound . . ." Jacob inhales sharply, a terrified look creeping across his lined face. "A deep humming noise, as if the devil himself were inside. I felt sluggish—weighed down, barely able to move. It was all I could do to keep myself standing upright . . . and no one could use their ability."

Something inside of me breaks, and my chest erupts with a thrilling mix of cold adrenaline and fiery hot emotion. I grip the frame of the cot, and my hands turn white. I can't breathe. I can't think. It's as if I've risen up from the shell of my own body to stand on the sidelines as a witness to Jacob's story.

"The rumor is true," he says. "The government developed a weapon against us."

My mouth is suspended in shock, and after a few moments, my mind rejoins my body. "It's true? It exists?"

Jacob nods gravely. "Yes, the weapon exists."

"Do you know what it could do?" I ask, barely able to contain myself.

Jacob pauses, his chest heaving. He looks me in the eye, and a chill runs down my spine. "I don't know, child."

"But you said no one could use their ability."

He hugs himself, clinging to his clothing. "Yes, but I healed myself. I lived . . ."

I feel sick. Defeat crashes over me, but compassion kindles in my chest. Jacob's right. He survived. But what if that was simply a result of his particular ability? A freak accident—something the government never anticipated?

I look into his tired face, and behind his eyes, I see the weight of his story.

"I'm sorry that I can't say for certain," he says. "The one thing I know is that during the massacre, the government knew our every move—even of those who had gone into hiding. They could find us. Anywhere."

"So the weapon could find people with abilities?" I ask. Adrenaline fills my limbs and face. "But then . . ."

I trail off, struggling with this point. If that were true, why hasn't the government found the Diseased Ones down here?

"Yes. The weapon could find us," he says. "Nothing else could explain how they knew our every move, how they were capturing us by the thousands, even as we were scattering across the world."

Jacob's face is streaming. He is visibly angry with himself, and the color in his cheeks darkens.

"And somehow, I survived, with my cursed ability—to never feel physical pain, to never die—when I have watched so many perish around me. I can heal all of my physical wounds, but not the ones that have crippled my heart."

"But sir," I say, venturing forward cautiously. "Forgive my skepticism, but how can that be true? If this weapon can find people with the biomarker, then why haven't they found us? How are we safe down here?"

"What a brave young man," Jacob says. Tears trace his hardened face, forming lines that glisten in the candlelight. He seems to be lost in thought.

"Sir?"

"Let me tell you a story," he says. "It's the tale of a brave young man who sacrificed everything to keep us safe. He discovered the whereabouts of the weapon and did his best to destroy it."

"What?" Hopelessness crashes over me. "Was it destroyed?"

"I don't know," he says. "But from that point on, the government was unable to find us. Whether it was damaged or destroyed, this young man saved us all."

"What happened to him?"

"Likely killed," Jacob says. "What a brave young man—a true hero. Sacrificing his own life for the lives of others. He's the reason we're safe. The government can't find us. Not anymore. And so, my dear child, the secret weapon doesn't matter. What matters is that your life above ground was a lie, and I've lived through the aftermath of it."

Jacobs takes both my hands into his own, imploring me with his eyes. "I beg you," he says. "Start over here. Forget what you knew on the outside. Forget about your pain, your loss. Up there, all they care about are rules, order, accomplishments. But down here, you can experience family. Fall in love. Live a meaningful life. Find joy in the ability that makes you who you are, because what's in here, with these people, that's what true life is about."

He squeezes my hands firmly, and I give him a sad smile, trying my best to offer him comfort with my expression. But how could I possibly comfort a man who's lived a hundred years of pain when I've only experienced a few short months of it?

"I trust you to keep this in confidence," Jacob says. "For you have asked me under the pretense of seeking truth, and I have shared it with you."

"Yes, sir," I say. "Of course."

I sit there a minute before realizing that I ought to go. The conversation is over. I stand up, still gazing into Jacob's worn face, and empathy fills me to the brim. I'm hopeless to ease his suffering, and all that's left to do is leave.

"Mr. Ganiston?"

"Yes, child?"

"Thank you," I say. "You've given me a lot to think about."

I walk to the door, pull it open, and close it gently behind me. Taking a few steps down the hallway, I stop, placing my hand against the wall.

My knees give way, and I sit on the cold floor, dazed. The secret weapon was real. It could track people with the biomarker. It was damaged, possibly destroyed. But one phrase is seared into my brain: "no one could use their ability . . ." Can I dare to hope that this small detail is the key? I'm in shock, not only from Jacob's testimony but from my own boldness.

I stare at my feet, hands to my forehead, panting like I've run a mile. I have to make a decision. I need to stop riding the fence between worlds. I want to get rid of my ability. I want to go home.

"What's stopping me?" I whisper.

The voice in my heart screams: it's because you finally believe them. The government tried to kill you. You escaped with your life. You've seen the memories. You know the truth. Bear the ability. Learn to overcome the darkness.

But the—voice in my head—the one in my hands—that dangerous, inexplicable, sinister portion of me whispers: everyone is waiting for you. Your family misses you. Your life can go back to the way it was. There might be a way to remove your ability. You don't have to fear the monster beneath your skin. You don't have to hurt anyone else. You can go home.

"What am I supposed to do?" I say aloud.

I close my eyes, hoping that the solution will fall into my lap. With everything I've seen and experienced, I have to make a choice, and as I sit here, the answer comes to me in a moment of shining recognition.

I didn't choose this power, it chose me. It claimed me for its own. It's why I failed the Test. It's the reason I was kidnapped.

It's the force that's proven its volatility and strength—the biomarker that's destroyed my chance of having a normal life.

I don't want any part of it. I'm done. Perhaps the government was seeking to rid the world of the most powerful abilities for the betterment of humanity. I simply don't know.

I've heard the Diseased Ones' side. I've listened to their stories. I've learned about their world. But now I want to talk to the government. I want to hear their side, but not from the pages of a history textbook. I need to talk to someone in charge. I have to find this weapon, because if it can really take away my demon, the world will be better for it.

No one needs to get hurt, and the government doesn't need to know about this underground society. From what I've seen, these people aren't the ones I've been taught to hate. Whatever happened in the past, they've changed. But I need to free myself from this ability. I'm going home.

I stand with a determined spring in my step. I know what I need to do. I'm going back to the Testing Center. I'm going to see this weapon for myself, and if I'm wrong, then so be it. I can always come back. I can learn to live with this, but only if I have to.

The idea is so simple—so clear—and no one can stop me. My ability will make sure of that.

21

I CAN SEE CLEARLY NOW. MY TASK IS SET, AND I'M READY to pursue it. The muddled, questioning, nimble girl who arrived four months ago is gone, and a new one stands in her place. A calm sense of direction washes over me. I can finally get some answers.

I believe the Diseased Ones have changed for the better, but the truth of the past has no bearing on the present. The Terror War. The massacre. I still can't say which is true. All I know for certain is that I have a power far more depraved than theirs, and ridding myself of it is my only hope.

I jog back through the hall, down the metal stairs, and into the massive common room. I don't feel like joining in on any games. I wouldn't be able to focus. I'm exhausted.

I'll be dragged into playing if I'm spotted, so I place myself strategically between the tables, walking opposite the recreation area. After navigating through the dining section, I make my way to the set of metal stairs in the farthest corner. I'm eager to get to my room.

Climbing the steps two at a time, I hold the handrail like a lifeline. I'm still not keen on heights, even behind a barrier. After reaching the top, I stride through the hallway, counting each room I pass.

"Hollis," a girl's voice calls out to me.

I stop my quick pace, grimacing. I don't want to talk to anyone. I just want to sleep, but I retrace my steps, turning back to the previous bedroom.

"Hey, Tiffany," I say, leaning against the frame of the doorway.

She smiles at me from her cot. "What's up?"

"Heading to my room to get some sleep. I'm exhausted."

"I bet. You did really well in that last training session. You've improved a lot."

"Thanks." I give her a thumbs up. "Oh, and thanks for saving me. I completely forgot to work on my fine motor skills."

"No problem. I figure you'd find the time."

I smile sheepishly. "Yes, I will."

"Like now." She jumps up and stuffs her feet into a pair of fluffy green socks.

I gape at her, bleary-eyed. "Now? Like right now?"

"Why not?" she says, shrugging. "Were both up, and you're already behind. Jonah thinks you've got this down."

I give her a disgruntled look, but she's right. I should've learned how to do this by now, and considering what I've decided to do, I need practice. She waves me through the door.

"Alright, we get to work on these freaky powers of yours." She flitters her fingers over her head, as if playing an invisible instrument.

"Hey, I'm not that much of a freak," I say.

Tiffany's hand gesture intensifies, and she leans forward, puckering her lips to produce a spooky sound.

I wave her down. "Okay, fine, my powers are freaky."

She laughs. "Just giving you a hard time."

I walk over to the cot and sit on the edge gingerly, tucking my legs up crisscrossed. I rest my head on my hand. "Okay, what should I do?"

Tiffany points to a pair of blue shoes in the corner of the room. "Make me put my shoes on."

I look between Tiffany's eager countenance and the worn pair of blue shoes.

"You want me to put the shoes on and tie the laces?" I bite my lower lip, staring at the tangled mess. Determination pulls me up from the cot. "Right. Good plan. Let's do this."

"Whenever you're ready," says Tiffany in a passable impression of Jonah's voice.

I snicker. "Not half bad."

"I know, right?" She grins.

I hold my palms up, rooting Tiffany to the spot. Channeling my ability into her, I point her toward the corner and say, "Go pick up your shoes."

Tiffany obeys, moving mechanically forward and grabbing her shoes. My fingertips twitch, and she turns back to face me. I stand straight and mirror her, picturing what I have to do in my mind's eye.

I lock Tiffany's movement to my own, sitting on the floor. She follows me in time, perfectly synced.

My fingertips vibrate and power seeps out, but I keep it controlled. It's crucial to coordinate each movement cautiously. To my surprise, after a minute of trudging through the motions, Tiffany's feet are stuffed into the shoes, her green fluffy socks askew.

"Perfect. Now those damn laces," I mutter.

Passing air through my lips, I stare intently at the shoes, furrowing my brow in concentration. My ability buffets my hands forward, and I yield to the power. The buzzing makes me feel alive. Nothing but my newfound determination could have tied those laces, and as I finish, I sit back, reveling in the accomplishment.

"Symmetrical bow loops and all," I say smugly.

"You did it," Tiffany beams. "Wow, good job. See? I knew you could do it."

I roll my eyes. "Right."

"I did," she says. "You want to let me go now?"

"Oops." I swipe my hand, releasing her from my ability. "Sorry."

I lean against Tiffany's cot, sitting on the floor and feeling utterly drained. It takes so much of my energy every time I use this power. My eyes droop from fatigue.

"I think I need to call it a night, Tiffany." I yawn. "I'm so tired."

She stands up, and hops back onto the cot, folding herself up. "Lucky . . . I have insomnia. I can hardly ever get a decent night's sleep."

"That sounds awful."

"Yeah, it's not the greatest. But I manage."

I move back to the foot of the cot, joining Tiffany. I could crash right here, but a thought occurs to me, and it jerks my brain out of its tired fog.

"Hey, Tiff?"

"What's up?"

"Do you go on every rescue mission? You know, when the Council finds someone with an ability?"

Tiffany hugs a rather large pillow, rocking forward and staring up at the ceiling. "Well, I do now."

"Why's that?" I ask.

"It's much easier to get back here with my ability, isn't it?" she says brightly. "It used to take teams a lot longer before I joined, and it was really dangerous."

I give her a strange look. "How so?"

"Well, the people we were trying to save would attack us with their abilities," she says.

"Why would they do that?" I ask, alarmed.

Tiffany, no doubt noticing my apprehension, speaks quickly. "It makes sense. They're frightened. A group of strangers approaching their hideout—that would be enough to scare anyone. It used to be dangerous, but now that Ashton and I have joined the team, it's safe and efficient."

"Ashton?"

"He's really valuable. He's the reason that rescue missions are safe now," she explains, leaning back against the wall. "Ashton suppresses the person's ability while we talk with them, and then I teleport the team in and out. It's a really polished system."

A pit forms in my stomach, but Tiffany's let slip what I needed to hear. I stare at my fingers, picking at them, and ask my next question with a guarded tone.

"Do you force people to come here?" I look up to meet Tiffany's dark brown eyes. "Like Vianne Evolet?"

"No." Tiffany's voice is soft and gentle. "But once they see that we have abilities, it gives us a lot of credit. They know that we can't be from the government. People *want* to come with us. Honestly, they can't believe there's an entire group of us living underground. That's what happened with Vianne after we found her out there. She chose to come with us."

"But . . . you made me come here, and then you forced me to stay. You locked me in that room."

I stare at her. A terrible feeling washes over me, and I'm sick to my stomach. Here I am, face to face with my kidnapper, the same girl I call friend, and I can't help but feel at war—torn between worlds once again. What she did to me wasn't right. But was it wrong?

"I know," she says. Her face deepens in sorrow. "Hollis, I'm sorry, but you didn't understand at the time. They would have shot you. If I hadn't brought you here, you'd be dead. You know that now, right?"

"Right . . ." My fingers knot together. I'm trying to stay

calm. "You did what you were trained to do. I get that. I really do. If there's anything I understand, it's that. Doing what needs to be done is how I was raised. It's in my blood. It's how I learned to control my emotions. It's how I became a society member."

I try to look kind, but she appears stricken. Her eyes are glistening, and I look away, staring at the floor.

"Hollis, I know that our world is still new to you, but I'm really glad you're here." She falters a moment, biting her lip. "And I understand it's difficult, but you're doing something incredible."

"And what's that?" I ask, looking up. "What's so amazing about losing my home?"

A tense moment follows this, and I immediately regret what I've said. I know that Tiffany was following orders when she rescued me. It's not entirely her fault, but on occasion, spite rears its ugly head when I see her.

"You're taking on a power that's far greater than anything I've seen," she says. "And you're absolutely mastering it."

I don't know about that, but I smile at her, attempting to make nice after my vicious comment. "Mastering it is the plan."

"You've only been here four months, and you've demonstrated the proficiency of someone who's had their ability for a few years. Jonah's impressed."

"Really?" A warm feeling enters my chest, and for a moment, I feel proud of what I've accomplished with this power, terrifying though it may be.

"Yeah," she says, giving me a nudge. "You're his star student."

"Well," I say, in a playfully conceited tone. "I was top of my class out there, so it only makes sense that I've got you beat."

She grins. "You haven't beaten me at anything, Timewire."

"Star student," I say in a sing-song voice, pointing at myself.

Tiffany throws her pillow at me, whacking me in the face. It topples off the cot and onto the floor, nearly taking me with it.

"Hey!"

Tiffany points to herself and copies my tone. "Killer aim."

I jump down, scooping the pillow up from the floor and holding it threateningly above my head. Tiffany laughs. "I've seen you play pool. Don't bother."

I chuck the pillow, but it misses by a foot. "Damn."

Tiffany snatches it from the cot and holds it to her chest, a satisfied look plastered across her face. "Impeccable aim, but you're out of pillows now."

I cross my arms. "You know, I could take that from you," I say. "Wouldn't even be hard."

"Whatever," she says, laughing. "You still couldn't hit me with it."

I sigh, sitting down. "You're right. I have terrible aim."

My spirits have lifted. The tense conversation is finished, and once again, weariness takes over. I need to sleep. With so much to think about, a decent night's rest will do me some good. I've heard what I needed to hear and practiced a little as well.

"Thanks for your help," I say. "Seems I've nailed tying those shoelaces."

She gives me a goofy thumbs up. "Seems you have."

"You're so weird."

"Best compliment you could give me." She scoops her radiant black hair over her shoulder. "Maybe we could practice again tomorrow?"

"Yes," I say. "I'd like that."

"Great. Get some sleep."

"You don't have to tell me twice."

I jump off the cot, scamper through the door, and wave goodbye over my head. I've got big plans for the morning.

22

THE NEXT SEVERAL WEEKS PASS BY IN A BLUR. I'M WORKING so hard on my ability that I've scarcely had time for anything else. Every day I push myself to the limit, honing my power and bringing it to new heights.

It's been a curious journey, moving from timid and fearful to power-wielding and triumphant. I've changed more than I thought a society member could. It's surprising, and every time I use my ability, the carefully hidden feeling within me grows a little stronger. My power is bringing out what society has locked away, and I'm not resisting it. It's wonderful and unexpected, and as time progresses, I realize I'm taking Jacob's words about finding joy in my ability to heart. It's alarming, but utterly magnificent. Every time I use my power I feel alive.

I've spent nearly every waking moment by Jonah's side, and I'm seeing massive growth, but what I really need is consistency. That's my guarantee.

"I want to try thirty people," I say to Jonah one afternoon.

Jonah looks up at me, startled. "Thirty?"

I nod. "Thirty people. I'm ready."

It's my ticket into the Testing Center. If I can reliably control a group that large, then I'll have no trouble with my quest.

"Alright," he says. "I'll need to find thirty people willing to participate."

"Of course."

I don't have to wait long. The next day, thirty people have gathered on the training platform. Apparently many of them volunteered out of curiosity. I don't blame them. After all, I am the girl who 'failed the Test.' This title doesn't give me much credit, but it does afford me hushed whispers and staring eyes, most of which I hardly notice anymore.

Ashton's been asked back for this little venture. I can tell that Jonah is nervous, and as I glance around the group, I'm put off by the task. Thirty people. More than the Testing Center. But I've done this on purpose.

"Whenever you're ready," Jonah says, giving me a stiff nod.

We lock eyes, and I clench my hands into fists, determined. Jonah isn't sure I can do it. I can see it in his face. If I'm honest with myself, I'm not sure either, but I know that I need to get this. Everything depends on my ability. If I can't control a group this large, then going back to the Testing Center is out of the question.

I stand across from them, feeling overwhelmed, but I close my eyes, taking a moment to myself. I can do this. All I need to do is recreate the moment I experienced nearly five months ago—the moment in the lobby where I escaped two dozen men with guns.

I open my eyes. "Can you all walk around?" I ask. "In front of me and behind me? Just around the platform?"

No one moves at first, but after a few seconds, they oblige, dispersing about the platform. Clumps of people move around me, walking back and forth.

"And keep walking around," I say.

I shut my eyes tightly, blocking out the distractions. For this, I'm going to need all the power I can harness. I think back to Jonah's instructions: "You need to think of something equally as powerful. You've been allowed to express emotion. I want you to focus on the way it compelled you . . . and when you're ready, let that experience help you pour out your ability."

Keith. The boy who opened my eyes to something I never thought possible. The boy who held my hand for the first time. The boy who made me feel as though I'd woken from a deep slumber. The boy who kissed me. Keith.

An enchanting sensation rises in my chest, and with it, my power awakens. My eyes fly open, and my hands launch to either side, fingers splayed. I grasp for them as the power explodes from me. Every person on the platform freezes mid-step, completely still, without so much as a falter.

I gaze around, panting heavily. My arms are still outstretched, and as I lower them, a sense of victory congratulates me. I have thirty people under my power, and I did it on the first try.

I swipe, releasing my captive audience, and turn to my teacher, who stands speechless. He bears an impressed look, and his expression is mirrored in the crowd, but I don't look to them. I keep my attention fixed on Jonah because he alone understands what I've accomplished. He's the only one who can truly appreciate it.

"Beat my record," I say, still panting. I smile and shake my head, placing my hands to my forehead. I'm in disbelief. "Did you see that?"

"Young lady," he says. "Of course I saw that. Well done."

I grin. "Thanks."

"Well, I think that will do for today," Jonah says. "No need to push yourself any further."

"Yes, sir."

▪ ▪ ▪

The dining hall is ablaze with activity, and as usual, I sit next to Keith, listening to the lively conversation of Ben and Candice, and only catching half of it. Keith is discussing game night with Darren. Tiffany, Rosalie, and Audrey are across from me, involved in gossip about some boy.

I tune it out, staring across the tables. I'm lost in thought, and I have hardly touched my lasagna. I'm still in shock. I did it, and that means that I'm one step closer to my goal.

"Hollis, that was impressive," Darren says.

"Really crazy," Rosalie adds.

"Impressive crazy," Ben says.

Tiffany chuckles. "I knew she could do it."

I snap out of it. "What?"

"Have you ever put that many people under before?" Darren asks.

I look up from my plate, fork in hand. "No. There were more people today than back at the Testing Center."

"More?" Ben repeats. He slops some grape juice down his front.

"Nicely done," Candice snorts.

"Well, I guess. I didn't exactly stop to count," I say. "Could have been less. It's hard to tell."

"Well, I'm impressed," Darren says. "My ability is a lot different than yours, but I can appreciate how much power that must've taken."

"Thanks," I say.

"Same," Keith says, bowing his head. I smile, and my eyes dart back to my lasagna. "I've noticed that you've been working hard, so no surprises there. You earned that stunt."

"Yeah, I noticed the same," Candice says, jumping in. "You've ditched game night a few times. Any particular reason you're working so hard?"

I shrug, grabbing my glass of water and downing it in one go. This is the last thing I want to talk about, so I ignore Candice's question and turn to Ben, smirking. If anyone can change the subject of a conversation, it's Ben Bryson. I just need to loop him in.

"So, Ben," I say. "I see your hair is back to normal. How much product did you use to get rid of the pink?"

I nudge Candice, and her look of glee says it all. "You know,

Hollis. I'm beginning to like you more and more."

Ben folds his arms across his chest and leans back in his seat, squinting. "Vianne changed me back."

"Did she now?" Candice says, snickering.

"And what did you have to do?" Audrey asks.

"Give her flowers? Sing her a song? Write a note?" Candice bats her eyelashes, and the girls giggle.

Ben's face turns pink. "For your information," he says, sending his fork clattering to the floor, "she just kept her end of the deal. She said I'd have it for a day, and I did. Then she changed me back."

"Alright," Darren says, scooting back from the table and holding his hands up. "Take it easy, Benny boy."

"Ben fancies her," Candice whispers to the group.

"I do not!" he roars.

Candice turns to him, clapping her hands together. "Then she likes you. No wonder your hair is back to normal. She changed you back because she *loves* you."

Ben's pink shade deepens.

"What a lovely couple they'd make," Audrey says, mopping her eyes in fake admiration. "Just lovely. Don't you think?"

"Will I be invited to the wedding?" Candice asks.

"There won't be one," Ben says.

"I could be the wedding planner," Candice says brightly. "Wouldn't that be magical?"

"No."

Audrey's expression changes to soppy sadness. "Oh come on. Why not?"

"Because," Ben says, turning to her crossly. "I don't like Vianne."

"Well you like someone," Candice says. "I know you too well, Ben. I can see it."

Ben is beside himself, an embarrassed hue lingering under his features.

"Candice," he says, gritting his teeth.

"What?"

Ben lets out a frustrated noise. "Why do you have to . . . can't you just . . . give it a rest?"

"Give what a rest?" she asks, a little too seriously. She raises an eyebrow. "The wedding plans?"

Ben stands up, knocking over his glass. "I don't like Vianne!"

Candice jumps up as well, pointing a finger at his chest. "That's bull and you know it," she says. "You've bumped into that girl so many times I've lost count. You like her. So why don't you just admit it? Why can't you just—"

"Because I like *you*!"

There's a collective gasp from our table, and Candice's mouth drops open. Several rigid seconds follow this, and I don't know whether Candice is going to speak or hit him in the face.

Ben, taking the moment in stride, disentangles himself from the chair and walks around the table, directly up to Candice. He stares at her, a determined look plastered across his face.

"Never thought I'd have the guts to do this," he says softly.

"But I like you. I have for a while now. And all that nonsense with Vianne . . . I was honestly just bumping into her."

The biggest smile lights up her face. "You're *that* clumsy?"

"I'm that clumsy."

He grabs Candice's hand, and the two stand face to face, inches apart.

"Well," Candice says, staring into Ben's eyes. "It's about damn time."

She grabs the front of his shirt and pulls him in, kissing him with abandoned passion. My jaw drops, as does everyone else's, and after a few fierce moments, the two break apart. Candice's face turns as pink as Ben's.

Everyone cheers, and soon half the dining room joins in. People are even standing on chairs to get a good look at what all the fuss is about. Ben and Candice sit down, completely flustered.

Darren claps his hands together, looking between the two, a wicked grin spreading across his face. "Well, now I think it's appropriate to ask. When's the wedding?"

Candice hides her face in her hands and says nothing. I think it's the first time she's ever been speechless.

"Hey Keaton," Darren says, looking to Keith. "You owe me two weeks of meat rations."

"Shut up," Keith says.

Candice turns to her brother and hits him on the shoulder. "You bet meat rations on me? Seriously?"

"Well—"

"Figured I make a profit," Darren says, cutting him off. "It was only a matter of time before you two kids got together."

"What?" Candice says, affronted. "No it wasn't."

"I bet it would be this month," he says. "But your brother thought you'd hold out longer."

Keith looks sheepish. "Yeah."

"It was so obvious," Darren adds.

Candice looks around the table. "It was obvious?"

Everyone answers at the same time, nodding vigorously, and saying things like "saw it coming," "so much flirting," and "do you even have to ask."

■ ■ ■

The evening moves on, and after all my nightly duties are complete, I make my way to the vacated dining area to sit in one of the booths. I need a minute to myself.

Tonight made me happy. I'm happy that I have friends here. I'm happy that I've accomplished a task I thought impossible. I'm happy for Ben and Candice. I'm happy with Keith. I've experienced so much joy in a place I never knew existed, with people I've been trained to hate. If my life above ground is truth, then what I've experienced here shouldn't have happened.

"What am I doing?" I whisper. I bow my head, resting it in my hands, my elbows propped onto the table. "What am I doing this for?"

But the reason eludes me. If I'm honest with myself, my time here has been nothing like the horrors I imagined. I have Jonah, the man who stood by my side and walked me through every step of this frightening ability. I have Tiffany, the girl who encouraged me and never gave up on me. I have Keith, the boy who made me realize just how wonderful expressing emotion can be.

I sit, staring at the smooth wood of the table, counting the lines that weave across its surface. This small act grounds me, and instantly, a sense of calm hits me.

"Hey there."

I jump and slide back against the booth, clutching my chest.

"Sorry," Keith says. "Didn't mean to frighten you."

"You seem to have a knack for that."

"I guess so," he says, grinning. "Mind if I join you?"

"Not at all."

He scoots into the booth and sits next to me, tapping his hands on the table. He smiles that charmingly boyish smile and brushes his dark hair from his eyes. My stomach flutters.

"Is this where you come to think?" he asks.

"Well, I can't fly," I say. "So yes."

"Seems suitable to me." He looks up at the ceiling. "But people can't see our feet if we're sitting all the way down here."

I shake my head. "Nope. They definitely can't."

"Well, that settles it then." He peers out across the room.

"Settles what?"

"The cave in the ceiling is clearly the better thinking place." He nods knowingly. "People can see our feet from up there."

I laugh. "Well, that *is* the criteria."

I follow Keith's lead and look out at the room. It's peaceful now that most people have cleared out.

"Can I tell you something?" Keith asks.

"Of course."

He turns to me, and his brilliant blue eyes take my breath away. "I don't know all the details about what you went through to get here, but . . . I'm really glad you're here."

I give him a warm smile. "Thanks, Keith."

"It must have been hard to leave your life up there," he adds. "I can't imagine being pulled away from the life I have here . . . so, I want you to know that I think you're really brave."

Guilt guts me. "I . . . I wouldn't call myself brave."

"I'm serious," Keith says. "You're an incredible person. You've braved a world you've been taught to hate, and you've come out stronger for it."

"It's very different here," I concede. "And I've learned a lot."

Keith grabs my hand, sending an electric pulse straight through me. "I just want to say that I'm happy you're here, and I'm happy I know you."

"Me too," I say. "You're . . ."

Our eyes hold each other for what feels like an eternity before I finally break away. He squeezes my hand.

"I'm . . . ?" he says.

I tilt my head to the side. "Fishing for a compliment?"

He chuckles. "You're the one who stopped talking."

"Well, some things are best left to mystery. Don't you think?"

"You're funny," he says.

I laugh. "Ben's funny. I'm boring."

Keith shakes his head. "Hollis Timewire, you are not boring. You're one of the most interesting people I've ever met. You have a crazy life story and an impressive ability that easily challenges anything I've seen down here. That's the complete opposite of boring."

I drop his hand, flustered by the compliment. "I don't get it."

"What don't you get?"

"You look at me . . . and you see someone that's not there." My voice cracks. I swallow painfully, and my eyes begin to water.

"You want to know what I see when I look at you?" he says softly. "I see a person who has overcome adversity, who's broken barriers, and who's done incredible things."

"But how can that be me? I don't understand. I don't see it."

My hands are trembling, and guilt overwhelms me. I look at Keith's kind face, and my heart breaks. He doesn't know what I've planned. No one here does. I hang my head, wanting to vanish.

"I don't see it," I say again. "I don't see what you see."

"That's because you're not looking for it," he says. "And I don't know if that's because you're working out how you feel about this place, about having powers, about expressing emotion . . . but I know that you've done something very few people have done. Be proud of that. Own that and give it time. You'll see it one day."

Keith places a soft kiss on the back of my hand, and I'm overcome with remorse.

Everything washes over me. The late-night pool games. The magic tricks. The laughter. The training. The freedom of expression. The display of powers. Jonah's words. Jacob's memories. It all hits me in a moment of wonder, and the last reservation within me breaks. And suddenly, my own longings—the plan to go home, the desire to find the secret weapon, the wish to rid myself of my own power—it all amounts to nothing but a foolish fantasy, brewed in the mind of a naïve girl.

Keith is right. I haven't been looking for it. I haven't even tried, and as I sit here, staring at this wonderful boy, I hear Jacob's earnest words: "Start over here. Forget what you knew on the outside. Forget about your pain, your loss . . . experience family. Fall in love. Live a meaningful life. Find joy in the ability that makes you who you are, because what's in here, with these people, that's what true life is about."

A single tear courses down the side of my face, and I wipe it away with my free hand. I take a deep breath and say the words I've been fighting for the past five months.

"I want to stay here," I say.

Keith's mouth parts ever so slightly and a curious expression crops up in his face. "You want to stay?"

I nod slowly. "Yes."

Deep down, I know what this decision means. I can't go back home, I'll never see my parents again, and I must learn to live with the curiously dark ability beneath my skin. But when it comes down to it, I know in my heart that I can't give up what I've found here. Keith, Jonah, Tiffany, my friends—

they've become my family—one I never thought possible. I've experienced more joy and freedom in five months down here than in sixteen years up there. I can't go back to the mundane, identity depriving, suppressed, and muted life I once knew. I've tasted the exhilaration of my power, the intensity of pure passion, and the kindness of true friendship. I've found a new home, one that has embraced me, despite everything. I'm where I'm meant to be . . . and as I realize this, my desire to return to my old life fades away, like the lingering images of a bad dream.

Abounding energy ignites my resolve. I feel free, lighter than air, happier than anything words can describe.

"I want to stay," I say again, staring into Keith's wonderful blue eyes. I grab both of his hands, searching his face. "I want to start over. You're right. I've been missing it. This. Right here. Life. Feeling. All of it. It's right here, and I've been missing it because of my past, but that doesn't matter anymore."

He smiles and squeezes my hands gently. My fingertips tingle with energy.

"And you know what?" I say, beaming.

"What?"

I take a deep breath, allowing my ability in, and uncontainable joy surges through me. "I'm a Diseased One, and I'm okay with that."

"There it is," he whispers. "I knew you'd see it."

He leans forward, his lips brushing my own, and we sink into a wonderful moment of bliss. Everything disappears, and the spark of passion reignites, filling my soul to the brim. Happiness. That's what I've been missing.

We pull apart, smiling and looking at each other. I take in every detail. His dark hair. His beautiful eyes. His goofy grin. His strong hands. Everything about this moment seals my decision. I've changed my mind. I can't go through with it. Not anymore. I'm staying here, with these people, and this life.

"You're wonderful," I say. "That's what I was going to say before."

He chuckles. "That wasn't left to mystery for long."

"Wonderful."

Keith smiles, stretching his arms above his head and leaning back in the booth. He yawns. "Well, the night is still young, and the gang is playing pool. Want to join them?"

"The night is young?" I say, peering around the corner of the booth at the deserted space.

"Relatively young."

"I think I should get to bed."

"You sure?"

"I'm sure."

Keith leans in and kisses me on the forehead. "I'll see you later, Hollis."

He jumps up and walks backward a few steps. I wave at him as he retreats. He waves back, turns over his shoulder, and jogs away. I watch him for a few moments and then sink against the booth.

Another wave of remorse hits me. I feel sick to my stomach. There's one more thing I have to do before I join their world for good. I have to tell Jonah what I was planning, and I need to accept the consequences, whatever they may be.

23

THE NEXT MORNING, I WAKE EARLY AND LIE IN BED, STARING up at the ceiling and contemplating the task ahead of me. I'm going to come clean to Jonah, and I feel nauseous. It's like the morning of the Test. I have no idea what to expect, and just like before, the outcome of today decides my fate. I want to join their world, but I need to do it properly. It's the right thing to do.

"No more lying, Hollis," I whisper.

I dress silently and bundle up, stuffing my feet into shoes. I want to catch Jonah before the morning Council meeting. Something in my gut tells me this can't wait. I have to tell Jonah as soon as I can.

I jog down the hall, through the door, and to the metal staircase, making my way into the massive room.

It's loud. I'm greeted by an onslaught of echoing voices, and as I scan around, I notice clumps of people running back and forth. Why are people up right now? It's so early.

I jump down the last step and slink along the wall to keep out of everyone's way. A large group brushes past me, chatting rapidly, and as I turn over my shoulder to listen, I crash head-on into Rosalie. She yelps, and we both end up in a heap on the floor.

"S-sorry," I say, stammering. "Wasn't watching."

"Oh, Hollis. That's okay," she says, jumping to her feet and tottering a little. She extends her hand to me. I take it, and she pulls me up with a surprising amount of strength.

"What's going on?" I ask.

"We found someone," she says. "Those electrical storms near Area 2, it's someone with an ability. The rescue team should be leaving anytime now. Sorry, but I have to go."

"Oh." My stomach turns uncomfortably. "Where's Jonah?"

"Training platform." She points behind me and then skips off.

"Thanks."

I arrive at the training platform a minute later, completely out of breath. Tiffany and Jonah are standing across from one another, and small scraps of paper litter the mat. Tiffany vanishes, reappearing at Jonah's side.

"Good," he says. "Now remember, always focus on the number of people you're teleporting."

"Of course," she says.

"This time I want you to teleport with me. Hit the paper at the back corner."

Tiffany grabs his arm and they both vanish, reappearing

across the platform on the mark in the back.

"Good. Your control has improved," Jonah says. "Alright, you're set. I need to brief Pierce, and then we'll be on our way."

"Yes, sir," she says, hopping down from the platform, and nearly colliding with me. "Oh, hey Hollis. Sorry, excuse me."

She trots past me, tucking her black hair up into a messy bun.

"Hi," I say distractedly. I grab the edge of the platform and pull myself up, approaching Jonah. I'm struggling to control my tone. "Jonah? Can I talk to you?"

"Hollis, I'm afraid that now is not the best time," he says, moving around the platform to collect the small scraps of paper. He tucks them into his pocket. "Can we talk later? I don't know if you've heard yet, but we've found someone new, and the rescue team is leaving soon."

I nod, swallowing the horrible lump in my throat. "Of course. I'll wait."

"Thank you, Hollis."

He turns away from me and continues to gather the paper scraps. I retreat from the platform and sit on the nearest table, attempting to calm myself by counting the chairs around me.

It doesn't help. I'm on edge, and as my mind wanders, my heartbeat quickens. The nasty feeling in my stomach won't let up. What will Jonah say when I tell him? What will become of my place here? How long will it be before they regain my trust? I don't know . . .

"I can't sit here anymore," I mutter to myself.

I slip off the table and walk through the dining area, my

hands sliding along the tops of the chairs. The dread of this conversation is sickening. I'm lightheaded and my knees feel weak.

I continue to meander through the room, moving in no particular direction. Pacing seems to be helping me more than counting.

A familiar, jeering voice issues from straight ahead, and I stop in my tracks. Ashton is just beyond me, leaning against a booth. Vianne Evolet is perched inside, huddled to herself, hiding behind a book with papers strewn across the table. I edge closer.

"So, I guess Ben and Candice are an item now," Ashton says. "Too bad for you, Evolet."

Vianne looks up from her book and scoffs. "Why do I care? I never liked Ben."

Ashton laughs. "Oh, right. Of course not. You only knocked into him every chance you got. It's kind of pathetic, to be honest."

Vianne sinks into the booth, averting her eyes. She stares at the papers but then sits up again, glaring at him. "Don't you have to go? Aren't you on the rescue team or something?"

"Oh, but this is touching," he says, ignoring the question. "You like him, and now he's off with some other girl. Too bad for you."

"I don't like him."

"Liar."

"Will you leave me alone?"

She pulls the papers closer and buries herself deeper into

the book, lowering her head. Ashton grabs a chair from the nearest table, turns it around, and sits on it. He leans forward, a taunting smile smeared across his haughty face.

"What are you reading?" he asks.

"None of your business." Her hair flickers, changing to a shade of light blue.

"What's that color mean? Lovesick?"

Ashton leans over the backrest of the chair, staring at Vianne. "Come on, Evolet. What are you reading?"

"I said none of your—"

Ashton plucks the book from her hands, and my jaw drops. I take a few steps forward, but hesitate, unsure of what to do.

"Hey! Give that back." Vianne reaches across the table, but Ashton pulls the book away, thumbing through it rapidly. His face lights up, and he chuckles.

"You're an artist. That's cute," he says, mockingly. "Look at all this. This is nice, Evolet."

"I said, give it back," she snarls, and her hair snaps to a shocking white.

"Feisty color."

Vianne stands up, sending papers flying everywhere. She swipes for the book, but Ashton jumps backward, evading her easily. "Oh, come on Evolet. I just want to see your art."

"Give it back."

She steps out from behind the booth, and Ashton dodges her, moving around the next table and rifling through the pages.

"What don't you want me to see?" he asks. "Bet you have sketches of Ben in here."

"Ashton, give—"

"Bet you have your initials penciled into a heart."

She lunges, but Ashton is too quick. He skips past her, positioning the next table between them, and grinning wickedly.

"Bet you kiss your drawings of him too," he coos.

Vianne's hair turns from white to blood red, and her pale cheeks change to match. "You're vile," she says coldly, "and I bet the only reason you're picking on me is because you know I wouldn't talk to you otherwise. Is that why you're such an ass? Because it's the only way you can get a girl to acknowledge you?"

Ashton's expression falters. "No one asked for your opinion," he replies darkly. "You stupid little metamorph."

Bang.

Vianne's hands move in a flash, and an intense cloud of purple smoke erupts from her. I gasp, my hand slipping from the adjacent chair.

Ashton's appearance changes radically. His nose, pressed flat against his face, is angry red. His lips, fat and disfigured, protrude from his face, and orange hair extends down the back of his neck. Yellow teeth bulge at odd angles from a distorted mouth. Vianne seems to have transformed him into the semblance of a mutated dog.

Ashton drops the book, howling in discomfort and clawing at his face. Vianne stoops, snatching it up and retreating. I breathe a small sigh of relief. At least Vianne can hold her own, though 'her own' is a bit disconcerting.

Ashton drops his hands and speaks in a frightening voice.

"You bitch." He advances on her, and she steps back, tripping over a chair and dropping the book on the floor. "I know what you are. I know what you hide with that stupid ability of yours."

Ashton's hands slash through the air, his deformed appearance vanishes, and Vianne's face erupts with several horrific scars. They line her cheeks in jagged slices, extending down to her neck, raw and deep.

Vianne stumbles back into the booth, holding her hands up to her face in an attempt to cover it. She whimpers, pulling her sweater above her nose.

"See?" Ashton growls. He points directly into her face, getting offensively close. "That's what you are. That's what you cover up. Without your ability, you're hideous and disgusting, and no one in the world would ever want to be with that."

The monster in me awakens. Raw tingling consumes my entire body. Like a dam bursting at its seams, I explode forward, lunging toward Ashton with a surge of incredible power. Every sinew of my being is electric, and my hands launch from me, encasing him in my vicious grasp.

Ashton screams.

I twitch my hand, pulling him to me, and forcing him to his knees. I curl my forefinger, and Ashton's head jerks upward. I stand over him, dark rage filling me to the brim. I speak in a venomous tone. "You shouldn't have said that."

I'm overcome by the entity in me, numb to everything else. My hands move with calculated control, and the sinister voice of my ability speaks for the first time since the Testing Center.

This boy. The nerve of this boy. The blatant hate he displayed.

My fingertips extend, and Ashton's eyes bulge. Blood trickles from his nose. I stand in front of him, shaking, an uncontainable fury pouring from me.

"Hollis!" Vianne shrieks, jumping up and tugging my arm. "Stop. You're hurting him!"

My ability erupts, gripping Vianne and throwing her against the tables with a thunderous crash. She crumples to the floor, unconscious. My eyes never leave Ashton.

Disgusting, vile boy, the voice says.

I'm quivering, power emanating through me, alive and invigorating. Ashton is screaming.

Let him writhe.

Blood pours from his nose at an alarming rate, and disgust roars in my heart. My hands move together as a unit, striking Ashton like a viper, and his eyes light up in agony. I've never experienced such rage. The demon deep within me has awoken to pour out wrath, and I am simply its faithful vessel, delivering judgement.

Kill him, Hollis. He deserves it.

I hear a faint voice in the back of my mind, quiet and muffled, but present . . . Hollis, stop. You're hurting him. Stop. Hollis, you have to stop. This isn't you. Don't do this. Fight it. You have to fight . . . It's my own voice, battling with the creature that's overtaken me.

My ability snarls, drowning it out and consuming me once

more. I'm overcome by it—utterly overpowered.

You know what you have to do, the darkness growls, *kill.*

Screaming. Everyone is screaming at me. It's issuing from all sides. It's in my head and in my ears. People have crowded around me, yelling at the top of their lungs. There's so much noise, but somehow, it's dulled. I feel nothing but anger and power. Nothing exists but savage rage.

Finish him, Hollis.

The buzzing in my fingertips comes to an abrupt halt, and the power vanishes from my limbs. My ability has been wrenched from me, and Jonah is at my side, breathless. His hands are extended over me, having just cut through the air. He's suppressed my ability.

Ashton falls from his rigid form and collapses to the floor, gagging. Blood soaks his front, and his body heaves. He's wheezing, struggling for breath on all fours and clutching his chest. He wipes the blood from his face, trembling.

"She's a demon! A monster!"

I look down at my hands, rising out of the trance-like state and coming to my senses. I gasp, as if surfacing from a long dive. I'm back, and I look around me.

Keith. Candice. Ben. Audrey. Darren. Rosalie. Tiffany. Jonah.

They're all wearing the same look. It's the look I saw in the eyes of the nurse. The one I witnessed from the man I threw into the pillar—the same expression I perceived after my mishap at the marble game. Fear.

I gaze at my hands, trembling violently. What have I done? My breathing is shallow, and my heart rate is soaring. I lost control. I hurt them. Adrenaline thunders through me and stars pop in and out of my vision.

I'm going to be sick. Eyes streaming, I turn away and run blindly through the room, up the stairs, and through the heavy metal door. I pelt down the concrete hallway and charge into my room. I barely make it through before sliding down the wall and bursting into tears.

I'm gasping for air, clutching at my neck, as if I were drowning. Hugging my knees, I rock myself back and forth. The spring of hot tears continues to fall. I take one heaving breath after another, trying to find something solid to hold onto.

What happened to me? What did I do back there? Why couldn't I stop myself?

I cower on the floor, paralyzed with the gravity of what I've done. I almost killed Ashton Teel. My chest feels as though it might explode. I close my eyes, trying to slow my pounding heart.

A jarring knock sends me to my feet. I spring back, shaking from head to foot.

"W-who is it?"

The door splits open, banging against the wall, and Tiffany enters, disheveled. She shuts the door behind her, and we stare at each other.

"What the hell was that?" she demands, her voice stricken.

I can't speak. I stand limply against the cold stone, unable to move. My deepest fear has been realized. I've lost control, and it's this moment that seals my fate. My plan must happen. I need to act. Right now.

An unnatural calm descends on me, and despite the

coursing adrenaline of my pounding heart, I gain a sense of purpose and clear direction.

"Tiffany," I say. "Listen to me. You need to teleport me back to the Testing Center."

"You want me to what?" Her eyes register a slight shock.

"Teleport me back to the Testing Center," I say again.

She gapes at me. "Hollis, are you out of your mind?"

I clench my hands into fists. "No, listen to me. They might be able to help me. They might be able to cure me."

"No," Tiffany says. "They'll kill you."

"Tiffany, the secret weapon is real," I say in an alarming tone. "It's real. Jacob saw it, and it might be able to remove my ability. Don't you see? I hurt people. My ability hurt them. I lost control."

"Hollis, listen to me," Tiffany says. "It was an accident. We can figure this out. Jonah can help you."

I shake my head. "But it wasn't an accident. My ability took control of me! It forced me to hurt Ashton, just like I hurt all those people at the Testing Center. Only this time, it wanted me to kill him! It wanted me to kill Ashton. The power has grown stronger!"

"Jonah will help you," she says. "We can—"

"No. I can't stay here." Adrenaline thunders into my ears and my vision turns sharp. "Don't you see? I didn't ask for this. I don't want it anymore. I've lost control. I have to go back to the Testing Center. I have to see for myself. If this weapon can get rid of my ability—then I owe it to everyone to end this. I'm dangerous, Tiffany. My power is too strong."

"Hollis, no," she says firmly. She backs away from me, pressing herself against the door. "If you go back there, you'll die. Don't you understand? They believe you are diseased. They'll kill you. You failed the Test. You have the biomarker."

"Tiffany—"

"I won't do it," she says.

My heart sinks. It was silly of me to believe I could truly overcome this ability. How foolish of me to think I could join their world. My power has finally proven itself to be what I feared, and the only way to stop it is to snuff it out, permanently. I can't risk hurting anyone else.

"Hollis, you can't leave."

I look at her, deep sadness overcoming me. "I wasn't asking . . ."

I flick my fingers and Tiffany stiffens, completely still, perfectly under my control. She gasps, a horrified look seizing her.

"Hollis, don't do this," she begs. "Listen to me. We can fix this. It's not too late. Please, you don't have to leave. Please, don't do this."

Her frame shivers. She's fighting me. I can feel it in my fingertips. I take a deep breath, channeling my ability into her and extinguishing the quiver. She's completely under my power now.

"Hollis, please," Tiffany whimpers. "You can't leave. They'll kill you."

"I have to."

Tiffany begins to scream. I raise my hand, palm forward,

and close it into a fist. Her jaw snaps shut. I've silenced her, and a single tear traces a path down my face.

"I'm sorry," I whisper.

I turn away from her, letting my ability enter my chest. I drop my expression, reverting back to the society member I was trained to be. The Testing Center requires utter control. Everything must happen according to plan.

"Teleport me to the Testing Center," I command.

I feel a hand on my back, and then I'm plunged into complete darkness.

24

MOMENTS LATER, MY FEET SCRAPE ACROSS SOLID GROUND. With an unpleasant crunch, I stagger forward, and cold air whips my hair askew. I feel like I've just been crushed.

Tiffany stands a few feet behind me. We're alone, and the towering marble steps of the Area 19 Testing Center rise before us. Massive pillars, crystal glass, and golden decorative trim shimmer in the light of a setting sun.

I look back to Tiffany's terrified, tear-stained face. Her mouth is still pressed shut, but the shiver has returned. She's physically quivering, fighting me, but she doesn't understand. I brought her with me because if the government can truly take my power, then she's my only way out. I feel sick to my stomach for endangering her like this, but I need her. Maybe I can stay with the Diseased Ones, but I have to kill the monster in my hands first. It's the only way to protect them.

I look away, unable to face her, and my fingertips move,

pulling her under again. The quivering stops.

My moment of hesitation is gone, and I drop my expression to match. I flick my fingers. "Follow me."

She obeys, falling into step beside me as we climb to the entrance. The glass double doors glint, leering at me, and my hand hovers over the handle. Once I step foot in here, there's no going back.

Gritting my teeth, I pull the doors open, and we pass through the entrance into the grand lobby. It's as if I've been thrown back into my worst nightmare. Images of machine guns flash in the back of my mind, but I drown them out. I have a task to do, and I must stay focused.

I walk straight to the receptionist's desk. The woman seated there is dressed in a simple white uniform, her chestnut hair done up in a tight bun, with a red pen propped behind her ear. I tap on the desk. The woman looks up, startled.

"Oh my." Her perfect control slips momentarily at the sight of Tiffany. "My dears, what are you . . . ?"

An inkling of recognition flashes behind her eyes. She knows who I am. Her mouth opens, and my hand springs forward, encasing her in stillness. I clamp my fist shut, gagging her with my ability. I can't let her warn anyone.

"Take me to the Chief Overseer of this facility," I say, channeling my power into her with full force. "And don't even think about signaling anyone for help."

My ability jerks the receptionist to her feet, and with another flick of my hand, she totters to the side of her desk. Her eyes bulge as she moves next to me.

"I don't want to run into any crowds," I say, "so don't lead us to the lift."

She takes several mechanical steps forward and then breaks into a brisk walk, chauffeuring us to the side of the lobby. I follow, twitching my hand to command Tiffany again. She steps behind me, and I feel a tug through my palms. She's still fighting me, but I push back, allowing the power to fill me, and the tug vanishes.

The three of us walk in eerie silence. It attacks my senses, and once more, visions of military men and weapons remind me vividly of the morning I failed the Test.

We enter through a heavy metal door. I flinch as it clangs open, banging against the concrete in a thunderous chorus. I hold my hand aloft, forcing the receptionist ahead of me, and up the spiraling staircase.

Our footsteps ring out in the echoing space, and sickening memories crash into me like a wave. Five months ago I ran down these steps. Five months ago I emerged into a room full of machine guns. Five months ago, the military broke into my home.

I stop walking, throwing my hand forward to halt the two helpless prisoners bound under my power. I clutch the railing, trying to breathe properly, as the smallest moment of panic overcomes me. What am I doing? But Ashton's terrified screams replace my doubt. I lost control. My ability wanted me to kill him. I know exactly what I'm doing. I'm here to get rid of this blood-thirsty demon.

My fingertips dance, and we continue up the steps. The

stairs go on and on, spiraling upward like a snake until we reach a door just shy of the top flight. The receptionist places her hand against a panel to the right. It flashes, opening to reveal a long, white hallway.

"Move," I say, pushing her through with a twist of my hand.

I step forward, closely followed by Tiffany. Proceeding cautiously, I scan the hall ahead and spot another facility worker. He's meandering toward us. I tense, panic threatening to close my throat. He looks up, and his blank face wavers.

"What are you doing up here?" he asks, addressing the intake receptionist, but just as in the lobby, his eyes move, first to Tiffany, then to me, and fearful recognition springs up across his face.

My hands cut through the air, silencing him before he can shout. I pull him in line next to the others, my power pulsing through every part of me. The terror in his face turns my stomach, so I look away.

"Take me to the Chief Overseer," I say, thrusting the two employees forward. They obey, compelled to action by the force in my fingertips.

I follow them to the end of the hall where they stop at a wide, ornately decorated golden door. The receptionist places her hand to a side panel, and after it lights up, the heavy door opens to a large, shockingly white room.

The walls are lined with screens, and a grand arching desk sits at its end. A sharply dressed woman is seated in the chair behind the desk, and a dozen military men line the sides. The atmosphere is stifling, and the sickening odor of sterile chemicals stings my nose.

At first, no one moves. The room appears surprised by our odd group. The woman gazes at the receptionist and the facility worker with muted confusion, and then everyone in the room looks at me.

The guns raise, the woman stands from her desk, and I step in front of my captives. My palm launches from me in a torrent of adrenaline fraught power. I grasp every person in the room, freezing them into perfect statues. My fists close, silencing them, and I lower my hands. The men mirror me in perfect time.

"Put your guns on the floor," I say, a powerful surge coursing through me.

They submit, and in a synchronized movement, the guns are discarded. I kneel, forcing them to their knees, and then flick my hands, leaving them bound there.

I approach the woman behind the desk, squaring my shoulders. Her abnormally dark eyes pierce me, and her silver hair, pulled into a neat bun, glimmers in the lighting. Her cornered spectacles twinkle, catching my eye like a knife. Her uniform is pure silver, clean, and pressed—utterly flawless. She looks terrifying.

I gulp and gather myself, twitching my hand to release the woman's thin mouth.

"Are you in charge?" I ask.

The woman says nothing. She simply stares at me, a strange glint behind her eyes.

"Are you the Chief Overseer of this Testing Center?"

The woman looks me up and down with pristine control.

"Hollis Timewire," she says, her voice silky and perfect. "What an unexpected surprise."

I falter, words momentarily out of reach. I gape at her, taking in the majesty of her societal stare, the chicness of her attire, and the utter void of her countenance. Nothing in her face moves—not even a quiver of expression. She gazes at me, her perfect features overwhelming, but her cold, black eyes keep me at bay.

"We've been looking for you, my dear," she says softly.

"Why?" I ask, snapping out of the trance. "So you can finish me off?"

She tilts her head to the side ever so slightly and stares at me with unblinking eyes. "Now what could possibly make you think that?"

"Isn't that what you tried to do five months ago? Kill me when I tested positive for the biomarker?"

I watch her features like a hawk, trying to pick up the slightest hint, but her control is flawless. She moves her head to the other side, methodically, studying me with unwavering attention. Her dark eyes don't leave mine.

She speaks in a poignant tone, drawing me in with her enchanting voice. "Is that why you have come?"

"I . . ." My voice fails, choked out by an unpleasant feeling of dread.

"Tell me, Hollis," the woman says, her eyes burrowing into me. "Who's your friend?"

I glance at Tiffany for the briefest moment. The desperate look of anguish on her face sears my insides like a hot fiery torch. I look away from her, turning back to the woman.

"She's like me," I say. "She has an ability."

The smallest flash appears in the woman's eyes, but it vanishes quickly. Her mouth curls as a hungry tone issues from her delicate lips. "Another Diseased One?"

"Don't call her that!" I snap.

My tingling hands shiver, and several of the military men collapse on all fours. I flatten my palm, pressing them into the floor. The woman seems unphased. She simply bows her head gracefully, still maintaining eye contact.

"Of course," she says. "My deepest apologies."

"They're not Diseased Ones. They're people. They're human beings," I say, through gritted teeth.

Again, the tiniest flicker appears in the woman's gaze, and then it's gone. "They?"

My stomach lurches. "H-human beings," I repeat, stammering slightly.

"Tell me something, sweet child," she says, her eyes softening. "Why have you come here?"

Her question pierces me, and everything I've done consumes me once more. Horrible memories flood my mind. The crack of the skull. The crash of the tables. The dark voice, and the blood. Ashton's pleading eyes. His writhing, curdling scream.

I hang my head, barely able to bring myself to speak. An incredible weight presses on my chest and my voice breaks.

"Because . . . I hurt them."

"Who did you hurt?" the woman asks gently, peering at me.

"I hurt some of them . . . with my ability," I say. "But I never meant to. I never meant for any of this to happen. It was an accident. It's my power. It's evil . . . a monster."

The woman's soft tone holds me tenderly, as a mother holds her child. "Of course you didn't mean for this to happen, my dear."

"I couldn't stop it," I say, whimpering. "It took control of me. It forced me to hurt them . . . but I didn't want to. I tried to stop myself, but I couldn't."

The woman nods, and though her face remains impassive, understanding blossoms behind her eyes. "Of course not," she says. "I know how you were raised. A model society member with incredible potential, and flawless control. Your father saw it in you—what a glowing recommendation to the military elite."

My lower lip trembles. "My father?"

"You were brought up in a respectable home." Her eyes search mine. "Your parents were devastated when you went missing. I can't imagine the trauma you've experienced. I can see the emotion saturated in your face. You've been infected."

I furrow my brow, shaking my head. "No, it isn't like that. You don't understand. It isn't all bad. Some of it's incredible—like nothing I've ever experienced in society. Feeling isn't a disease, it's alive. It's . . . wonderful." I drop my head in defeat. "It's my power. That's what's evil."

"Then tell me, child, why have you come?" she asks.

Burning desire ignites my resolve. I ball my hands into fists and speak with all the daring I can muster. "The secret weapon of a hundred years ago."

Her lips press into a thin line. "The Terror War," she says gracefully. "The death. The destruction. The horror of those creatures."

She cocks her head to the side, contemplating me like a predator does prey, her soulless eyes drilling into me. A shiver runs down my spine.

"But the memories," I say, struggling with myself, as if truly considering the truth of the matter for the first time. "I've seen Jacob Ganiston's memories. I've seen what it was like a hundred years ago. It wasn't a war, it was a massacre. The government rounded them up and slaughtered them. Why? How do you explain that?"

"My dear child," the woman says. "You have been deluded and brainwashed—force-fed lies. You've let your emotions run rampant. Your blood is infected, and your brain is diseased. Why should you trust anything you've seen from these creatures?"

"Prove it," I say defiantly. "Prove that your version of history is right. Prove I'm wrong."

I try desperately to read her face, but nothing comes of it. Her expressionlessness is perfect.

"You can't, can you?" I say, stepping away from the desk. "You were going to kill me when I failed the Test. You were going to inject me and kill me."

"I can show you," the woman says, and she lights up with

sickening delight. "If you will allow me." Her eyes cascade down to her frozen form, and I stiffen.

I shake my head, backing away from her, panic seizing me. "No."

"No tricks," she says, intense control infused into every word. "Just the truth. That is what you're after, isn't it?"

I hesitate, biting my lip. "Yes."

"Then let me show you."

"Show me what?"

"The boy from twelve years ago," she says, and this time, her face erupts into expression, and a terrible wolf-like smile twists her features. Her black eyes hover over me, chilling me to the bone.

My ability buzzes through my limbs, electrifying and cold. I'm sucked into the moment, unable to take my eyes off of the beady ones in front of me.

"What did you just say?"

"I can show you the boy from twelve years ago."

"What? You mean the one who failed his Test?" My hands turn to ice, and I begin trembling violently. "The one you injected and killed in cold blood?"

"No," she says softly. "The one we restored to society."

25

ALL OF THE BLOOD DRAINS FROM MY FACE, AND MY mouth turns to ash. “What?”

A sinking feeling forms in the pit of my stomach. It’s as if the air has been sucked from my lungs. I clutch my chest and look to the woman, whose glaring features light anew.

“Would you like to see?”

I study her face cautiously. “No tricks?”

“Just the truth.”

I consider the woman for a moment, then raise my hand, palm forward. My heart pounds against my chest relentlessly. But before I can free her, an incredible tug jerks my hand down, and a muffled scream issues from behind me. I turn around.

Tiffany is physically shaking, struggling against the bonds of my ability, her eyes streaming and her pressed lips trembling. Another powerful pull yanks my hand again, but before she can break free, I extend it, freezing her in place. Her whimpering stops and everything turns still once more.

We stare at one another for a few dreadful seconds, and then I turn away. I can't face her. I hate that I'm forcing her under my power, but I need to see this.

My fingertips flitter, and I release the woman. I keep my hand trained on her as she walks around the desk. I move back, giving her a wide berth.

It's only as she steps down from the platform of her desk that I realize how tall she is, easily six feet to my petite 5-foot 3-inch frame. Her towering presence commands respect, and something more: fear.

She approaches the nearest wall screen and begins to tap on several buttons.

"What are you doing?" I demand.

The woman stops, turning to me. "If you'll allow me to access the footage from the security archives? It will only take a moment."

I nod, trying to squash the unsettling feeling in my stomach.

The woman finishes tapping on the screen and then steps back, bowing her head in a reverent manner. "This is the record of that day twelve years ago," she says. "I am showing you the truth about the Test, Hollis."

The screen expands to either side, and footage appears with the year imprinted in the lower right-hand corner: 2635. Twelve years ago.

I approach the screen, unable to believe my eyes. I recognize this. It's the room with the metal throne—the room where they tried to inject me five months ago. I stare at the footage, taking it in. The metal throne has been pushed forward and the countertops are askew, but it's the same room.

The feed continues, and several doctors, military men, and scientists enter at a hurried pace. Their lab coats contrast vividly against the dark and terrible room. Murmuring issues from the audio of the tape, but I can't hear anything coherent until the door bursts open.

A boy my age is pushed through the opening. The military men move with precision, arresting the boy and dragging him to the metal throne. A chill travels through me, and I watch, crippled with fear.

"What?" the boy demands, the societal control of his tone fracturing. "But you said I passed."

"Unfortunately, Mr. Deluca, you did not pass."

I'm completely numb, watching the footage helplessly. It's as if I'm reliving it.

"Get off me!" The boy struggles against the military men, putting up quite a fight, but there are too many of them. They force him into the seat and begin to fasten the cuffs to his wrists and ankles.

"Strap him down, securely Lieutenant," one of the doctors says.

"Yes, sir."

"No. This must be a mistake. I'm not a Diseased One," the boy says, flailing against his captors, his voice laden with panic. "I can't be a Diseased One."

"We do not make mistakes, Mr. Deluca."

"Let me go!" He thrashes within his restraints, twisting himself and pulling one of his arms free.

"I said secure him," the doctor growls.

Abruptly, one of the military men hits the boy in the stomach with the butt of his gun. The boy yelps in pain, slumping forward in a stupor, temporarily stunned. The rest of the men restrain his free arm and push his head back against the throne, placing a leather cord across his forehead to keep him upright.

"Let's get this done quickly," the doctor says, monotone, as if he were about to accomplish the most mundane of tasks. "I'd like to finish this before lunch."

A sickening murmur of agreement floods the room, and the doctor pulls out the syringe filled with green fluid. He gives it several hardy flicks with his gloved hand and then pushes some of the liquid through the tip.

The boy stirs in his restraints. "Wait. No. I'm not a Diseased One," he says, pleading with the doctor, his voice desperate. "This is a mistake. Please don't do this! Please!"

The doctor ignores him, wiping the flat of his arm. The boy begins to writhe in his restraints, contorting his body and screaming at the top of his lungs.

"Lieutenant," the doctor snaps. "Please, control him."

The boy receives another sharp blow to the gut, and a wad of cloth is stuffed into his mouth, gagging him. The doctor holds the needle above his arm and sticks him with it, emptying the entirety of the contents.

I gasp, hand over my mouth, my body completely numb. I'm rapt into the scene, unable to take my eyes away. The boy's tense frame relaxes in the metal throne, now quite still.

"But . . ." I say weakly. "You killed him. You—"

"Watch," the woman says, pointing her long, delicate finger at the screen. "It isn't over."

The feed continues, and the doctor cleans up, dumping the syringe away and wiping the surface of the countertops. After this, the group stops their work and stares expectantly at the large door. A harsh knock issues from the audio, and I jump, clutching my chest.

The scientist nearest the door grabs the handle and pulls it open. "Please, come in."

I squint at the screen, taking a few steps toward it. A small boy, about age five, enters the room accompanied by a smartly dressed nurse. He stands timidly behind the nurse's leg, peering up at the military men with his big blue eyes. He rubs his nose, his blond curls brushing across his face.

"Just as we discussed, sweetheart," the nurse says, coaxing him forward. She brings him out from behind her leg and leads him to Deluca, casting a wary eye at the military men. "Never mind them, dear."

The little boy looks at the nurse and then points to the boy fastened to the throne. "Is he the one?"

"Yes, dear," the nurse says.

"Okay."

He bobs his little head, trotting over to the boy cuffed to the throne, a cheerful delight etched in his demeanor. He takes his tiny hand and places it on Deluca's knee. The moment he touches him, a wonderful surge of golden light erupts between them, filling the entire feed.

The light extends from the boy's palm, expanding into the room, and lighting up the air. I watch, mesmerized, as it arcs between the little boy's hand and Deluca's knee. The golden glow persists for several seconds before it folds itself up into the boy's palms.

"Well done, sweetheart," the nurse says. "Come along now. These people must get back to work."

The woman leads the little boy back through the door, and the feed cuts out. I stare at the black screen, blinking rapidly, as if waking from a nightmare.

"What was that?" I ask, turning to the woman. "Who was the little boy?"

The woman draws herself up to her full height, towering over me, her features alive with triumph. "The secret weapon of a hundred years ago."

My eyes widen, and my mouth drops. "The secret weapon is . . . a child?"

"A child with the ability to remove another's power," she says. "Permanently."

Icy cold feeling hits me with unbearable weight. The secret weapon can remove someone's ability. I'm trembling from head to foot, unable to believe it. After all this time, after everyone I've hurt, after all I've done—at last, I have my answer. It's possible to remove this cursed monster. I can be free.

"But," I say, struggling to find the proper words. "You injected him."

"Merely a sedative to make the process run smoothly," she says. "Mr. Deluca does not remember this unfortunate event. As far as he and his family are concerned, he passed the Test with full marks, and he was returned to his family later that day."

"And . . . that's what would've happened to me?" I ask. I'm shaking, barely able to keep myself upright.

"My dear," she says soothingly, her perfect tone razor sharp. "Society does not abandon its own."

"But how is this little boy still alive?" I ask.

"We keep him safe in a cryogenic stasis, perfectly preserved and perfectly healthy."

Jacob's hoarse words ground me in a moment of clarity: "a huge, glass-like coffin with an intricate button panel. I saw it when my hood slipped. And that sound . . . a deep humming noise, as if the devil himself were inside."

"Jacob saw the cryo chamber . . ." I whisper.

"Incredible technology, isn't it?" the woman asks.

My stomach turns. Something isn't right. The woman's story doesn't make sense.

"But, isn't the weapon supposed to find people with abilities?" I ask, eyeing her cautiously. "What about the man who damaged it? The secret weapon was damaged, and after that, the government couldn't find anyone with the biomarker. That's what the rumor says."

The woman's countenance changes, the wolf-like smile returning. "Would you like to see?"

"See what?"

"Tell me something, Hollis." She walks through the room, standing a few feet from Tiffany, her gaze cascading over her still form. The woman's black eyes dart back to me. "What did they tell you about this man—the one who damaged the weapon?"

"That he's a hero," I say. "Jacob told me that he's the reason the government will never find him again. He's the reason that everyone is safe."

The woman's wolf-like smile grows. "I want to show you something."

She moves with calculated speed, tapping the screen again and stepping back. Another feed pops up, the date embossed into the frame—2547. A hundred years ago.

"Watch," she says.

It's a room filled with tinker toys, blocks, and books. Two children sit among the toys, playing together. Their little voices carry on the recording. Too young to conceal emotion, their laughter lights up the audio. They're smiling and talking to one another in sweet voices, dreaming up magical make-believe. It's enchanting.

I furrow my brow, squinting at the footage and scrutinizing the little boy's face. "That's the boy from the previous tape," I say. "Who's the little girl?"

"Twins," the woman says.

"Twins?"

"Watch," she says viciously.

A commotion from beyond the room spews from the feed.

The children stop playing, and a bright light flashes. Several moments pass, and the metal barrier bursts open to reveal a disheveled man. He slams the door behind him, sealing himself in and panting wildly. Blood runs down his cheek from a nasty gash above his brow, and sweat drenches his clothing.

The children scream, clinging to one another and staring up at the man with terrified eyes. He stops, taken aback by the sight of the two little ones cowering before him. His face turns ashen, and he begins to tremble.

"It's kids?" he says, utterly stricken. "They're kids? It's not possible."

Bang.

The noise from the hall beyond bursts through the audio again. The man holds his palms up, spraying the door shut with a strange metallic substance. It spews from his flesh, covering the seams of the entrance and sealing it.

He runs his grimy hands through his black hair, a sick look plastered across his face. He paces back and forth while the pounding grows. The door is physically shaking. He turns to face the children, grief in his eyes. But something more overcomes his features, as if, for a moment, he was no longer himself...

In a quick burst, he moves toward the little girl, and to my horror, his hand extends, and silvery metal issues from his skin, knocking her backward.

I watch, tears searing the sides of my face, burning my cheeks.

The little girl screams in agony, trying to shield herself from the onslaught of molten metal, but she crumples against the opposite wall with a loud crack, her tiny body splayed out across the floor.

The little boy shrieks, rushing the man and clamping onto his arm with vice-like fists. The golden light bursts between them for several seconds and the man yells, attempting to pry the boy from him, but it's too late. The golden stream slinks back into the little boy's hands, and with it, the man's ability.

Bang.

The door reverberates on its hinges, splitting the seams of the plastered metal.

The man shakes the boy from him and totters back against the wall, staring at his hands, wide-eyed.

"What have you done to me?" He thrusts his fists forward, but nothing comes. The man lunges at the boy. "What have you done?" he screeches. "You've ruined everything!"

Bang.

The door splits open, shattering the silvery substance into a hundred pieces, and military men flood the room. The man staggers back, shot repeatedly in the chest. He slumps to the floor, his body still, his limbs at awkward angles.

The boy rushes to his sister. His cries echo off the walls as he hugs her, laying himself over her tiny frame. His wailing, tearful lament guts me, and then the screen cuts to black. The images are gone.

I stand there, mouth open and hands shaking. Warm salted tears stream freely. My knees buckle, and I kneel on the floor, staring up at the woman. Tingling enters my face, but it's not from my ability, it's from shock.

"Twins," the woman says, a silky victory entering her delicate words. "The boy with the power to remove abilities. The girl with the power to locate those with abilities. The golden pair. The perfect weapon to aid us in the war against a hateful, murderous race."

"Twins." I clutch my chest, wiping tears away with the back of my hand.

"Now you see the truth," she says. "Proof of their murderous ways. Evidence of their altered minds. Killing a poor, innocent child. Killing her in cold blood."

The woman kneels down in front of me, her dark eyes glistening. She isn't crying. She isn't even portraying emotion, but something deep in her soul connects with mine.

"Everything the government's done has been to protect its citizens from the horrors we faced a hundred years ago," she says softly. "The Test is designed to eliminate the biomarker and restore young people to society. No one should have to suffer the delusion of bad blood and a mutated brain. You said it yourself, Hollis. You couldn't control it. You hurt them, but you didn't mean to. It's the biomarker—the delusion. Not you."

My mind races, running through the footage I've just witnessed. The boy who failed the Test. The secret weapon. The twins. The little girl. Everything about my world crashes over me. My education. My upbringing. My parents. My carefully crafted expressionlessness.

Maybe it's better this way. Maybe lack of feeling is the only way to prevent senseless murder and hatred. I run it over in my mind once more: emotion leads to conflict, and conflict leads to war. Wars have been fought over hatred, jealousy, power, wealth, love . . . neutrality guarantees equality. I understand it now. I'm not a murderer, but this ability almost made me one.

I rise from the floor, and the woman follows me, standing up and bowing her head. "Now you have seen it for yourself. Now you've seen the truth, Hollis."

26

I'M HURTLING THROUGH TIME, FLASHING BACK TO WHAT started this nightmare: failing the Test. My mind replays the story: freezing the men in the lobby, cracking the skull, running through the streets, vanishing from my home, learning about my power, experiencing feeling, attacking Ashton, forcing Tiffany to bring me here, learning the truth. All of it seems utterly clear now.

"You were going to help me?"

"Of course we were," the woman says. "We are not like them." She glances at Tiffany and then back to me.

Tiffany's eyes meet mine. I don't believe that she and the others are evil. Not anymore. But it seems that the Diseased Ones from a hundred years ago are exactly the monsters I've been taught to fear. That man murdered the little girl . . .

"So," I say, fighting my constricted tone. "Five months ago, when I failed the Test, you were going to remove my ability and send me back . . ."

"Home," she says. "To your family. To your parents. The Testing Center is society's most noble institution. It has one purpose and one alone: to help those who have been cursed by this horrific biomarker. As I said before, society does not abandon its own."

I stand there, my arms limp at my sides, completely overwhelmed. I don't know what to say. There's too much going on in my mind.

"Hollis," the woman says. "Would you like to go home?"

"Home," I whisper, blinking several times. "I can go home?"

"You can go home if you want to," she says, coming to stand behind Tiffany.

The woman places her spindly hand on Tiffany's shoulder, and my mouth drops open. She just touched her. I'm so shocked by this that I momentarily forget what the woman's asked me. I gawk at the two of them, unable to speak.

"Tell me, Hollis," the woman says. "What does your friend do?"

I close my mouth, snapping out of it. I hesitate, but only for a fraction of a second. "She . . . she can teleport."

The woman cocks her head to the side, studying Tiffany. "Is she the one who took you?"

"Yes."

"You don't have to live in fear of these creatures anymore," she says, clutching Tiffany fiercely, and although Tiffany is still bound under my ability, the smallest shiver courses through her. "You don't have to go back there. They're murderers and liars, after all."

Tiffany and I lock eyes, and I see the anguish in her face. A single tear drops down her cheek and lands on her sweater. I flick my hand, releasing her mouth, and approach her, staring deep into her face.

"You lied to me," I say. "How could you lie to me? You said the Diseased Ones never murdered anyone. You said your people were slaughtered, but that man killed that little girl. He murdered her. He never even gave her a chance."

Tiffany begins to cry, and the sound assaults my ears. I feel sick. "Hollis, listen to me. I didn't know."

I scoff, pacing back and forth. "How convenient."

"Hollis, this woman is manipulating you!"

"So far, she's the only one giving me any answers."

"Because she's the only one you're listening to. Those videos don't prove the massacre never happened. They don't prove anything. Hollis—"

"That little boy," I say, cutting her off. "He took away Deluca's ability. You saw it for yourself. Why would the government do that if they were just going to kill people who failed the Test?"

"They killed him and took away his ability for good measure," Tiffany retorts. "It's like Jacob. They killed him, but they couldn't truly kill him. The government doesn't know what powers will manifest, so they have to do both. They kill someone *and* take their ability. Don't you see? Deluca was dead before the little boy came in. She's lying to you. That green vial wasn't a sedative."

Jacob's chilling words come to me again: "I felt sluggish—weighed down, barely able to move. It was all I could do to keep myself standing upright . . ." He must have been drugged . . .

"How can you possibly know that?" I say.

"Hollis, she doesn't want to help you, she wants you to give up your ability so she can kill you!"

"No," I say, shaking my head.

"Hollis, please—"

"No, that can't be true," I say. "The biomarker turns us crazy. It makes us murderers. You watched the footage."

"Even if that were true, it isn't anymore!"

"Isn't it? Look what I did to Ashton," I say desperately. "Tiffany, I almost killed him. It makes sense now. The government needs to get rid of the biomarker to restore people to society. You saw what that man did! He murdered the little girl—he even fought the urge to do it. Didn't you see his face? He changed. Like his ability was controlling him!"

Tiffany trembles and I feel a pull through my hands. "That was one man. One man who made a mistake. One man who committed an atrocity," she says bitterly. "But that man doesn't define an entire group of people. Hollis, listen to me, we're not the bad guys. We rescued you!"

"You kidnapped me."

"We took you in. We helped you."

"You lied to me."

"No," Tiffany says. "We told you the truth. Whatever happened in the past, whatever casualties were suffered—our people were not the murderers. Our people were slaughtered. The biomarker doesn't make us kill people. That's a lie."

"You don't have my ability!" I snap. "You don't know what it's like! I'm fighting a demon voice in my mind! How is that *not* a brain mutation? It told me to kill Ashton—it wanted him to writhe. I don't want this power."

"You can still fix this. Come back with me, please. Jonah can help you."

I shake my head, heart falling. "Tiffany, I can't . . ."

"What about Keith?" she says, shaking violently, and my power slackens. She's fighting me again. "Is he murderous? What about Jonah? Would he kill? What about me? We're not dangerous."

"Even if you're right—"

"Please come back. It's not too late. We can help you. We're your family."

"Tiffany," I say, an overwhelming sadness crushing me. I choke on the tears smeared down my face. "Even if you're not dangerous . . . I am . . . and that's why I can't go back. I have to do this. I have to get rid of it. I can't let it hurt anyone else."

Something within me seals, and I back away from her, hanging my head. "I'm sorry, Tiffany. Thank you for showing me your world. It was wonderful . . . but it's not my home."

"No, Hollis, please—"

With one swift movement, I close her mouth, and intense control washes over me once more. She stops shaking, and I turn away from her, and back to the woman.

"I don't want this anymore. I don't want my power. I just want to go home."

She gives me an understanding look. "My dear Hollis, you've made a wonderful choice."

Relief floods me. I can finally go home. It's over. They are going to free me from this dark urge—this terrible power. They can cure my bad blood. I bury my face in both hands, too overwhelmed to speak.

"My dear, would you please release my men?" the woman asks kindly. "They need to go and fetch our little friend."

I drop my hands, looking to Tiffany once more, and a powerful surge fills me. "On one condition."

"What is that, my dear?"

"Tiffany leaves here and no one touches her. She goes free. This doesn't concern her."

The woman bows her head gracefully. "Of course. You have my word," she says. She walks into the midst of her bound military men and speaks in a cold and severe tone. "No one is to touch the girl. That is an order."

My fingertips tingle, and I relinquish my grasp on the room. The men fall forward, sputtering and coughing on their hands and knees. Tiffany, however, remains frozen in place. I've done this with intention. I don't want her to grab me and teleport me back.

I walk up to her. We are both crying. I lower my voice, speaking barely above a whisper. "I'm sorry." My hand twitches and I command her with my ability. "Teleport yourself back."

The last bit of anguish glints behind her eyes, and then she is gone. I stand in the place she's vacated, slightly dazed. The military men begin to line the end of the room, blocking the door from my view, and the woman comes to stand by my side.

She looks down at me, and with a motherly tone says, "you've done the right thing, Hollis. I can see the pain you carry, but you don't need to suffer anymore. Two of my men have gone to get the boy, and then this nightmare will be over."

"Okay."

"It will be quick and painless. Easier than falling asleep. I promise."

I nod, hugging myself and trying to breathe. I hang my head. I'm devastated by what I've done to Tiffany, but it was the only way to discover the truth, and more importantly, it was the only way to protect them. I nearly killed Ashton, and if I stayed, who knows what else I could have done.

I'm ending it. I'm removing the beast—not only for my own sake but for the sake of everyone I've come to love. My parents. My friends. My teacher. This will all be over. I can go back to my life. I can go back home. I can forget.

For one shining moment, the most wonderful thought occurs to me. I don't have to feel anymore. I don't have to delve into my emotions. I don't have to know pain. I can forget and go back to the life I've always wanted—a graduated society member, a valued addition to the world, striving toward a career that suits my gifts and talents.

The door opens with a soft click, and the military men move to either side. I watch the opening intently, and the boy from the footage enters the room, accompanied by a nurse. He blinks in the bright lighting, his little hand rubbing at his nose, and his blonde curls falling askew across his forehead.

"Here we are, sweetheart," the nurse says. "Go on."

He approaches me, peering ahead curiously, and I sink to the floor, kneeling down to his level. We lock eyes.

"Hi," he says, and his sweet voice carries in the large room.

"Hi."

"Are you the girl?"

I nod slowly. "I'm the girl."

"Okay," he says. He looks back up at his nurse.

"Go ahead, sweetheart," she says.

The boy turns back to me, a pure smile on his face, and he places his tiny hand on my forehead.

The spark of golden light arcs between us and a curious sensation seizes me. Warmth is leaving my fingertips, and the tingling pulses erratically. With every heartbeat the power vanishes. The sensation emanates from the pit of my stomach, up through my chest, and into my forehead. It continues for several intense seconds, and then the golden light retracts, tucking itself back into the little boy's palms.

I gasp, clutching at my heart. I feel like I've just been dunked under icy water. I flex my hands, and for one awful moment, the boy appears to stiffen, as if captured under the ferocity of my ability. But then the boy smiles and steps backward.

I breathe a sigh of relief. My power is gone, the tingling has stopped, and the deed is done. It's finally over.

"Alright sweetheart," the nurse says. "It's time to go."

The boy moves back to her, looking up and wearing a joyful expression. The two of them retreat through the group of military men, into the hall, and out of sight.

The woman points to the men, giving them a stiff nod. "You know what to do. As quick as you can."

All of the men exit the room in an orderly fashion, leaving us alone.

"Now I can go home," I whisper.

The woman strolls gracefully to the curved desk at the back of the room. "Hollis," she says. "I want to thank you."

"Thank me?" I look up, confused. "For what?"

The woman opens a drawer. Staring within, she carefully selects something from its depths and closes it. She moves out from behind the desk, gazing at me with her black eyes.

"Before tonight, we were unaware that more Diseased Ones were infesting our world."

I stare blankly ahead, and my lower lip trembles.

"And now you have led us right to them."

I'm flooded with adrenaline, and a cold sensation spreads to my knees and face. I stumble backward, my heart ramming itself against my ribs. Sheer horror rips through me like a hot, fiery knife. "No."

"Your friend," the woman says. "I placed a tracking device on her clothing. We will have thousands of our military there within the hour. You have made me a very rich woman, Hollis Timewire."

"No!" I cry, gripping my throat, unable to think, unable to breathe. "No! You can't!"

The woman moves with unbelievable speed, her teeth bared. "You wonderful, foolish, idiot girl," she leers, advancing on me. She grabs my arm, yanking me forward. "You and your kind have soured us."

Instinctively, I throw my hands up, spreading my fingertips, but a horrible gut-wrenching pang slices through me. I no longer have my ability, and I will never feel that power again. I'm helpless, less than myself—torn and utterly broken.

I gasp as the woman lifts me from my feet, her black eyes bulging behind her wicked smile. "Society must rid itself of the infection that threatens to kill. The Diseased Ones must be wiped from the face of the earth, and you have helped us accomplish this."

She throws me to the floor with incredible strength, and my hands smack into the tiles. I skid a few feet, crashing into the wall. Pain springs up in every part of me to a degree I never thought possible, and fear explodes through my chest.

"No, you can't! You can't!" I scream, springing to my feet. I'm shaking, and tears stream down my face, hot and dreadful. "You can't kill them! Please! Don't do this! I beg you, please!"

I lunge at the woman, wild and grief-stricken, torn to the depths of my soul, crazed. This is my fault, my terrible mistake. I've betrayed them.

I halt, stopping dead in my tracks, as the glint of a gun flashes. The woman points it directly into my face, a demonic smile emerging from her features.

Now I know the truth, and I know it for certain. And all of the family, the friendship, and the freedom of the world below—

all of it flashes before me. It's so clear. So real. And I'm a fool...

The gun fires, and everything is crushed into complete darkness.

ACKNOWLEDGMENTS

To my husband: Steven, thank you for your relentless support and love. I appreciate all of the late night brainstorming sessions, countless read-throughs, and endless edits. You're my partner in crime and my best friend. I couldn't have done this without you.

To my parents: Dad, thank you for bugging me to get published. I needed the push. Mom, thank you for always taking an interest in my stories. I love you guys more than words can say.

To my siblings: Michelle, thank you for inspiring the cover of this book. You're an incredible, creative soul! Luke, thank you for instilling joy in the process. I love our writing conversations. Gabby, thank you for insisting that this book turn into a series. I'm forever indebted to you. You did good, little sis!

To my editor: Holly, you turned this painting into a beautifully colored masterpiece. Thank you for your thoughtful feedback, your difficult questions, and your attention to detail. I'm so blessed that we met at the SCWC. You're a gem!

To my original beta readers: Molly and Skyler, thank you for sticking with me, encouraging me, and supporting me in my pursuits. Your feedback made this book shine. Love you two.

To my readers: Thank you for giving me a chance. Writing allows us to expose the magic in our souls. So here's a little piece of mine.

To my Savior: Jesus, thank you for giving me this incredible opportunity.

www.ingramcontent.com/pod-product-compliance
Lightning Source LLC
Chambersburg PA
CBHW030527310726
48979CB00010B/1823/J

* 9 7 8 1 9 4 7 3 9 2 7 0 0 *